i

ANASTASIA

LOUISE FURLEY

Anastasia

ISBN- 978-1-7349807-6-9 (Paperback)
ISBN- 978-1-7349807-5-2 (eBook)

Cover design by Pixel Mischief Design

Also by Louise Furley

Solitar

Halo Valley

Isle of Orainn

The Kissing Number

Distilled Duplicity

The Poser

Wrath of Wolf

Devil's Prince

Devil's Seed

Anastasia

Chapter One

"I'm here," Vinca Nivelli announced. Not waiting for consent to enter the study, he strode right in and went straight to the wet bar.

Passing over the assortment of spirits showcased in front of the green mosaic backsplash, he opened the small stainless steel fridge and removed a beer. The pendant lights over the bar highlighted his dark auburn hair and rolled over thick shoulders, he was a big muscular male. A highly trained, amoral, lethal asset.

At his desk, Nero Lamontagne typed a few words on the laptop. He reviewed what he wrote, satisfied, he closed the lid and reached for the cigar perched on the crystal ashtray. Not as buffed muscular as the big man, Vinca Nivelli, still, Lamontagne filled out his suit with a husky build and above average height.

Reclining in the burgundy leather chair, Lamontagne pushed the computer off to the side scraping over papers on the immense elk-wood desk and watched Nivelli pop the top off the bottle then slug down half the beer.

The corner of Lamontagne's mouth cut in expressing his disgust. "Always the peasant, Vinca. You can dress the man in Armani, but the suit doesn't change the brute longshoreman."

Vinca arched a brow at Nero then glanced down at his blue blazer, white shirt and black slacks. With his thick almost curly hair, Roman nose and full, sculpted lips he resembled a brutish Michelangelo's David.

Guzzling the rest of the beer, sounding slightly affronted, he replied, "I haven't been a longshoreman since I was in my early twenties Nero. You've never made any complaints about the dirty work I do for you." Leaving the empty bottle on the black marble counter he got himself another one.

Ankles crossed, elbow on the countertop in a narcissistic pose, before taking a drink he scowled. His tough chin in the air he said, "You think it wasn't tricky taking out the top two CEO's of Scarfeld Industries and making them look like accidents? Prominent men making millions have security, bodyguards. But," the scowl turned to a smug sneer, he bragged, "I did it. And you were able to slide in during the chaos and finesse a slick take-over." The second beer went down faster than the first.

Nero rolled his eyes, Vinca loved to blow his own horn, and he wasn't done. Bored eyes perusing Vinca, Nero palmed his sleek black hair back, crossed his long legs and toked on the cigar with irritated draws. He had the heavy face of a Rottweiler but the temperament of a savage pit bull complete with bloody fangs.

Vinca went on, "Yeah, due to my eliminating the CEO's you were able to coerce- *terrorize*- the remaining executive in charge to use information asymmetry to lower stock prices. The company panicked enabling you to buy them out at a ridiculously low price." Finishing his second beer and reaching for a third, Vinca smirked. "Admit it, Nero, you need me."

Nero tapped the end of the cigar on the ashtray with a muttered, "Whatever." Propping his elbows on the desk he leaned forward. "Now about this new venture. I gave you the information on the employee I want you to compel to work for us."

He waited until Vinca grunted his acknowledgement with his sculptured lips on the bottle's rim before continuing. "We discussed what I want. If you have to wrench every single tooth out to get the compliance, do it. Start with the back molars, I don't want anyone noticing the person suddenly has missing teeth and growing suspicious."

Vinca frowned. "You already have eyes in the lab. Why do you need more?"

Nero's head came up, his brows lowered. "I don't like to be questioned, Vinca, even by you. My spy gathered the initial Intel that the professor and that girl, the young chemist are working on an antidote for Falk's oil bacteria. The word is they're close to a breakthrough.

"Reviewing the dossiers, it's more likely the Brainiac behind the antidote is the professor as he is older and would have the experience and know-how. But my spy can't get into the inner circle to steal their data and learn who the actual lead is for sure."

Vinca opened his mouth, but squinting a reproachful eye at him Nero said, "Don't question my logistics again."

"Okay, keep your shirt on, cripes, touchy much?" Vinca leaned a hip against a table. "Go on."

Nero responded wryly, "Oh, thank you for your permission. Now, I want everything you can get on the professor, ah," he pulled the laptop back over, lifted the lid then scrolled through his online notes. "Connor Chandler. Start with him. If we get nothing out of him then you go after," he read the monitor, "Anastasia Athens. If the professor doesn't pan out, make him disappear then I want Athens' notes on the formula and I want her."

Vinca opened his blazer and pulled out a small notebook and pen. He wrote down the two names Nero gave him then tucked the pad and pen back in the inside breast pocket.

Nero informed Vinca, "I have a confederate at the lab that can scope them out, but the other mark can get in closer. I want both the professor and the girl watched, see where they stow their notes and computers. The info may be at the lab or in their homes. Get Fisher and Twizz to help you, I want eyes on them 24/7. Tell me when you have the professor's computer and the notes. After I review them then I'll give you the order to take him. We clear?"

"Why don't we just snatch the girl, the weaker link and make her give us her information?"

"Because Chandler's data may be more precise. I can verify the validity of his computations then force him to complete the formula for us. Governments and everyone involved in the oil and gasoline business, including vehicle factories and businesses, shit, so many things governed by oil, that people, companies, will pay millions, even billions for the damned antidote. Now, you think you can handle the tasks?"

A loud belch, Vinca tapped his fist on his abdomen and burped again knowing it repulsed Nero. Setting the empty bottle on the glossy ebony bar he reached for another. "Yeah, yeah. I may be a brute, but I know how to get the job done. I'll find out where the mark with the soon to be missing molars parks their car. I'll set Fish on the professor and Twizz after the girl, our hack boy Kori Kaymon can get more in-depth workups on them. It'll be an easy grab."

"I want smooth, Vinca, no fuck ups. I want both their records and then the professor. Be painfully crystal with the mark, I do not want them blabbing to anyone but us. Make them too afraid to even consider going to the police."

A slow grin crept over Vinca's self-assured centurion face. "I can do smooth, Nero, and I'm looking forward to working the girl over for you." At Nero's frown, he said with a sigh, "Okay, fine, the dude first."

Cigar tucked between his teeth, folding his arms behind his head, elbows winged out, Nero leaned back, the chair rustled leathery with his weight. "When you grab the mark, tell them I want all the data within 48 hours. Call me when you have the information. Don't take the professor until I give the order."

Vinca nodded. "No problem. Tell me why you want me to start with the teeth and not something more fun, something I can slice?"

"I would think it would be obvious, I already said that I don't want anything visible that someone might question. You can do whatever other coercion you want as long as you leave no visible marks. Now, get out."

Vinca saluted Nero with two fingers and a jaunty grin and left with the beer.

Chapter Two

"Drat," Anastasia Athens muttered, her eye pressed against the microscope. She scribbled notes on a pad beside the scope.

Snickers came from across the lab. "What, Stassi?" Research chemist assistant, Dixy Lee taunted, "Sleeping with the boss got you the job but you don't have the IQ points to actually produce results?" When she wrinkled her snub nose freckles hopped across it. They joined the rest of the little brown spots dotting her face, curly blonde hair on the edge of frazzle bounced around her round head.

Dixy did extreme dieting and bought only couture, unfortunately you can take the farm girl out Iowa but you can't take the farm out of the girl. She still looks like she should have a bucket in one thick, white pasty hand and an udder in the other.

"Yeah, he's only interested in your secret project Stassi. It's certainly not your looks." Juliette Moore shared a sneering grin with Dixy. "If it were, everyone knows I'd steal him from you too." The voluptuous woman fluffed her red hair. She obtained her position as an organic chemist assistant at Exbiotics Laboratory, a highly accredited leader of environmental chemistry labs in America, through her uncle. Uncle Felix, an esteemed scientist is a co-owner of the lab.

Stassi didn't need any reminders of her past college days when she was deeply in love with Glenn Dyke, the man she'd planned on marrying. That was until she came upon Glenn and Juliette humping in the middle of her living room floor. Glenn hadn't known she was getting out of school early that day, but her roommate Juliette did.

Glenn swore up and down later that it wasn't his fault. He came by to wait on Stassi and Juliette pounced on him naked as a jaybird, took him by surprise. She had opened the door to his knock wearing nothing but six-inch heels.

His excuse was that he'd just gone brain dead, acted totally on instinct, like a reflex. Men were wired that way to keep the human species thriving. It was a male thing he said. Stassi, as a female without those instincts should still understand it was out of his control. Blame it on testosterone, not him. Besides, he had complained, Stassi wasn't giving it up to him yet, so he needed an outlet for his manly needs.

Right, Stassi thought, freakin' animal instinct like an alley cat. Glenn told her it hadn't meant anything to him, it was just sex, he insisted he was in love with Stassi and she should forgive that one indiscretion. He said this as they were standing outside on a warm autumn day on the vast grounds of Rathburn University and his gaze was glued to a co-ed's swinging hips as she strutted by.

Stassi moved to a studio apartment and chalked up the incident to her motto; you can't trust anyone, ever, and therefore, don't. Completing grad school, leaving Glenn a distant pang in her heart, she took a few years off to earn money, but she had to work with Juliette if she wanted to stay at the prestigious Exbiotics.

Her eye was still pressed against the scope but Stassi wasn't looking into it. She was struggling to keep from throwing the damn thing at Juliette.

She sighed in exasperation, it was her own fault, she should have known better back in those college days. She should have learned from her own home life that humans just didn't have it in themselves to be devoted. Love and honor and bravery were as real as unicorns and elves. No, she would concentrate on her career, put all her love and trust into science. Black and white, cut and dried.

Currently Stassi was working on her PhD in environmental chemistry. Of course she hadn't had sex with their direct supervisor, Brantley Douglas Stoworth III, but her denials fell on deaf ears because he did everything he could to make it appear they were a couple. It was as if he thought if he acted like her lover, it would be so.

"Stassi."

Speaking of the devil, Brant hovered in the doorway of the lab.

Dixy Lee blinked brown cow-eyes at him, her crush on the senior scientist no secret. From a corner in the room, tracer chemist Donovan Crane never moved his attention from the dual computers he studied.

Juliette arched her spine so her breasts would thrust out and up, hopefully attracting Brant's notice. His eyes flicked to her but he trod over to where Stassi was closing her notebook.

Before Brant could speak to Stassi, Juliette sashayed over and moved between them. Running one finger down his blue tie, she cocked her head and peered coyly up at him. "Hey, Boss, we're going to Brontysaurus' outside patio for drinks and ribs after work, you comin' along, honey? It's Friday, it'll be packed, everyone will be there."

Brant's eyes lowered to Juliette, then further to her cleavage then he looked to Stassi. "As long as my sweetie comes, I'll go."

Stassi rolled her green eyes and frowned at him. "Really, Mr. Stoworth, please don't-"

Moving away from Juliette he positioned to stand near Stassi and cut her off. "Call me Brant, Stassi," he scowled at her, then quickly cleared his irritated expression. "I told you we're informal here, call me Brant." He reached his hand out to touch her but she shifted away from it. Hiding his annoyance, he smoothed the top of his wavy, dark blond hair instead.

Without responding to him, Stassi took the slide out from the microscope, set it inside a clear container with a label describing what it was, sealed the container and put it inside a large cooler that took up part of a white wall.

Biting back his chagrin at her basically dismissing him, Brant coughed and said, "I need you to come to Francis' office. He's waiting for us."

Stassi grabbed up her notebook, tucked it in a big pocket of her lab coat and headed for the door. Not expecting her to move so quickly, Brant hastened after her.

"Brant," Juliette called, hurrying to place herself in front of him making him stop abruptly.

He was tall, but so was Juliette, with heels they met almost eye-to-eye. She picked up a lock of her red hair and wove it around her fingers. Large lips painted ruby red like the tight dress she wore under the lab coat tipped up. "You know, I am qualified to work on your…the…yours and Stassi's project. I can sign a nondisclosure contract. I would love to help out."

He slid his right hand on her waist and squeezed. His gaze dipped to where her lab coat parted exposing the front of her dress. A good-looking man with blue eyes, Brant smiled in appreciation. The bodice was shockingly low cut. Speaking to her large breasts, he said, "Maybe later when we're further along, sweetheart, I might talk to Crick."

Insinuating a possible quid pro quo, his hand slid up to just nudge the underside of her breast and he squeezed again. "I'll see you at Brontysaurus." His voice lowered, "We'll see what the night brings, eh?" Then he dropped his hand and followed Stassi out the door.

Brant had to hurry to catch up with her. Stassi was striding quickly down the beige tiled floor and was almost to the elevators. She nodded at several employees that passed by.

Brant reached her just as she stepped into an opening car. The building was two-stories high and set on four acres with more space below ground. Stassi pushed button # 2. Offices, meeting rooms, lockers and the cafeteria were located on the second floor. Reception and some of labs were on the first, the bulk of the labs and storage areas were situated below ground.

Brant hurried inside the elevator just as the doors were closing. He moved to stand close to Stassi, complaining, "Hey, why didn't you wait for me? I'm in the meeting as well."

Crossing her arms over her chest, Stassi stared up at the buttons indicating the floors. She shrugged. "I didn't know you wanted me to wait for you, you only said that Mr. Crick requested my presence."

The elevator stopped on the second floor. Brant stood aside for Stassi to exit first and they moved down the tan carpeted corridor together. Passing several doors, they turned into Francis Crick's office. His assistant, Karine Benton looked up from her desk.

The anteroom had white walls with white and beige carpeting. Clusters of comfortable chairs with blue and beige plaid cushions sharing small tables filled the space. Karine's glass-topped desk with gold curved legs was placed a few feet in front of and to the side of Mr. Crick's interior door. She typed a few words on her computer then waited.

At the ping of the responding email, Karine rose smoothly to her feet and greeted the pair with a polite smile. "Good morning, Brant, Miss Athens." She wore a form-fitting emerald green dress, her golden blonde hair in a neat chignon. Slightly slanted exotic eyes skimmed coolly over the pair. With the figure and posture of a model's, the thirtyish woman nodded regally and paced a model's walk to the door. She knocked then opened the door. "Go right in," she said, gesturing to the office.

Juliette Moore's Uncle Felix was a co-owner of the lab, but Francis Crick held the majority shares, he was really the boss. The man in charge. Brant set his hand on Stassi's lower back and ushered her through the doorway.

Francis Crick, long and lean, wore a dark designer suit, red tie, and expensive tasseled loafers. In his forties, he had a full head of brown hair without a streak of grey. Cryptic eyes regarded the couple through glasses as they moved into the room. He half-stood in greeting and motioned to two chairs that sat in front of his huge desk, then re-seated himself behind his desk. The desk held a landline, three laptops, two cell phones, and piles of papers that were mostly graphs and charts.

Brant waited for Stassi to sit before he claimed the other chair. He watched her cross her shapely legs and glanced over at Francis, who was also staring at her legs. Crick raised a brow to Brant with a hint of a knowing smile. Settling herself, Stassi glanced around the room not seeing the look they shared.

Crick's huge office boasted a large window that overlooked acres of neatly mowed, velvet green grass. Precisely trimmed shrubs bordered a pavered square where two benches sat opposite each other with a small fountain between them. Machines of all sorts lined his office walls, and even with the computer age, filing cabinets took up a corner.

Crick looked to Brant then tendered Stassi a cool smile. "Ms. Athens," he said, negating Brant's insistence that the lab was run informally. "Although you have only been here a short time, I have asked you here so you can fill us," he nodded to Brant, "in on your progress to date. Brant assists you, but you keep your records completely private and under tight lock and key. No one knows your precise data and of course we want no leaks. Even I am not privy to it."

Stassi felt the rapt attention of both men on her. She knew her cheeks were pinking by their dual indulgent expressions. She tugged her notebook from the jacket pocket, but didn't need to open it. "Well, it's, um moving along, however, slowly." She squelched a wince at the flash of anger that crossed Crick's face.

Crick abruptly pushed his chair back and stood up. Leaning over, he set his palms on his desk, his arms rigid, and drew a harsh breath. "Ms. Athens. Our investigators learned of the bacteria created by Talis Falk. Allegedly, the strain he invented can deliberately, from far distances be funneled then leached into oil fields in Venezuela, Saudi Arabia and Alberta as well as other major distributors. Once in the land we're told it changes the chemical makeup of the oil, that when it is introduced to heat, batteries, even electricity, it causes the oil to break down and become useless."

"Yes, sir, I know-"

Crick cut her off. "Whoever owns the formula for this devastation, can make many oil fields obsolete, thereby forcing consumers to only be able to use certain oil. Then this person, or persons, that possesses the bacteria can make it so that only the particular oil fields they own are clear of this bacteria, and thereby, conceivably own the world. The entire damned world."

Stassi shifted in her seat, uncrossed then re-crossed her legs. "Yes, sir, I-"

Crick leaned over further, his stare daggering straight at her, brows a deep V between his angry eyes, he said, "We contacted you when we heard through the grapevine from universities, then via your professor, that he believed you were developing a formula that could counteract the alleged bacteria." He took a breath, Stassi remained silent, since he clearly wasn't giving her a chance to respond.

He went on, "There is only speculation about this bacteria, nothing has been proven, put out there yet to verify this, however," his lips pursed, shoulders hunched, "our sources claim Talis Falk is the driving force behind the creation of this bacteria. If that is so, and we believe it is fact because Falk is a genius scientist but also a frighteningly wicked force to be reckoned with. One of the premier scientists in the world, and one of the wealthiest, and," he took a breath, "one of the most ruthless and violent men on this earth. If anyone was capable of developing this bacteria, it would be him."

"Frank," Brant mumbled and shifted to the edge of his chair. Crick sent him a discouraging glare. Brant folded his hands together, placed them on his thighs and didn't move.

"Ms. Athens," Crick said, whipping his fierce stare back to her. Again, Stassi had to strain to hold back a flinch. "We believe if this bacteria is real, and you have developed a formula that can be added to gas tanks and such that would remedy the bacteria ineffective, there will be dangerous people seeking to have that formula, they can make a fortune off it. We need to set wheels in motion. So, have you created this antidote, or have we made an enormous error in bringing you on board?"

"Um," Stassi opened her mouth, but he cut her off again.

"Is all of this just a- a fairytale? Just a made-up threat to throw the world into a panic?" Crick stood erect, folded his arms aggressively over his chest and beamed his furious gaze at her, "Is any of this supposition real? Was your professor telling the truth?"

She waited to see if he was done or had more to say. It was embarrassing and humiliating to have him ask her a question then not allow her to respond. When he clamped his angry mouth shut and just glowered, daring her to deny or affirm his words, stroking her palms down her skirt as if it needed neatening she cleared her throat.

Brant squirmed awkwardly in his seat, restlessly clawed rigid fingers through his light hair.

"Mr. Crick," she answered, her gaze aimed back at him just as level as his was to her, "we believe it is fully fact that Mr. Falk has developed this particular strain of bacteria. He-"

"I don't want theories or guesswork, Ms. Athens!" he roared, slamming his hand on his desk. Stassi didn't jump but Brant twitched. "I want utter confirmation of this! I brought you here under the assurances of my people that you can defeat this bacteria, that you-"

Stassi stood up, clutching her notebook in one hand. Her voice steady and polite, she cut him off this time, "Mr. Crick, if you won't allow me to speak, then this is a waste of time and I need to get back to work. Excuse me." She half-turned, Brant got up, put his hands out to stop her. "Stassi, wait-"

A hint of amusement in his voice, coming around the side of his desk, Crick said, "Okay, Ms. Athens, you have the floor."

She paused to see if he was going to jump down her throat again. When he merely smiled patiently at her, her stiff stance relaxed and she told him, "It is all true, sir. One of the science professors at Rathburn has a- a- I guess he would be called a mole in Mr. Falk's labs and he was able to sneak a miniscule vial of it out. We tested it, and it does as promised. We put oil in an engine and switched the ignition on and the oil basically evaporated."

Losing some of the tension in his shoulders, Crick adjusted his slipping glasses. The edges of his lips curled up slightly. "Yes, your Professor Chandler is quite shrewd," he said. "I've provided an office and workspace here for him as well. I plan on having him work on reproducing the bacteria. So, if you possessed some of this formula you can recreate it and then we could possibly-" he stopped when he saw her shaking her head.

Long curls of reddish-brown hair swept back-and-forth across her chest, she unconsciously shoved locks behind her back with a flick of her hand. Large eyes as green as crystal glass shone her sincerity. Small yet full lips pulled in with a bump of one slender shoulder. "There wasn't enough. There was barely enough to conduct the experiment. We tried to keep at least a speck, some residue, but the sample was just too small.

"And, it degraded on contact with the oil so we couldn't even separate its elements from the oil's and go that route. After the initial experiment there was basically nothing left to work with. Professor Chandler will have to start from scratch. That will take years, if ever, no one outside of Mr. Falk knows the formula. Plus, that tiny sample wasn't enough to conduct full experiments and studies to solidify the full comprehensive, accurate results of the product."

Crick opened his mouth to cut in but she compulsively shoved her hair back again and kept speaking. "We need to discover any effects of other things than just the oil, such as the danger to the drinking water supply in those areas it contaminates, destruction of the land, long term effects of the pollution and how to combat that. You see, there are many things that need further investigation."

Crick looked to Brant for any confirmation of what she said. Brant turned his palms up. "I spoke with the professor and the other chemists working the initial experiment and they corroborate what she's telling us. I was going to tell you this at our afternoon meeting but you requested this meeting now."

Crick's attention back to Stassi, he said, "It sounds like I was wise to jump the gun and bring you all on board so quickly before waiting for any verification of any of this." At Brant's nod, Crick said to Stassi, "Then this mole can obtain a larger sample for us to-"

Shaking her head, Stassi told him, "Not at the moment. It seems this…person, has disappeared. No one has heard from him since a few days after he slipped Professor Chandler the sample."

His arms crossed, Crick stroked his chin in contemplation. He said to Brant, "He stole from Talis Falk. Falk would not hesitate to…dispose of him."

Stassi's eyes rounded. "You mean he had him arrested?"

Both men turned to her with that indulgent look again. Brant said, "No, honey, he means he had him killed."

The color drained from Stassi's face, and Crick snapped at Brant, "You idiot. She doesn't need to know that shit."

"Are we all in danger, Mr. Crick?" Stassi's hand pressed over her mouth.

His face softened at the sudden fear lancing through Stassi's voice. "No dear, of course not. The person worked for Falk and double-crossed him. An unforgiving man, Falk is known for…ah, let's say, taking matters into his own hands. He does not tolerate people stealing from him."

Brant agreed. "Or anything else. Falk delivers swift punishment. They found that guy," he looked to Crick, "you remember, the one who slept with Falk's woman de jour, in a drainage ditch. The woman's torso has never been found but her head was-"

"Brant, shut up!" Crick bellowed, his face darkening with ire. He held a hand out to Stassi, when she ignored it he reached out and grasped her hand and held it. With a gentle smile, his voice warm, he told her, "We have nothing to worry about, you are safe. Falk wouldn't have any reason to come after any of us. We haven't done him any wrong," the word *yet* hung at the end of his sentence.

"But, Mr. Crick," Stassi hoped the anxious fret was not audible, "what about when the antidote is-"

"All right," Crick spoke sternly, the subject was closed. "That's settled. Now, speaking of the antidote, onto your part. Your professor advised that you were working on the formula that could destroy the bacteria." He held up a hand as she started to speak. "No, not working on, he said you were on the verge of completing the formula. That's why we brought you here. If all this is real, true fact, you will provide us with it as quickly as possible. Well?" His brows arched in confrontation. He straightened his lean shoulders and tugged at the cuffs on his suit.

Holding her notebook to her chest, Stassi replied carefully, "That is true. I believe I can complete the formula we've named BE-x, but I need more time."

"BE-x?" Brant inclined his head to Stassi.

Stassi gave him a slim smile. "Yes. Bacteria Eating Extract. The letters also denote its chemical makeup."

Brant laughed. "It's also close to the name of our lab, Exbiotics. Was that deliberate?" he asked with a smile to Stassi.

She returned his smile but shook her head. "Just a coincidence. When I determined the chemical makeup I worked up the name to match both the action of the formula and the letters. But it all should tie nicely together when some form of marketing is created."

Crick studied the young woman as she turned back to face him. "Your professor told me that you are brilliant. You entered college at a young age and excelled in the sciences. More so, he told me you completed your master's in half the average time with Honors. He said he challenged you with validating the bacteria and then developing a counteragent to the bacteria as soon as he'd learned of it."

Stassi blushed, she didn't reply but inclined her head slightly at the compliment her professor had stated to Crick.

"Your professor said that your initial trials astonished him. But that you needed more time to complete the formula, but, he felt you would be successful. When I spoke with him you hadn't yet validated that the bacteria was 100% real." He didn't tell her that the professor wanted a deal. He wanted a percentage of what the antidote would bring in. Because Stassi was working for the lab she would only receive a wage because the formula belonged to Exbiotics.

His face pinched in consternation. Smoothing his expression, Crick straightened his glasses with a finger and thumb on the frame of one lens. Peering at her through the specs, he inquired with suspicion, "Since you were only able to prove the bacteria existed but not able to replicate it, how are you able to create the antidote?"

Stassi's shoulders relaxed a smidge. With zero boasting she told him, "I worked with the substance long enough to get a grasp on how it destroyed the oil that I believe I can figure out how to counter-activate it. There are principles, you know."

Taking in the sincerity of her words, under hooded lids Crick silently observed Stassi for a minute. When he had first met her, he didn't believe such a beautiful package could hold such a brain. Sexist, yes, so what? And just like Brant, he'd wanted a piece of her.

So far he hadn't had the opportunity to get near her, be alone where he could press his suit. He was growing tired of Devon his current mistress. He decided Stassi would make a perfect, younger replacement for Devon.

Talk about launch a thousand ships, the cliché notwithstanding; Anastasia Athens could launch a million rockets. She was the type of woman men fought duels over. No way a classic beauty, that would be boring, no, her face was wonderfully mesmerizing.

Surprisingly, as quiet and unassuming as she was she had a backbone, and sass. She was no shrinking violet when riled. That was hot. He'd heard through staff gossip that she had no interest in male companionship. She wasn't lesbian, she just did not want to get involved with anyone.

He continued surreptitiously examining her. Although she went to lengths to hide it, the girl rocked a body made for sin, her green eyes were tantalizingly gorgeous, but they turned ice-cold in a snap and shut a man right down. But Francis Crick wasn't just any man.

Chapter Three

Stassi planned on grabbing a quick drink to appease Mr. Crick who had been adamant about her taking a dinner break and joining the rest of the staff at Brontysaurus. There was a crowd congregated outside behind the restaurant. Twinkly lights strung through the trees and music playing in the background made the courtyard festive. The patio was teeming with beer-chugging, rib gnawing, guffawing tipsy people.

Tangy barbecued ribs and pungent spicy wings sifted up her nose and rumbled her empty stomach. She had worked through lunch again. Stassi made her way through the boisterous crowd to the bar. The two bartenders, one male the other female were filling glasses with dexterity and laughing with the customers. The male bartender caught Stassi's small wave and came right over.

"What can I get ya, sweetie?" In his late twenties, his gaze roved down Stassi's figure and back up bringing an admiring grin to his surfer boy handsome face. He set a cocktail napkin in front of her.

Nearing winter in northern Nevada, the air was crisp but with the grills steaming and the crowd, Stassi's short-waisted leather jacket was warm enough. She'd changed into jeans, a long-sleeved t-shirt and ankle boots with a narrow two-inch heel to blend in. Even with her body hidden under the jacket and her long hair tied back in a thick braid, she still drew most men's notice. Some just discreet brief glances, others tracked her every move.

"Um, just a cola, please." Stassi smiled politely and opened her purse.

"Sure thing, babe," the bartender replied, shooting her a cheeky wink. He was back in seconds with a glass filled with soda and ice. He set it and a straw in front of her. "That's three and a quarter bucks, honey."

Stassi frowned at his honey, sweetie, baby tags, but knew he would just laugh off her rebuke, and only do it more if she complained. "Thanks." She nodded and set four, one-dollar bills on the bar. Removing the paper from the straw, she plunked it in the glass then took a sip.

Picking up her drink, she strolled away from the bar and searched the patio. "Great," she muttered. Brant was sitting with a group at a huge round table and waving like a madman at her. He was her boss, she could hardly blow him off. She threaded through the partying crowd to his table.

"Hey, Stassi," Brant greeted her, standing up. He snagged a chair from another table and motioned the people on his right to move over to make space for her. "Glad you made it. Here, take a seat," he gestured to the chair.

Stassi set her glass on the wood-topped table and sat down on the chair he offered. Brant grinned ear-to-ear and plopped down beside her. A sturdy wind rifled through and everyone made mad dashes to grab flying napkins. Stassi brushed at loose tendrils that dallied over her face.

Juliette Moore, Dixy Lee, Donovan Crane, chemists Jody Ricketts, Troy Marshall, Charlie Shaw, and admin assistant Valentina King filled out the table. Everyone greeted her except Juliette who stuck her nose in the air and nudged her chair closer to Brant's other side. The table was littered with gooey ribs, chicken wings, layered cheesy nachos, fries, onion rings, drinks, stacks of napkins, and bowls brimming with gnawed bones.

"So," his lids thick and low over bleary eyes, Troy Marshall looked like he'd been at the restaurant for a while, dark hair messy and needing a trim, he slurred, "how's the big secret, ah, experiment going?"

Jody Ricketts poked him in the arm with her skinny elbow, her hands drenched in barbeque sauce. "It's called a secret for a reason, dope. You know she can't talk about it." Inelegantly, she licked her sticky fingers one-by-one.

His hand wrapped around a mug of beer, Troy shrugged. "How 'bout a little hint, Stas babe? Wassa big deal anyhow?"

Brant shifted his chair nearer to Stassi's and told her, "Ignore him, honey, he knows the project is confidential. Listen," he laid his arm around the back of her chair. Lowering his voice to a whisper, he leaned close to her ear, and said, "As soon as you're done why don't we go somewhere more…quiet. Ah, my place has a great view of Venice Peak."

A server interrupted him to take Stassi's order.

As she gave her order of a shrimp po'boy and macaroni salad, she subtly inched her chair a hitch away from Brant.

On his other side, Juliette set her hand on Brant's arm to draw his attention to her. Thankfully, she kept him engaged in flirtatious conversation while Stassi quickly gobbled her dinner.

"Hey, Stas."

Stassi turned to Valentina's warm smile. Val's lush, chestnut brown curls waved over her slightly plump shoulders, round brown eyes sparkled with mirth.

"Hi, Val." Stassi returned the friendly smile. "How's your little sister doing?" She took a bite of her sandwich.

Val lifted her beer, took a healthy sip, set it down and scrutinized the giant burger in front of her. Removing the top bun, she replied, "She's much better, Stas, thanks for asking. She appreciated the flowers you sent her. How are things with you? I heard you had a meeting with Mr. Crick earlier." She squeezed a glob of ketchup on the burger and replaced the bun. Picking up the burger with both hands, she opened her mouth super wide to chomp off a hunk of it.

Stassi shot Juliette and Dixy a glare. Tattletales. The staff spent so many hours at the lab most of their lives revolved around it so gossip was rife, the dirtier the better. Nodding, she stuck a fork in her macaroni salad. "Yes, he was checking on my progress."

Speaking while chewing, Val asked, "What about your family, Stas? You always ask about ours but never share anything about yours. Your face gets all pinched and grim whenever anyone mentions them and you change the subject." She leaned in and said quietly, "It's evident that you had a hard time of it. I'm a good listener," she hinted.

Stassi watched Valentina swallow the burger and stuff several ketchup-laden fries in her mouth. "There's nothing to tell, Val, let it go, okay?"

"Ha, the typical sexually abusive childhood," Donovan Crane tossed in with a sneer of disgust. "You're just another statistic." Like his name, he had a long thin neck. He twitched nerdy black-framed glasses up a long blade of a nose and reached for a stacked nacho with tapered fingers. Opening his thin lips wide to take a bite of the nacho, it splintered when he crunched it and a gunk of guacamole spurted out landing in a splotch on his white shirt that was buttoned up to his rangy jaw. He didn't notice it and crunched on.

Stassi felt her neck burn. She thought he was a friend. Although Stassi was a noted loner, whenever they worked very late nights together they shared burgers and beers at The Bull, the sports bar down the street.

He taught her about football and she vicariously lived his life through his tales of growing up. He had a large, close-knit family that nosed into his business. His older sisters teased him, and his mom bossed him around while setting him up on blind dates with all her friends' daughters and nieces.

He complained, but Stassi would have given anything to have a nice normal family that cared about her. She blasted out without thinking, "If you must know, my dad was a knockdown, drag out bully who only spoke to me with his fists."

"Oh honey," Val said softly.

The biggest geek of the group, his hollowed cheeks colored slightly in guilt, Donovan tendered in his defense, "You never said anything about that to me. Didn't your ma or whatever step in?" He picked jalapeños off another nacho dropping them on the platter then lifted the nacho off the plate, a string of cheese clung to the plate all the way to his open mouth.

"Huh." Stassi snorted, the deeply buried rage bubbled, threatening to rise and burn like acid up her throat. "No. My ma ran and hid in the bedroom when he beat me, my older brother always left the house, the coward. He joined the army at 16. I hate them both, I haven't seen or spoken to my mother or brother in close to ten years." Her lips compressed tightly to hold the rage down, it wanted to boil over, gouge out more inner scars.

Val asked softly, "Your dad? Is he still around?"

The rage boiled hotter, scalding her esophagus, shrinking the hole where her heart should be making it tinier and tinier. Her eyes glazed with repressed memories, Stassi spoke haltingly, didn't want the words to come out, but they had a mind of their own and fought to break free of the cage she'd locked them in long ago. "On my fifteenth birthday, my father died of a heart attack while screwing his mistress in a hotel room. My brother was in the Army and I couldn't bear to look at my mother who never stood up for me. Even after my teacher-" She broke off, and sucked in air.

What the heck had she just done? She'd put that part of her life behind her. They hadn't stood up for her, interfered, called the police on her father, nothing then, she sure as hell didn't need them now. After her father died, her mother became ill and Stassi had gone to live with an aunt in Utah where she stayed until she left for college at an early age. She didn't need to think about her family. And she didn't need these people's pity or lurid interest.

Before she could be questioned further, she said quickly to Charlie Shaw, "Charlie, how's the baby? And Melinda? You guys getting any sleep?"

Charlie blinked at her, he was on the phone but he grinned at Stassi.

Everyone at the table paused, forks raised, eyes darting around at each other, seeing her mortification, letting the subject go, they averted their gazes from her blatant pain.

Oblivious to what had just occurred, Charlie hung up his phone. He had that new dad happy, dazed, sleepy look about him. His shirt was buttoned wrong and there was what looked like baby drool on the collar.

He pushed his poker-straight light brown hair back but it flopped back over his eyes, he grinned. "Need a haircut, right? Cody seems to eat little but poops a lot. Looks just like me, gonna be a football player I'm sure." Husky and cheerful, the chemist smiled proudly. "Melinda is wonderful. She's a trooper, gonna be a wonderful mother. *Is* a wonderful mother."

"You guys sound happy," Stassi said with affection. She'd known Charlie from study groups in college. He was the kind of guy who gave you the shirt off his back, and his pants and shoes too if you needed them. Everyone says call him in the middle of the night for an emergency and he'd be there for you in a blink. Stassi had attended their wedding two years ago.

Charlie nodded then yawned. "Yeah, we sure are. We are so blessed." He poured a packet of sugar in his coffee and stirred it with a spoon. "You coming to the Christening and the after party? We sent you an invite." He set the spoon on the saucer.

Speaking through a mouthful of shrimp and mayo, Stassi nodded, "Wouldn't miss it."

"So," Charlie started, took a sip of his hot coffee, then blew on it. "What about your love life? Anything hot going on with you? You bringing a plus one?"

Setting her sandwich down, Stassi shook her head.

"No," Valentina answered for her, "she's allergic to men. Besides, working 16 hour days, she has no time for dating." She curled her lip at Stassi then winked.

"Last time I set her up on a blind date, well, she wasn't aware it was a date. As soon as she started counting the guests, boy-girl-boy-girl, it dawned on her. Never seen someone eat so fast and have a 'sudden emergency' she had to leave for. But," she waggled a finger at Stassi who was rolling her eyes. "I'm not giving up, count on that."

Rolling her eyes again, Stassi begged in fun, "Shoot me now, someone, please."

Charlie threw his arm around her and gave her a hug. "Come on, Stas, take a leap. Look how happy Melinda and I are. There's a good guy out there for you."

Stassi patted his husky chest. "I think you were the last one and Melinda got you, so, I'll live happily ever after on my own."

"Alone?" Valentina asked with wide eyes, ketchup dribbled down her chin.

Stassi wiped her lips daintily with a napkin. Folding then setting the napkin on her plate she said with a shrug, "I'll get a dog."

Charlie chuckled. "You don't have time for a dog. They need attention, walking, feeding, you're never around long enough to take care of a dog."

"Okay." Stassi sighed with amusement. "I'll get a cat. Cats don't like people, they don't require company and a lot of work."

"Hey!" Miffed, Donovan Crane stated firmly, "I have cats. They're great, loving, snuggling, petting-"

"Cats?" Troy sneered with disbelief, his tongue sticking out. "How many cats you got?"

Donovan's nerdy neck turned red. He answered with a sheepish toss to his head, "Uh, five."

"Five? You have five cats in your tiny apartment?" Troy's drunken splutter expressed how preposterous he felt about the idea. The two men then engaged in a heated discussion about the merits of dogs vs cats.

Conversation flowed, Stassi made sure she was always chatting with someone to dissuade Brant's unwanted attention. Fortunately, Juliette was great at garnering most males' interest.

When Brant and Juliette were occupied, their heads close, their whispers growing heavily flirtatious, Stassi got up, waved silently to the group at the table who were now engaged with their own conversations, and she hurried off wending her way through the bustling guests and harried servers.

She found her server, paid her bill, and started to walk around the side of the building to go out front where she parked her car, but the way was blocked by what appeared to be a bachelor's party getting rolling. A jostling band of men joked and slapped each other on the back. She quickly swerved and hustled to go around the other side. An alley separated the restaurant from a shop that was closed for the night.

Stassi paused at the neck of the alley, unsure if it was wise to venture into the dim corridor. The sun was lowering rapidly and the alley would be darker. Creatures lurk in the dark.

Shaking her head and straightening her shoulders, she laughed. "Oh grow up, Stas, girl, it's just an alley. You watch too many horror movies."

Still, she moved quickly and cautiously, her ankle boots tapping on the asphalt she made her way down the dirty clammy alleyway.

Almost to the end, she heard someone cry out. She paused. Should she stop? Was it safe? Hearing the cry again, she knew she'd have to see if someone was in trouble. The alley forked and Stassi found herself moving quietly boxed in on both sides with brick.

Following the sounds of distress, she reached the end of the side alley, and saw there was yet another branch. And that's where the noise was coming from.

Stassi peered into the dimness, her hand resting on a cold brick of a moldy wall and leaned in. It smelled musty and of rotting garbage. "Maybe it's just a couple of noisy lovers looking for priva-" Her gasp sounded like a cymbal clash in her ears. Way down the end of the alley, Stassi could just make out two men in the gloom. One man was sitting on the ground, slumped against a wall, and he was begging.

"Please, man, no more, *please*," he wailed. The other man was crouched in front of him bashing his fists into the man's face. The attacker looked like he could crush a rock in one hand. In this case, it was a man's face, and he was making it look like a crushed rock.

In a thick, scary accent, the assailant commanded, "Tell me, Jasper, tell me where he is," and he pulled a knife from his boot and slashed a shallow slice across the man's neck. The man screamed and so did Stassi. Both men looked up at her.

Slapping a hand over her mouth, Stassi turned and ran.

The man with the knife shouted, "No! Wait!" Jabbing the blade into the man's shoulder, the assailant barked, "Tell me now or die!" The victim cried and burbled out an address through bloody broken teeth.

The attacker jumped to his feet. "Goddammit," he cursed, then yelled down the alley, "get back here, dammit!" He slammed his fist into Jasper's head knocking him out cold. He rolled him onto his belly and snapped plastic tie cuffs on his wrists, then sped after the witness.

Hurtling around a corner, Stassi pulled her phone from her pocket and while running, dialed 911. "Help! Help!" she shrieked into the phone. "A man is killing another man!" The dispatcher told her to calm down and tell him where she was.

"At-at-at," Stassi huffed and tore back down original alleyway. Hearing the man's feet pounding after her, she shouted, "The east- uh, yeah, east side of-of the Brontysaurus rest- restaurant, hurry!" She raced to the restaurant looking for people, hoping the man would see other people around and leave her alone. But no, just as her foot hit the parking lot, her arm was grabbed and she was hauled back, hard.

So hard she fell into what felt like a granite wall. It was a chest of steel, two hands clutched her arms and steadied her. Her purse crossed over the front of her slapped into her hip.

"Let me go!" she screamed. Kicking at his shins, Stassi kept screaming. Trying to twist out of his grip, she continued kicking at him but he dodged her feet and her knee that jerked up between his legs.

"Listen, girl," he huffed with a wince as her shoe connected with his shin. He still held the knife in one hand he'd wrapped around her arm. In that same scary accent he ordered, "Stop, let me explain. You can't call the cops, I need to-"

Sirens came wailing down the street. The police station was located near to the restaurant. "Oh fuck, damn," he cursed, his grip was crushing her arms.

"You're caught now, you- you hoodlum!" Stassi struggled in his grip.

"Shit," he spat, "I can't go to jail, you dumb bitch," he released her and turned to run, and came to a dead halt. Two men were standing with guns aimed at him. His hands shot up by his shoulders. "Wait, I have to go, it's a matter of life or death, I need to-"

"You ain't goin' nowhere, mister, the cops are here." One of the armed men turned to Stassi, "You okay, there, miss?"

Quivering like shaken jelly, Stassi wrapped her arms around her body and nodded. A bit breathy, she managed to get out, "Yes, yes, thank you, thank you so much, you're so brave," gratefully she praised her rescuers.

"You stupid, interfering broad," the man with the knife cursed at her. "You're gonna be so fucking sorry, I'm gonna make you pay," he swore oaths in a foreign language.

Roaring engines sounded then several doors banged closed and loud footsteps hit the pavement as police officers rushed up to them. One of them uttered in a low shout, "What's going on?" He ordered the men with the guns," Put them down, boys, get on the ground, right now." The other officers had their weapons drawn. "You too, put the knife down," one of the cops ordered the attacker.

"Listen," the man with the knife said, "I can explain-"

"Down, drop the knife and get on the ground!" the officer shouted with his gun aimed at him. "Everyone, down on the ground!" He said to Stassi, "You, ma'am, step over to that car," he nodded towards one of the police vehicles parked close to them.

"Oh, okay," she murmured gratefully and hustled to do as he said, thankful she didn't have to lie down on the dirty cold tar.

Twenty minutes later, the police had Stassi's and the two rescuers' statements and released them. They had handcuffed and placed the man with the knife in the back of one of the police cars. Stassi tried not to look at him while she was explaining what happened.

The man was frightening, even without witnessing him beating that poor guy in the alley, he had a harsh accent and a rough, dangerous look about him. And his glare at Stassi promised a deadly end if he ever got his hands on her.

Two of the cops raced off to where she said the victim had been being beaten by the man with the knife. She didn't look at him, but she could feel his menacing glower burning threats into the back of her neck. She resisted the urge to raise her hand to cover her neck.

By the time they were done and the man with the knife was taken away, the lab staff had joined the crowd congregated at the scene. They gathered around her asking what happened.

As she told them the story, Brant reached out to Stassi and took one of her cold hands. Rubbing it to warm it, he said, "I'll see you safely home, Stassi."

Shaking her head, Stassi mumbled, "No, I'm fine. I'm done here, I'll go to my car." She tugged on her hand but he wouldn't let it go.

"No, Stassi, you're shaken up, you've had a fright, hell, you're still trembling. I'll take you-"

She wrenched her hand free and dug into her purse for her keys. "No, I'm fine," she said firmly, "thank you, Mr. Stoworth." As she spoke, Juliette snaked up and slung her arm through one of Brant's arms. She sniffed her disdain at Stassi. "She said she's okay, Brant, come on, you said no one could see us if we were on the balcony while we-"

"Shut up, Julie," Brant swung on her with a growl. At that moment, Stassi spun and hurried off to her car.

Chapter Four

Stassi could practically feel them breathing down her neck. If Brant wasn't hovering, then it was Mr. Crick frequently passing by her station. The lab was so big and spread out that numerous studies and experiments were ongoing at all times. Each senior chemist had his or her own office, all the others had assigned cubicles. Stassi seldom sat in her cubicle. She had an urgent, earth-shattering solution to complete that kept her active on her feet and in the actual laboratories.

She was standing in front of one of the centrifuges, the alarm was about to beep announcing its completion although it was still spinning. Suddenly she felt heavy hands land on her shoulders and lips pressing against her temple.

"Stassi," Brant whispered in her ear, "how about we grab some dinner together in a few?"

She jumped at this touch but he tightened his fingers. Last thing she needed was for anyone to see her in an amorous clutch with her boss. First, they'd confirm she did sleep with him or Mr. Crick or both to get her position, and she would never be taken seriously again, and secondly, there were likely rules against fraternizations between staff and subordinates. Of course that wasn't stopping Juliette from pursuing Brant, or Brant from hitting on Stassi.

Bristling, Stassi plucked his fingers off her shoulders and quickly stepped out of his reach. "Please, Mr. Stoworth, I've asked you not to touch me and ask me out. I am here to do a job, not to be fooling around with my supervisor." She pivoted and strode quickly out of the lab and down the hall to where her cube was located.

"Aw, come on, Stas, don't be so unfriendly." Brant hurried after her.

Her long curls bouncing on her back, her lab coat flapping, she kept walking until she entered the area where her cubicle was grouped with others in the huge room with only a few windows.

"Stas-"

"Oh my gosh!" Stassi exclaimed in shock. She came to a hard halt at the opening to her cube. Drawers were open and hanging askew, papers were scattered on her desk and the floor, even on her chair. "What on earth," she bemoaned, her hand went to her throat as she gawked at the mess.

"Stassi, I only wanted to- what the hell?" Brant stopped beside her. "You cleaning house or something?"

Astonishment rang through her voice, "No, I didn't do this. Someone has broken into my locked drawers," she looked up at the row of cabinets lining the low wall that fenced her space, "and the cabinets." Feverishly she glanced around, "It's not here, it's gone," she proclaimed in dismay.

"What? What's gone?"

Stassi moved inside the cubicle pulling open crooked drawers that had been pried open, to peer inside. She checked inside each one, and then the cabinets then under the desk. Surprisingly her purse was in the drawer she'd left it in. She pulled it out and rummaged through it to see if anything was missing. Nothing had been taken. She continued searching the small space.

His hands on his hips, Brant hovered watching her in puzzlement. "Stassi, what are you looking for?"

She wiped her sleeve across her eyes and turned to him, her eyes stunned. "My computer. My laptop is gone."

Brant frowned and glanced around like she had. "Are you sure it was here? Maybe you took it to the lab, or left it home?"

Shaking her head vehemently, Stassi denied this. "No, no, I always leave it here and lock it in a drawer when I'm working." She spun still looking for the computer as if it would suddenly materialize on her desk where she left it.

"Fuck," Brant cussed, pulling out his phone. "I'll call security." He spoke into the phone as Stassi, still stunned stared at her trashed cubicle.

They waited off to the side as two security officers searched the small area but didn't turn up anything that could point to who would have done such a thing. Both male officers were indistinguishable from each other, both in their twenties, clean shaven, trimmed hair under caps, brown uniforms.

One of the guards stepped over to where Stassi and Brant waited. "Miss," he said politely, his gaze flashed down her body and quickly back up. "We'll ask around, see if anyone saw anything, there aren't any cameras here, just outside the building. No one, ah, expects this sort of thing, it's never happened before." Pulling his cap off he scratched his head perplexed, the corner of his mouth tugged in. "We'll need Mr. Crick's permission to search other staffs' desks and lockers."

Brant and Stassi stood nodding in anxious bewilderment.

"Well," the guard said, "if we come up with anything we'll be sure to let you know. If you think of anything, or anyone that could have done this, contact us right away. I'll speak with Mr. Crick about calling the police to make a formal theft report. In case they want to take fingerprints, you should probably not go back in the office or touch anything else." He and the other guard left.

"Stassi, it's late, we might as well leave. I'll take you to dinner, help you calm down." Brant went to cup her elbow to lead her out of the room.

She pulled her arm away. "No, I'm going to remove my solutions from the centrifuge, lock them up and go home." She turned towards the exit.

"Seriously, honey, you're shaking like crazy, you are in no condition to drive. I'll drive you home-" he was talking to air, she was already halfway across the room. He chased after her, but gave up when she hit the stairs to go down to the labs.

After she locked her work up, Stassi drove towards her apartment as if in a trance, murmuring disconcertedly, "Why would someone do that?" She pondered all sorts of theories all the way home. Everyone at the lab was issued a laptop, why would someone need to take hers?

Besides, it was right on the desk, why break into and rifle the drawers and take nothing else? Her notes on the work she was doing were encrypted and in her own personal code. It would be useless for someone to try to break into the computer to garner the information.

Parking in her assigned spot, the company had paid to move her to Nevada when they brought her on since she lived Texas. People commented on her faint accent. It was a soft twang, she worked to erase it, but it was still discernable. She wearily dragged her feet up the stairs to her apartment.

Opening her purse, she realized her hands were still trembling. It was shocking, someone breaking in and going through her things. People say they feel violated, that's exactly how she felt. Especially since it was undoubtedly someone that worked at the lab. Maybe someone she knew. There were seldom visitors, and they would be continuously escorted.

It was a large lab with a lot of employees, since Stassi stuck to her station she seldom met anyone else except the other chemists that worked in her area. There was a cafeteria but she generally ate a sandwich while working.

Sticking the key in the door, she sighed, there was so much more work she could have gotten done at the lab, she wondered out loud, "Was someone trying to steal my work, or was it someone like…Juliette who just wanted to scare me, annoy me, cause me some trouble?" Brow furrowing when she realized the key wasn't opening the lock, she looked down and saw it had been broken.

"What…" She pushed the door open and stepped inside, and gasped. Her apartment looked like her cubicle had, ransacked. Furniture was moved around, some slashed, drawers pulled out and tossed all over, items dumped on the floor. "Oh, no," she cried, alarmed at the sight of her wrecked living room. Stassi staggered against the wall, then the thought that the perpetrator might still be inside made her hurry back outside and call the police.

After the police came, took her statement, crime scene techs had finished examining the apartment, a policewoman said to her, "We're done for now. You said you didn't notice anything is missing. Your manager said tomorrow he'll put a new lock on the door. The offender probably won't return, but you should stay with a friend for at least tonight. Your manager told me there are no surveillance cameras, and we spoke with everyone in the complex and no one saw anything amiss, no strangers skulking about, no one near your apartment, so they claimed. If we come up with anything on the prints, or whatever, someone will give you a call."

Stassi had dashed in and packed an overnight bag while the police were still present. She did not want to be alone in the apartment. Since she basically had no friends except Charlie and Valentina from work, she stayed in a hotel. Charlie had a new baby, she couldn't impose on them, and Valentina sort of had a revolving door with men.

Although on the plump side, the pretty brunette had no trouble picking up a man. Before Stassi had left the restaurant she noticed Val gazing coyly over at the table next to them. A cute guy was smiling broadly at her. No, Val would be busy tonight, Stassi would not intrude.

Chapter Five

After a restless night in a stark hotel room, Stassi made the trek back to begin straightening up her apartment. A shiny new lock was on the door, the manager gave her new keys. He apologized up and down but the deed was done.

She worked like a drone all weekend, throwing out damaged chair cushions and putting things back in place. At least the drawers had only been tossed, not broken. She put everything back where it belonged. Normally she would have been at the lab, but the apartment had to be dealt with. The apartment was plain, utilitarian that's it. Furnished with motel-like pieces, walls off-white, carpet brown. Small kitchen, small bedroom, which was all fine as she spent very little time there.

A creepy feeling tickled across her shoulders as she worked. It felt like she wasn't quite alone. No one could see her inside the building, but still… Retrieving a broom and dustpan, she scolded herself for being nervous. *Yeah, but, maybe my instincts are right*, she thought. Bolstering her instincts she said, "I feared the alley and there was trouble there after all. First my cubical and now my apartment, what are they looking for?" Keeping the curtains drawn and the doors locked while she worked didn't take the edge off the disturbing feeling that someone was watching her. Could it be that knife-wielding attacker prowling around waiting to pay her back?

Monday morning, before she could get started, Stassi was summoned to Mr. Crick's office. Unnerved by the break-ins, her heart raced, now another meeting with Mr. Crick. It didn't bode well for the beginning of a new week. Then she brightened, maybe they caught the person who ransacked her belongings!

As soon as Stassi entered the reception area to Crick's office, his PA Karine Benton lifted her phone and pushed a button with a manicured nail. She spoke quietly into the phone and then did as before, got up, paced her model's walk the few feet past her desk.

Knocking softly on Crick's office door, she opened it and nodded for Stassi to pass through. Today Karine wore powder blue satin that hugged her lithe figure, blonde locks in the regular chignon, makeup perfect, face and figure flawless, she looked like she should be on the arm of a dashing movie star.

Feeling plain and grubby after watching Karine's svelte saunter to the door and back to her desk, as she stepped over the threshold, Stassi saw that Brant was present.

Both men stood as she entered. Tucking her hands in the deep pockets of the lab coat, Stassi looked from one man to the other. Their expressions were twin blanks, giving nothing away. They didn't appear to be about to tell her good news. She took the initiative and spoke first, "Sir, you asked for me?"

The two men shared an unreadable glance before Crick cleared his throat. He gestured to one of the four leather chairs in a semi-circle around a marble coffee table. His office was designed more as a CEO of a prestigious Wall Street firm rather than of a conservative laboratory. The large office bedecked with expensive furnishings, wood borders trimmed in ornate detailing, Turkish rugs, and premium masterpieces decorating the walls of antique white with silver embellishment wallpaper, fit the man who dressed and acted like a Rockefeller.

"Have a seat," Mr. Crick told her. His tone indicated she'd need to sit down for what he had to say.

Stassi glanced at Brant, but he was staring at the floor. "Okay," she said. A polite smile pinned to her face, she smoothed the skirt and lab coat under her as she sat in the chair Crick indicated. Perching on the edge of the cushioned leather seat, her spine erect, she forced herself not to fidget. A strand of hair escaped from the braid tickled the side of her face, she folded her hands in her lap to keep from tucking it behind her ear.

"Ah," Crick murmured, moved to stand in front of her and crossed his arms. Off to the side, Brant crossed his arms then realizing they looked like an intimidating pair of bouncers, he moved to set his hands on his hips. The longer they stalled, the more Stassi's gut tightened.

Clearing his throat again, Crick spoke evenly, "Your, ah, Professor, Connor Chandler, well he…" Crick trailed off.

Brant tugged at the knot of his tie that bumped with his audible swallow.

"Yes?" Her cinnamon brows arched with the question. A shade of trepidation primed with curiosity trickled up her spine.

Crick just threw it out there. "Chandler had gone missing. We weren't aware of it until late last night." His eyes flicked to Brant then back to Stassi. "Apparently, a few days before your office was ransacked, Chandler's was too but he didn't report it until a week ago, and then he vanished."

Blinking rapidly, Stassi asked, "Did anyone check to see if he went on vacation, maybe he ran off with a new girlfriend, he's been known to do that. I don't see what all the-"

"He's dead," Brant blurted out. He flinched at the dark look Crick shot him.

Stassi leaped to her feet. "What?" she spouted. "I don't understand. You just said he was missing?"

"Calm down, dear," Crick said, making a lowering motion with his palms. "He was missing for several days, but he was found by a kayaker paddling down the Four-Paw River in one of the most remote areas in the county."

"Found? He was found, so he's okay then?" Stassi queried, grasping at the hope, but Crick's face was grim as he shook his head.

"No," he told her, his voice stoic. "I said he's dead. He is dead. His body was found on a bank of the river. Appears he was likely tossed off a bridge at some point and dragged down the river by the rough current. The river thinned and grew shallow in an area and the body was left on the shore."

Looking from Crick to Brant, disordered by the news, Stassi asked, "An accident? Was he hiking and fell-"

"No, Stassi," Brant responded. "He was murdered. Tortured to hell first then sliced open, he was-"

"For God's sake, man, shut the hell up. She doesn't need to know the damned details," Crick barked in irritation at Brant. Red flushed up Brant's neck, he swallowed hard and shut his mouth.

"Murdered!" Stassi cried. Clutching her hands together she raised them to her chest, these kinds of things didn't happen to people she knew. "It can't be, are you sure?"

Crick nodded soberly, his voice somber he said definitively, "Yes, honey, they are sure. A detective came here earlier to ask questions, see if we knew of anyone who would want to hurt the professor. There's an article on it in the local paper. I assume you don't take the paper that's why we're telling you before you see it on the news or the net."

"Di- did he drown? Maybe he just accidentally fell-"

"No, the autopsy indicated he'd been cut. There were blade makes in his bones, they said-"

"Brant, for fuck's sake, man," Crick shouted.

"What?" Brant turned a frown to his superior. "It's all in the article."

Crick shook his head at him to tell him to zip it.

Her eyes wide as tears spilled, mouth open, Stassi turned to Brant, he nodded grimly. Then she whispered, "Oh my, does it have anything to do with…us? The formulas?"

Crick set a hand briefly on her arm in comfort, sighed heavily. "We don't know. The police are looking into it. They said they'd keep us up to date with the investigation."

Wrapping her arms around her waist, Stassi paced in a circle, swiping at her wet eyes.

"Listen, Miss Athens," Crick's voice strengthened as he watched her despair. "I know you were relatively close with Chandler."

"Yes," she sniffed, agreeing. "I've worked with him for a while. But," her head rose as thoughts tumbled around in her brain. "My desk was broken into, my apartment was broken into, searched and vandalized, and now the professor. Mr. Crick, should I be worried?"

He sucked in a deep breath. "I don't want you to worry about your safety. I'll have extra security posted, they'll walk everyone to and from their cars. You might want to take extra precautions when you're on your own. Maybe stay with a friend for a while."

Stassi's lips bunched, without a word she turned and headed to the door.

Crick and Brant looked at each other and shrugged. She was probably going to run off and cry her heart out.

Brant called out, "Where are you going, Stassi? Are you going home? Should we call a guard to escort you to your car?" He should offer, but he was as terrified as the next guy.

"I'm going to go to work," she tossed over her shoulder. "The sooner this formula is completed and handed over to the government, the safer we will all be." She didn't acknowledge Karine as she strode purposefully out of the reception area, pretending she didn't notice that the woman was standing as if she wanted to say something, probably to utter useless words of sympathy.

Chapter Six

Stassi worked hard every day as if her life depended on it, and it possibly did. She was coming closer to a conclusive formula, but it was still going to take some time. She had been moved to a different cubicle since hers was damaged, and assigned a new laptop.

She didn't leave anything at work anymore, even though Mr. Crick said she could lock things in his office or one of the labs that was strictly secured because certain formulas, and expensive or dangerous items were in there. It was well known that people would try to infiltrate, or just break into a building to steal a ground-breaking formula, or high level chemicals, drugs etc.

It was late, nine o'clock. Shutting down the computer, Stassi stuffed it in her briefcase. She kept her notebook in her lab coat, she wasn't letting it out of her sight.

"Hey, Stas, you still here?" Charlie popped from around the short wall and grinned tiredly at her.

"Hey, yeah." She noticed the dark smudges under his eyes. "What are you doing here so late? Melinda's going to kill you," she chided with affection.

"For sure. Little Cody has colic, keeping us both up at night. I left early yesterday to give Melinda a break, so I stayed later tonight to make up for it." He moved closer watching her close things up and lock drawers. Not that locking them would apparently make any difference.

"Terrible what happened to your professor, Stassi. I'm sorry for your loss," he said with compassion. "Horrible way to die, tortured like that. Uh," he could have bitten his tongue for saying such painful words to her. Stassi's grief was scribbled all over her soft face. "Aw gee, sorry, Stas, that was so offensive, forgive me."

He sounded so upset, Stassi smiled wearily at him. "It's okay, Charlie, we're all on edge. You see it on TV but you never expect it in your own home." She hung her lab coat on a hook and slipped her jacket on.

"Yeah, true that. Wretched business. Melinda is terrified for me to come to work. But the bills gotta be paid."

Nodding in agreement, Stassi removed her notebook from the lab pocket and dropped it inside her briefcase. Closing the case, she picked it up and slung it over her shoulder and grabbed her purse.

"You leaving now? I'll call security to escort you. I'm staying a little while longer to tie up a couple of loose ends." Charlie lifted Stassi's landline and pushed a number.

He held the receiver to his ear, the phone was answered right away. He said, "Hi, this is Charlie Shaw. Miss Athens is ready to be escorted to her car. I'm gonna need someone for myself in about thirty minutes." He nodded. "Yeah, we're the only ones left in the building."

"Thanks Charlie." As he hung up, Stassi sighed with the heavy emotion of Professor Chandler's death and the dark cloud of danger looming over them.

They chatted about idle things until a uniformed guard approached them. Dressed in the brown uniform, the guard, neat and clean cut, cap low over his eyes nodded at Charlie then Stassi, he asked politely, "Miss Athens?"

"Hi, yes, I'm ready to go." She turned to Charlie with a frail smile. "I hope this is all over soon, the stress is killing me."

"Yeah," he granted with a sigh, "me too. I'll see you tomorrow, take care, Stas." Charlie watched as the guard led Stassi out of the lab.

They took the elevator down to the 1st floor. The lobby was empty. As they walked to the exit, the guard said, "Terrible business, the death of that guy. They said you were close to him?"

"Hmm." Stassi didn't want to talk about the professor. Her stomach churned every time she thought about what Brant said about him getting sliced up, *God*, her hand splayed on her belly. She felt relatively safe with the very tall, strongly built guard.

The guard held the door open for her. The chill air swooped at them, flinging Stassi's knee-length dress and hair. Part of the driveway curled up to the front of the building for deliveries and to drop off people with disabilities. Everyone else parked in the lot to the side of the structure. They trod along a cement path that led through the grass to the lot.

"I'm over in that first row," Stassi told him as she opened her purse to get her keys. Of course her car was easy to see, the lot was empty.

"Uh huh," he mumbled. A white van was parked just at the end of the walk. When the guard veered to the van, away from the section she'd parked her car Stassi slowed her stride. The guard suddenly wrapped his hand around her arm.

"No, wait, I'm over there." She pointed, but he pulled her towards the van. As they neared it, the side door slid open and a frisson of alarm raced up Stassi's spine. Trying to dig her heels in and yank her arm from his grip, she shouted, "No! Let go of me!"

The guard spun her around, slapped his hand over her mouth, and she felt a sting in her neck, and then nothing.

Chapter Seven

Through a thick woozy fog, Stassi heard voices. Her body weighed a thousand pounds, her eyelids a hundred. Her tongue dry as old toast, and her head pounded with a fierce headache.

"You gave her too much, you idiot," an obviously angry male voice spoke nearby, as if he stood right over her.

Another voice, further away didn't disagree. "Yeah, maybe, I'm not used to dousing small women. I've only done men. She'll come around, Nero." The man sounded unconcerned that Stassi couldn't move a muscle. "There," he said cheerfully, "her eyeball twitched. She's awake."

She felt a gentle slap on her cheek, and moaned. Another slap, harder.

"Wake up, Miss Athens, I am not a patient man," a deep voice growled above her.

It took effort, but she didn't want to be slapped again. Her lids fluttered as she struggled to push them open. A man stood over her. He looked more curious than angry.

"That's it, little chemist, open those peepers."

Her lids were too heavy, they fell back down. And she received a sharp slap.

"Open your damned eyes," the man demanded, now sounding angry again.

"Geeze, Nero, give the broad a minute, she's doped up pretty good."

"No thanks to you, Vinca," the man called Nero remonstrated him. She heard his voice turn from her, then it was back. "Darlin'," he sounded hard, coarse. "I can hit you where it'll hurt worse. Now, open your eyes."

They felt like lead, but she pushed them open. The man still peered down at her. To the side and back a few feet was another man. A man with dark auburn hair, a really big man, he looked amused. His hair waved around of his head, dark chilling eyes expressed the amusement wasn't jovial humor. He was the guard who had been walking her to her car.

The man called Nero told him, "Help the lady to sit up, Vinca."

Vinca, grinned. "Okey doke," he said, and stepped towards the small bed Stassi realized she was lying on. She felt him stack pillows behind her head, then he rolled his arms under her and as if she weighed a feather, lifted her then set her down on the bed so she was sitting with her back and head against the pillows.

Stassi dragged both hands through her long hair pushing it back off her shoulders, it settled draping along the pillows in curls of mahogany. Someone had unbraided her hair. Rubbing her eyes, she drew in tight breaths.

She needed to clear the fog so she could think, although the fog was holding her fear at bay. A good thing, or she'd be out of her mind with terror right now. Lying on a strange bed with two very tough looking men staring down at her. They had obviously abducted her. Thoughts of Professor Chandler's demise floated through her mind chasing crawly chills of fright up her limp arms.

"That's better, Miss Athens." Nero's heavy face creased in a smile, although it was far from a pleasant one. The dark eyes that gleamed at her were empty of sentiment, just two black holes that promised terrible things were going to happen. To her.

"W- what do you want?" the words shivered out of her. She folded her arms over her front as if they could protect her from the two burly men. Her head bobbed slightly, still groggy.

Nero moved and sat a hip on the bed beside her, the firm mattress dipped only slightly with his weight. "Darlin'," he said with sarcasm, "the brilliant scientist I hear you are should have figured that out by now, eh?" He moved a hand out to touch her, she shrank from it. The edge of his mouth lifted in amusement, he dropped his hand.

"It's the formula," Stassi said frankly with a slight wheeze. There was no point in beating around the bush. The professor was dead, her laptop stolen and her office and home trashed, and here she was, kidnapped. Glancing down in slight relief she saw she still wore her dress although sans jacket and shoes, she hadn't been raped. Yet.

"Ah," he said with a smile, "see, you do have that big brain they claimed."

"That ain't all that's big," the man Vinca said snidely, his eyes on her chest. She raised her protective wall of arms higher, which only made him grin.

Nero cast Vinca a glare and turned back to Stassi, his face a mask of...nothing, no, she was wrong, there was darkness, a living seething darkness slithered in the elegant suit. Such profane darkness should have soiled the expensive garment.

Stassi shook her head at the fanciful thought, yet her heart squeezed in dreaded fear.

"So," Nero said, "this is how it is." All amusement left his voice leaving it stone cold, along with his eyes, like burnt chunks of hard coal. "I took your professor assuming he was the brains behind the antidote to the bacteria."

Narrowing her bitter gaze at him, she asked with accusation, "How do you know about the formula? There isn't even one yet. All this…subterfuge, murder, it's- it's outrageous!" Her hands fisted, jaw grit. "You're hurting people for no rea-*oh*-" He snatched up her chin.

Digging his fingers in her soft skin, he leaned in close and jerked her face up to his. The empty eyes were now blemished with inhuman malevolence.

Voice dusky with anger, he ground out, "I have people inside that lab of yours. They tell me everything. As soon as I learned of the bacteria, which was some time ago, I inserted spies into every major laboratory in America. Exbiotics isn't actually that supremely extensive, but it is highly accredited, cutting edge.

"I took a giant chance at it because your Mr. Crick," the side of his mouth nicked up, lids hooded with base admiration, "is a conniving, corrupt, genius at intercepting, stealing, whatever he wants, needs, even classified information to make money and become the powerful man he believes is his due."

Her eyes widened in disbelief, shocked at his words. She tried to move out of his grip but he cupped her jaw and tightened his fingers hard enough they hurt. Still she spoke in Crick's defense, "No, that isn't true, he's just a scientist like the rest of us. He wants to find remedies for environmental problems, he has a good heart." She winced at the bark of laughter that blasted from his mouth.

Nero's head fell back with his laughter. His smile condescending, he loosened his fingers and allowed her to move from his grasp. "Honey, what's it like to be that naïve? I think I was born with an immoral soul. I'm sure I never wore those rosy glasses you have on."

Wriggling her jaw, Stassi touched the side of it with trembling fingertips. She scowled at him. She hated to be talked down to like she was a child, or an inferior woman by a chauvinistic male. She graduated high school a couple of years early, and the same with college. She had interned for two years, with academic scholarships she earned two masters and is working on her PhD.

Sure, she'd lived a closed, sheltered life since leaving home. She'd wrapped herself in school and then work. Her brain was a sponge, God did she love to learn. One of the few friends she had in college that was majoring in psychology told Stassi that she buried herself in academia and work to shut off the grievous demons that still haunted from her ghastly childhood. That was the last time she spoke to that friend. She had a sparse social life because she didn't want any.

She asked Nero, "Who are the spies, your plants in the lab?"

Black hair slicked straight off his forehead gave the man a gangster look right out of the old mobster movies. His heavy black brows lowered at her question.

Her pulse quickened, if he told her, then that would mean he was likely going to kill her. If he didn't tell her, maybe she would get out of this thing alive. Still, kidnapping was a life sentence. It hit her like a punch to the gut, unless she managed to escape, he will kill her. And, her brain wept with fright, no one knew where she was, no one knew about him, except his spies, and they would be fools to tell, they'd only go to jail themselves, or be murdered by him as well.

He stood up, brushed his suit jacket down, straightened his tie.

The other man, Vinca, with the dark burgundy hair and Romanesque face wore a blazer with a white shirt and black trousers. He lounged silently against a wall watching the play between Stassi and Nero with a small smirk on his face.

Not answering her question, Nero tugged his cuffs down from the jacket sleeves, he said, "I have a lab set up for you. We'll get you something to eat, you can freshen up, then you will get to work." He glanced at Vinca.

Vinca grinned, ambled over, bent and scooped Stassi out of the bed and set her on her feet. He'd moved so fast, she was still light-headed from the drug he'd given her, she stumbled. But the big man held her tight until she steadied.

The grin widened when her hazy eyes landed on his, and she shivered at the pure hell that danced in them. He was the pull wings off pinned bugs kind of guy. He released her. Still feeling the pressure from his hard hands she rubbed her arms where he'd held them.

Thirty minutes later, after a sandwich and a soda, and freshening up in the bathroom Nero ushered Stassi into the lab. He owned his own laboratory and had strived to come up with the bacteria with his own scientists and his own skills, but was dismally unsuccessful. He had people try to steal the original formula, but Talis Falk lived in a fortress on a mountain with impregnable access. It was unthinkable that someone actually got some of his precious formula away from him.

But, Nero understood that the scientist who had blabbed about the bacteria hadn't been working in the fortress but in a satellite laboratory, he was a relative or something of Falk's so he had been trusted to keep the information confidential. No one expected him to steal a sample and sneak it to an outside lab. The relative was looking for his own big payday. That won't happen again.

No one has heard from the relative since he stole the formula and Falk would have tightened up security at the fortress, no one in, and no one out until the whole bacteria operation was done and on the black market to be sold to the highest bidder.

If Falk learns that Exbiotics is working on creating the antidote, he will assuredly go after them with all guns blasting. Literally. He would level Exbiotics until nothing and no one from the lab existed. Nero needed to get his hands on the antidote first.

Nero was unable to create the bacteria, therefore trying to develop an antidote himself was pointless. So, he did the next best thing, abducted the creator of the burgeoning basics of the antidote formula.

The bacteria destroys oil and once it comes in contact with any sort of energy or electricity. The antidote would make it ineffective before it enters a system such as a vehicle. Talis Falk created the bacteria, therefore he would totally own the oil industry, for the entire world. He would be king of the universe.

So far an antidote has not been created, but that's where Nero believes Stassi comes in, that she can develop it, then Nero would be the one to own the world.

His fingers wound around her upper arm, he led her to the lab where she would be working. It was large and white and steel with the latest and top of the line equipment that could be purchased. Machines with buttons lit in neon hummed along the walls, glass enclosed cupboards showcased every implement a chemist could imagine to use. Stainless steel sinks and resin counters surrounded an open work area that included several granite tables that had every device and instrument needed for just about any experimentation.

Six lab assistants in white coats stood at attention between a long counter and a wall. None of them made eye contact with Stassi. When she moved to speak to them, plead for their help, Nero squeezed her arm and said, "Don't bother trying, honey, it would be your life or theirs and they know it." He made a swirling motion with his hand and without a word the assistants turned in tandem and faced the wall.

Nero released her arm and stepped back. "Now, Miss Athens, may I call you Anastasia? Such a lovely name."

"No," she said flatly with a grimace.

His brows hopped in surprise, then he smiled. "Not the prim wallflower I had you pegged as, are you, Miss Athens?

What do your friends call you?" She stared blankly at him, he could see the wheels spinning in her brilliant brain on how to get the hell out of her predicament.

"Fair enough." He nodded. "But," he shook his head, then said, "not doing the long Anastasia or Miss Athens, let's see," he put a finger to his chin, then snapped his fingers. "Ah, I remember what I was informed they called you, Stassi, right? Yes, that's better. Anastasia brings to mind a tall, lean, regal, cool yet tough woman. When you are," he reached his hand to touch her face but she turned her head. He chuckled. "Yes, you are soft, delicate…very feminine. Darlin', I truly hate to have to break you," his voice hardened, the smile thinned to a callous line, "but I will if I have to."

She didn't say a word, just lifted her chin and stared at him with disdain. There was no way she could surreptitiously scan the area for a weapon or an escape, so she looked around boldly, not hiding her intent. There was one door and surely it would be locked while she was inside.

There wasn't anything large enough for her to grab and sling at his head so she could make a run for it. She assumed that big shadow loitering outside the door was that creep Vinca. The useless assistants were all cowering, shaking in their shoes, they would not help her.

Enjoying her display of contempt and the way she was obviously looking for a way out, Nero drawled, "Hmm, normally I like a little fire in my women, but, there'll be time enough for that later. For now, you will do as I say. Before you start thinking you can outwit me and take a long, stalling time developing a false formula, be warned. I have your notes."

At her gasp, Nero nodded at the table where her notebook and laptop lay. "I am quite a renowned scientist in my own right, you will be unable to fool me."

The fact that she really might never leave the lab alive was sinking in fast and frightening, along with total dismay and incomprehension as to his reprehensible acts. "Mister…ah, Mr. Nero, why are you doing this? Why are you hurting people for- for a stupid formula?"

"That's Mr. Lamontagne, but you may call me by my given name, Nero." He tucked his fingertips in the suit jacket pockets. Tilting his head, he regarded her as if he couldn't believe she didn't know why he robbed and murdered.

"I do it for the money of course, darlin', money and power. Power to make and break entire countries. I may not sell the formula; I may keep control of it myself and have the world at my feet. There are so many people and places I want to destroy, I'll have to make a list of which to go after first. I can decimate entire countries bringing their people to their starving knees. Once you create the antidote, then I will have you working on the bacteria, I will own both, and will be unbeatable." His dark eyes glowed with sociopathic greed.

Stassi recoiled, her mouth twisted in repulsion, she took a step back from the evilness that roiled off the man. "You are sick, insane. If you think I'm going to help you-"

Whack his hand lashed out and smacked her face whipping her head to the side. Her hair flew over her stinging cheek.

Forcing herself to not flinch at him, not show the pain he'd inflicted on her, she pushed her hair back and stiffened her spine. "Do what you will, you'll have to kill me because I refuse to help you hurt any more people."

His dark brows dug deep down between his angry gaze that strode down the length of her and back up. Broad shoulders raised up as he clenched his fists, a hiss released with his fury. His eyes narrowed to slits as he bore down over her, then, he took a breath, stepped back, smoothed his tie. "We will see about that, my dear. Some fates are worse than death. And I have time, I'm told Falk is still perfecting his bacteria, it may be many months or a year before it's completed."

He raised his arm and pointed at her, sneered, "Just a small female, you will break. Won't take long. So," he motioned to the lab station, "get to work and we won't have to see what a short time it would take to break you, hmm?"

For days, Stassi pretended to work, and Nero was not fooled. He paced around her, shouting, cursing, withholding food, threatening, hitting her, kicking her, yet she still refused to do what he demanded.

Finally, he said, "That's it. You're going into the cell. I will allow Rufus to do as he pleases with you. After deprivation, no food, little water, rape and beatings, we'll see how long you last. You will be screaming for me to release you once Rufus lowers himself between those lovely thighs of yours and splits you in half. That's after he beats you nearly to death."

Biting her tongue to hold in her gasp of fear, to swallow her pleading to be let go, to stop herself from agreeing and giving in, Stassi straightened her spine and looked him in the eye.

At her raised chin and determined defiant glare, he gave the order, and Vinca snagged her arm and walked her out of the lab.

He dragged her from the mansion across a yard and into a stone building. It housed a few rooms and half a dozen dirty cells. It was dark and dank, smelled of cold earth and urine, rank vomit. As they passed through the wooden door, past a leering Rufus, Stassi fought Vinca with everything she had. It was futile, she only injured herself on his stalwart body bringing enjoyment to his centurion's face.

Vinca tossed her into a cell, closed the barred door and locked it. "Tootles," he wriggled his fingers at her grinning. "I do hope Rufus leaves some of you intact, I still want my shot." He tipped his imaginary hat and took off. And Stassi's hell began.

Chapter Eight

A month or so later

The dead weight of his limp body so heavy on her frail form held her down, smushing her into the dirt floor. The smell of him would never leave her nostrils, her mouth, her soul.

He grunted, loud snores snorted in cacophony against her head, it took so much effort and time in her debilitated state, but she wriggled out from under his grimy slumbering grossness. It was hard, she was so weak, even drawing a breath took half her strength. Red-haired Rufus was a goliath, a fat, filthy pig, no, a wild boar of a stinking nasty troll.

Nero deliberately kept her half-starved, giving her just enough sustenance to keep her alive. Stassi pushed on the hard dirt to sit up slowly so as not to rattle the chain. Halfway up, she had to rest on her forearm and catch her breath, wait for the pain and dizziness to pass. Maybe while Rufus was out cold she could grab- A metallic squawk shook her, his radio, it poked into her leg.

A snarling snort and groan, and he rolled lumberously to his knees. Growling like an old bear, he scratched his red head, his barrel chest then his nuts. Squinting at her through rheumy bleary, bloodshot eyes, he sneered.

A long length of chain hooked to a steel clamp around her neck was chained to the moldy wall. He grasped part of the chain and yanked it, forcing her to fall forward, tumble right into him. He dropped the chain but before he could put his beefy hands on her she scrambled backwards.

His raspy guffaw bounced against the stone walls. "Come on, pretty thing," he mocked with a grin showing the few teeth he had. "We might as well try again." His blubbery lips drooped.

He came every day, Nero sent him, to rape her. Beat her into submission. Except Rufus was such a falling down drunk he couldn't get it up. Still, he hit her, ripped her clothes off, groped her, did things to her until either she passed out from the pain, or he from the booze. Thankfully, either was relatively quick.

"Fine," her voice weak, she moved to her knees. She knew fighting him was futile. It made him hot and angry at the same time, and he took both out on her. "But I need to use the bathroom first. You don't want any accidents on you, do you?" She cocked her head and gazed at him with what she hoped was a sincere sultriness when all she felt was pain and nauseated exhaustion.

Hopefully by the time she returned he would either be gone because he was constantly hungry and liked his ale, or passed out again.

An awful sound erupted from his big belly, he rubbed it with a wry grin. "Oops. Beer and beans, get ya every time. Okay, no tricks now. Last time you grabbed my radio and tried to conk me in the head with it, I had to really give you a beat down."

No kidding. Stassi's hand splayed over ribs aching in excruciating agony he'd likely cracked or broken in his fury, they pressed into her lungs making it laborious work just to draw a full breath. She couldn't think about the probable internal damage he'd inflicted. Constantly nauseous, just breathing hurt, standing for long wasn't an option. "No, no funny stuff. Just the bathroom."

There was no window and she never knew if Rufus came in the morning, noon or night, or all three, she had no idea how long she'd been imprisoned. Already slender, her dress now hung in tatters on her boney limbs. The only light came from the hallway outside the cell. She never heard any other voices, apparently she was the only prisoner being held there.

Nero made his way to her cell periodically to see if she changed her mind and would finally cooperate. When she shook her head, he'd beat her too, tell her that her time was running out.

The word was Falk was still tweaking his formula but before the end of the year it should be ready to blight the oilfields. Soon Nero would resort to real torture. The cutting off ears and lips kind of torture he'd told her. Thankfully, he hadn't been around for a while, Rufus told her he was out of the country. She had a brief reprieve; a time to enjoy that she still had all her limbs, fingers, tongue, etc.

Rufus pulled the chain again tugging her to him, breathed God knows what in her face as he stuck the key in the clamp around her neck. As soon as the clamp was removed he reached for her breast, she scuttled back and struggled to get to her feet. The pain intense, dizziness from the beatings she'd endured shrouded her mind making her stagger like a drunk.

He woofed with laughter as she toppled to her knees, her legs unable to hold her up. She crawled tortuously slowly across the rough dirt ground to the toilet. Small stones dug into her palms and knees as she dragged them along. The cell stunk badly enough, she didn't want her bodily waste to add to it so she forced herself to get to the bathroom.

It was only a tiny alcove with makeshift shower and commode. No hot water, and even the cold water he only turned on for her a few times a week. No mirror, towel bar, not even a lid on the toilet was there, nothing to be used as a weapon. Her palms and knees bled every time she dragged herself to the bathroom. So weak, she was out of breath by the time she reached the toilet. Rufus must have dozed off or he'd be there watching her pee.

Stassi gazed in longing at the shower. She was so grubby, her hair hadn't seen shampoo or a brush in who knows how long. But, she was lucky she made it to the toilet; the faucets in the shower were too far from her depleted power to get to. At least she'd been given a toothbrush she used with her one daily allotted bottle of water.

Completing her business, if only she could stand long enough to wash her face, her hands. But it had taken everything she had just to get there. She hadn't the energy to leave the bathroom. Didn't matter. When he grew impatient, Rufus would come get her. Try to assault her again, do hideous things to her when he couldn't. Tears welled at the hopelessness of her situation. Stassi shook her head. "No, I'll be damned if I let them break me down, I will not cry."

She could give in, produce the formula, but, Nero would only kill her when she was done. And she couldn't let him hurt so many innocent people. A rancid gleam lit in his eyes every time he talked about people he planned to dispose of, as in murder, once he was king. President wasn't good enough he'd told her while slapping her one day. No, he wanted to be the king of the world.

At least this way she had time to try to…what? Escape? A harsh laugh coughed out, it hurt. What a joke. No white knight was coming to her rescue, and she sure had found no way to get herself free. No, she- What was that on the ground by the arched opening to the alcove?

Stassi dragged her deteriorated body over to it. Something was in the dirt behind the opening. Hidden in the dark shadows, neither she nor Rufus had noticed it before. But sitting on the ground gave her a different perspective. Her stomach clenched in hopeful nerves when she realized what it was.

The edge of a rock was barely visible in the dirt. People moving back and forth in the cell must have worn the dirt down enough to expose just a glimpse, just a tiny point of the blessed thing.

Digging her fingers in the dirt around it, Stassi prayed over and over that it was big, big enough to- yes! It was bigger than her hand. Big enough to bash Rufus' skull in. "Oh," she mumbled with a grimace, "how low I've fallen, feeling boundless joy at harming another person." She pried the rock out and held it in her palms. "Screw it, this is life or death, my own. After what he's done to me…" she pushed to her hands and knees.

Then she realized, groaning helplessly, "How can I hold it and move too? And, even if I could carry it and crawl, I don't have the strength, the energy to stand and brain him. He's huge, a bear of fat and muscle. But," a small smile turned up the sides of her mouth. First time she'd smiled in…never mind. "He's all fat and muscle between his ears too. I can do this, I can," she bolstered herself.

"Girl!" Rufus shouted a grunt. "Get back here, now!"

Closing her eyes, Stassi steadied her racing heart, she needed to garner the bravery, the strength to do what she needed to. She called out weakly, "I can't, Rufus. It was all I could do to get here," she took a breath, it wasn't to fool him she was weak, it was because she needed it to finish the sentence. "I- I can't make it back out there."

"Fuck, bitch," he growled, "get yer ass out here. I don't want to have to go into that stink pit and get you."

Who's he kidding, he reeks worse than the scuzzy old toilet. "No, really, Rufus, I- I just can't do it," her voice faded away.

Mutters and curses rolled towards her, she heard his grunts and groans as he struggled to get his fat body up. "Yer gonna fucking regret this, bitch. I'm gonna drag you out by your hair." His heavy boots clomped on the dirt coming towards her.

This is it, brace yourself, Stas. It took everything she had to use the abrasive cement wall to climb to her feet. She propped her shaking body against it, clamping her lips tight to hold in the cries of pain.

His shadow passed the opening of the alcove; she could smell him before she could see him. He muttered and grumbled as he stepped through the opening, and Stassi stood on tiptoe and holding it with both hands slammed the rock into the back of his head. He was too tall for her to hit him on top.

Rufus stumbled with a howl, he dropped to his knees, his hand to his head, and Stassi lifted the rock with both hands and brought it down again and again on his head until he fell into a soundless slump. She gingerly leaned over him, questioned quietly, "Are you dead?" Could she live with another's death on her conscious? She'd have to because she was getting the hell out of there.

His barrel chest rose and fell, he was still alive. Stassi quickly, carefully dug into his pockets until she grabbed the keys. Adrenalin flowed, giving her strength as she clutched the keys and hobbled out of the toilet to the main cell.

Creeping painstakingly to the bars, she listened. No guards patrolled the stone building. They knew the chained slip of a girl wasn't getting away from Rufus or out of the cell. "Dumb-asses," she mumbled, "underestimated me because I'm female." Sticking her hand between the bars, she worked and wriggled until she got the key in the hole and cranked it. *Yes*! The lock turned and she pushed the barred door open.

A wave of dizziness passed through her and she had to lean against the wall or she'd fall. The keys slid from her numb fingers. The adrenalin was holding off the pain, but her body was going to soon fail. Summoning her will and strength, she stepped out of the cell. Her bare feet shuffling over the dirt, she moved slowly with her palms bracing along the wall as she headed to the sunlight.

Squinting in the bright morning light, she'd been in the dark for so long, Stassi paused by the doorway and peered out. Cold air struck her. "Darn," she groaned, there were men patrolling up by the main building where the labs were and Nero Lamontagne lived. Mulling over her position, she thought in despair, *how will I get out of here, to a main road?*

All she could see were miles and miles of wilderness surrounding the estate. Muttering silently, she agonized, "How many miles will I have to crawl to get somewhere and get help? That is, if I can even get away from the guards."

Glancing around the area, she searched for a place to run, to hide. She'd worry about what to do next once she was away from the compound. Rufus wouldn't stay out long, soon he'd sound the alarm that she'd fled, and they'd be after her. "Okay," she bolstered herself, "it's now or never."

Pushing from the doorframe, thinking she could run around the building and slip away from there, she lurched to the side of the cells. But there was a guard marching the perimeter that way. Gasping, trying to draw strength to her limbs, she started to dart in front of the jail, maybe she could make it to the forest before anyone sees her- and her feeble body seized up.

The damage to her body, starvation, pain, took their toll and she just collapsed like a bag of potatoes to her knees.

And she heard Rufus roar.

Chapter Nine

"It's vitally important Voltang that you do this for me."

"I told you to call me Volt, you say my name and people become wary claiming I sound like a dangerous foreigner or a fucking vampire."

A chuckle came through the phone. "You are a dangerous foreigner. You'll never eliminate that guttural accent, or the stealthy, lethal way you move."

Forking fingers through his thick dark hair, Volt scowled although the person on the other end of the phone couldn't see him. "Whatever, Kenan, I have other missions in the works. I don't have time to do it."

The chuckle gone replaced by a grim tone. "Volt, you know I wouldn't ask if it wasn't so vitally important."

Volt was taken aback. Kenan had never pled for his help before. "Ah," he groaned a resigned sigh. "If we weren't brothers in arms, K, then-"

"But we are. You know I would throw down my life for you, and you for me because we have. I'll give you the little bit of information I've comprised. There's no better tracker, hunter than you. The situation is precariously deadly, I need your expertise for this. You'll need to move fast, I don't think there is a lot of time."

Volt heard the urgency in Kenan's voice, he didn't offer up any more resistance. "I want dossiers on all involved. I want the surveillance videos from the building and the surrounding area, a ten-mile radius, names of witnesses, list of staff."

The air expelled on the other side of the phone expressed Kenan's relief. "Of course. I've already had it emailed to you."

Volt glanced down at his phone. "There's nothing there."

The chuckle was back. "Your 'business' phone, Volt."

There was silence while Volt went to his vault and unlocked it with the combination. He pulled out the cell tucked inside and turned it on. "You son of a bitch, you knew I'd agree. You sent this shit ten minutes ago."

"Yes, Volt," the voice turned serious, "you must be able to tell how important this is to me you shouldn't have put up the feigned balking."

He read the name of the target as the email came up. "Next time," Volt said with a sudden temper, "just tell me who right off the bat and we'll save time." Buried rage of an insufferable memory kindled cold embers to life.

"I've had to keep that part of my life separate, Volt, but as soon as I learned what had happened-" anguish tinged with regret in his reply. "I can't just stand by and let it happen, I have to-"

"Got it." Volt had read enough to understand the fear in his friend's voice. "I'll have Jubal Cain get me an aircraft, and call in my team."

A rumbled gruff from Kenan, he said, "Thank you bro, you don't know how much this means to me. Keep in touch, I want to know everything as you know it. I'm ready for whatever you may need me to do."

"Roger that," Volt responded then disconnected. Slipping the phone into his pocket, he strode into the room next to his den. Opening a closet, he took out his bug-out duffle. Checking the contents, he pulled out the variety of weapons to ensure they were cleaned and loaded, and sharpened. When he was done, he stowed everything back into the bag, then got his phone and dialed.

"Yeah, Volt," his friend Jubal Cain answered.

"I need a jet."

"When?"

"Now. I have a job."

"I'll call the boys."

"Right," Volt said, and hung up. He had a few things to do. Once he'd read the specifics of the email, he had been already thinking about who could be involved, and he narrowed it down to five. None of the five resided in the U.S., he knew he'd need the jet.

Chapter Ten

A cry of helplessness sieved from her injured lungs at the sound of Rufus' roar. On her ruined knees, Stassi knew she couldn't rise to her feet much less run. At Rufus' bellowing, a number of guarding soldiers' heads turned in her direction. Immediately they came charging at the same time as Rufus stomped out of the jail.

"You fucking bitch! You've done it now!" Rufus railed at Stassi as he stomped towards her. Blood leaking out of his head blended in with the thick red hair. Snarling curses, he threatened, "There'll be little left of you by the time I hand you back to Lamontagne when he returns from Russia."

The soldiers racing towards Stassi shouted to one another as they ran.

Stassi curled into a ball on the ground, covered her head, and prepared for the first bone-crushing blow. Rufus would pounce first, then the soldiers would join in now that she was out of the protection of the cell.

In the heat of the moment they wouldn't remember Nero Lamontagne and his orders. Gang-rape and more vicious beatings, they would leave her on her last tortured breath for Lamontagne to use. Her only hope at this point was that they would accidentally kill her quickly and end her torment.

A scream caught in her throat as she heard Rufus' booming curses nearing her as he raised his fist- she cringed waiting for his huge fist to bash off half her head-

Screams rent the air, sounds of fists hitting bodies resounded all around her. When the expected blow didn't come, she moved an arm to peek out expecting to see a boot or fist coming straight at her. But, her eyes widened in confusion.

Men dressed in camouflage swarmed the area and were fighting hand-to-hand with Nero's soldiers. One of them jumped in front of her and faced off with Rufus. He had black smudged all over his face to allow him to blend into the dark forest.

Rufus paused, dumb bewilderment crossed his meaty face. He snarled at the man in front of Stassi, "Yer day to die, motherfucker. Don't know who you are, but yer stickin' yer nose in where it don't belong. I'll take care of you then finish my bizness with this little bitch hen here," he lifted his chin in Stassi's direction.

All around them men rampaged at each other, fists flew, knives flung and stabbed, gunshots whizzing by had Stassi tucking her head back down.

Rufus roared like some Godzilla banging his fists on his big chest and then he hurtled at the man standing half a dozen feet in front of Stassi. The man easily side-stepped Godzilla's rush, and at the same time twirled and kicked a soldier coming up behind him in the head and stuck his knife in yet another attacking soldier's neck.

The soldier the man kicked in the head just dropped to the ground out cold, the man stabbed in the neck wailed and fell to his knees as he tried to yank the knife from his neck.

Rufus staggered to stop fast, caught his balance and turned back to the man. His thick face maroon he was so enflamed with rage, he roared, "Yer gonna die, boy, right the fuck now!"

and he ran at the man. The man again easily dodged him but this time he shoved his fist into Rufus' big belly. Rufus gasped, bent over clutching his stomach.

Shaking his massive head, Rufus dashed at the man again. The man appeared to have grown bored with the fight and decided it was time to end it and he lunged at Rufus. He let loose with punch after punch, Rufus' head slammed back and forth, blood and teeth spewed.

Stassi's mouth parted in astonishment at the ferocious brawling, the bloodletting, the fanatical killing that was going on in the yard of the empiric estate.

The man grew tired of playing with Rufus, he jumped in the air, wrapped his legs around Rufus' thick neck and brought him crashing to the ground. The man was almost as tall as Rufus' 6'6, albeit leaner yet with tremendous strength, powerful muscles bulged as he kept Rufus pinned to the ground. The man tightened his legs, crushing Rufus' windpipe.

Rufus struggled, fought, kicked his feet, clawed at the legs crushing him, hacked and gagged, but couldn't get a howl out. Soon, his body jerked stiffly then went limp, finally stopped moving and the man released him.

The man snatched a huge knife from a sheath tied to his leg and plunged it through Rufus' heart, staking him to the ground. Withdrawing the knife, he wiped it on Rufus' shirt, stuck it back in the sheath then he rolled to a standing position.

He looked over to Stassi curled up in mind-bending terror. His harsh face marked with black, sharp and threatening with the rising sun behind him shading his body making him even more deadly sinister. He took a step towards her.

Oh no! Stassi thought, this monster has come to take over Nero's organization and he's killing everyone in sight! With a tiny squeal, she fought to stand, to run from this new horror, but her knees buckled, her gravely injured body once again gave out and everything went dark.

******

"Shit," Voltang Saldano cursed. He assumed the woman would be in bad shape, but she appeared to be on her deathbed as she keeled over.

Volt sprang and caught her as she crumpled. Lifting her in his arms, he looked down at the filthy battered face. Delicate, fine bone structure swollen, covered in purple bruises and laced with lacerations, wholly emaciated, how had she survived this long?

He was so royally pissed he was forced to rescue her, this particular woman. He'd rather give her a whipping, but she wouldn't survive it now. Maybe later he'd get his revenge.

"All right," he called out to his men, "Lamontagne isn't here, let's go." He carried the woman to one of the jeeps and climbed in the back with her cradled unconscious on his lap. Even so, it was going to be a rough ride for the horribly damaged, frail female.

Jubal Cain hopped in behind the wheel and turned to look at their target. "Hmm, looks mighty pitiful, think she's gonna make it?" Dressed in camouflage with military boots, like all the men he wore a thick belt that held weapons and a holster tied to his thigh. Dark garnet hair cut short, dark blue eyes regarded the half dead girl with compassion.

"Don't know." Volt stared down at the pale brutalized face.

Rexal Jakes climbed in the front passenger seat, and twisted around, whistling when he saw the woman. "Doesn't look good, Volt," he remarked. "It appears we are too late." His genes from Black Ruś, his homeland were apparent in his black hair and hooded onyx eyes, his face sharp, and like Volt and Jubal, he was well over six feet with a barbarously strong physique that was necessary in their line of work.

"Yeah," Volt muttered. "Get us the hell out of here, Jubal."

Jubal stepped on the gas and swung the jeep away from the estate. The rest of Volt's men piled onto several other jeeps and followed in their wake.

Chapter Eleven

"Staring at her won't make her heal any faster, Volt."

Volt didn't respond to the woman entering the room, nor did he move his gaze from the wretched bundle lying motionless on the bed.

"Volt," the woman tsked as she set a tray on the dresser. The nightstand beside the bed was filled with medicine, water, thermometer, heating pad, ice pack, and other medicinal items.

"Sade, I'm not in the mood for banter." Wearing a long-sleeved black thermal and black Dockers, he was hunched over with his hands folded and his forearms on his knees.

In her early fifties, Sadie Durant took no shit from anyone, except Volt Saldano, and she was the only female Volt tolerated scolding him. He accepted little umbrage from anyone but his close friends.

A few strands of grey glinted in Sadie's dark brown hair. Lines around her brown berry eyes had deepened in the years she'd worked for Volt. A sturdy woman, Sadie had more energy than a tankful of guppies. She trod across the room and stood beside the chair he sat in and looked down at the woman in the bed.

"Looks like a little shattered porcelain doll. She any better?" her voice soft with compassion.

One shoulder bumped. "Hard to tell. The fever broke earlier, Doc said that was good. But," his mouth tightened, "she hasn't woken, hasn't stirred, he said that wasn't good. He thinks he's taken care of the internal injuries with the immediate surgery, taped her fractured ribs, he's not sure about concussion."

"The poor thing," Sadie said sadly. "To be so horribly abused like that, I wonder how she managed to survive."

Volt agreed. "She's a strong little thing, considering there was so much damage, she fought hard to stay alive. Both shoulders were wrenched out of their sockets, arms and legs had been twisted causing sprains along with neck and ankle sprains, even bite marks as well as the massive bruising and lacerations. Her knees and palms were scraped raw, it appears she was so wounded she could only crawl to get around.

"The doctor said it's hit or miss at this point whether she will survive. That fucker Lamontagne did a damned good number on her."

Shaking her head, Sadie wiped at an errant tear as she gazed sadly at the hideously battered young woman. "How monstrous can a person be to brutalize someone so delicate?"

Volt commented, "He's known for his heartless brutality. I wouldn't think he'd be so abusive to a female, but, a monster is a monster."

"Did you...avenge her?" Sadie knew the kind of man she worked for. She may not agree with some of his actions, but what he did wasn't any of her business. Her job was to take care of him and be his assistant.

His lips pressed into a hard line, brows daggered down in a grimace. "No. He and his killer dog Vinca Nivelli were out of the country when I retrieved her. He would have been mighty pissed to see his own soldiers about to destroy his planned moneymaker. The men were in a dervish bloodlust fury to assault her." The corner of his mouth nicked up. "They aren't anymore. We left few survivors."

"Oh dear." Sadie fussed with the items on the nightstand.

"I did take out the beast that she was running from." Reluctant pride for the injured woman crept in his deep voice, "Girl managed to escape from some deranged behemoth, probably the one that committed the wicked abuse. He was about to beat her to living hell when we arrived." Sitting back in his chair and crossing an ankle over a knee, he didn't look at Sadie when he flatly stated, "He's dead."

"Good," she said with a sharp nod.

The levity left as quick as it'd come. "Doc said he wasn't sure if she had been…raped. Said she had so much damage, was so…emaciated, she…" his big chest stretched the thermal then sunk with a heavy expelled breath. "If only the information about her being abducted had been learned sooner…"

Sadie set a hand on his shoulder. "You know I don't mind at all seeing to her, but how come the person who hired you to extricate her isn't seeing to her care?"

He grunted, his gaze glued to the incapacitated woman. "It's complicated. She's safer here."

"I see. Why didn't you take her to a hospital if she was in such bad condition?"

Volt's head twitched like a horse flicking off a fly. "She's clearly in danger. I couldn't personally guard her 24/7 in the hospital and I don't trust the hospital guards or the police. Vinca Nivelli is a viper that can slither through a keyhole. Doc Harper had everything he needed here. I brought in everything he said he would require, plus three nurses to assist him. Says he's done all he can, only time will tell if she recovers."

"Why did you dismiss the nurses? You're doing almost everything for her yourself."

"You know, you want something done right, do it yourself. They were in my way." In fact the nurses were more interested in him than the care of the patient. He had a dying female on his hands and each one of the nurses hassled him to have sex with them. What the hell happened to professionalism? Two of them were attractive, but the third was beyond plump and had twenty years on him. What made them think it was okay to hit on the man paying for them to take care of the injured woman? Especially when they didn't know what Volt and the patient's relationship was, for God's sake she could be his wife and they were hitting on him as she lay dying. "Anyway, you're equal to six nurses, you're doing your share of seeing to her."

Sadie observed Volt's relentless study of the woman. "You, ah, appear to have mixed emotions about her. When you left to extract her you acted angry, as if you…I don't know, hated her? But now, that anger has turned to something else, I'm not sure-"

He stood up. "Knock off the armchair shrinkology, Sade. You know me, you ever see me express any kind of emotions, ever?"

Her lips quirked at his denial. "Uh huh, a cold iceman you are, Volt." She continued watching him watching the woman. "I think we're getting a heatwave, maybe that ice is melting, hmm? You didn't see your face when you brought her home."

Sadie chuckled at his frown. "Anyway, I've brought some tea and a protein shake. Try to see if you can get anything in her besides water. The doctor said he'd have to hook her up to a feeding tube if she didn't get nourishment soon." She gazed down at the poor woman. "You didn't tell me what her name is."

His chest rose and he exhaled with vague irritation, he muttered, "Anastasia Athens."

"Oh my, what a lovely name."

Volt nodded absently, didn't notice when Sadie left the room. He went to the dresser and leaving the saucer there he picked up the teacup, he'd start with that. As he had been doing since he had brought her there, Volt sat on the edge of the bed and slipped his arm under the unconscious girl.

Carefully lifting her at an incline, he put the cup to her lips. "Okay, Anastasia, let's see if you can drink this, you did pretty well with the water," and he pressed the cup, pushing her lips apart, a small bit of tea trickled in.

It took him an hour to get the tea and the small protein shake into her. He gently laid her back down then pulled the blanket up to cover her devastated body. Sadie and one of the nurses had bathed the girl and then dressed her in a borrowed nightgown. She drank so little and sweated from the fever that all the liquid inside her came out her pores. They hadn't been bothered with her urinating on the bed.

"You did good, *tigris*," he praised her quietly, "got most of it down." His mouth bunched, a nickname? He gave this woman he hated a stupid nickname? He's getting soft in the head. Yet, he recalled when he arrived at the compound and saw her feebly escaping the building she'd been jailed in and struggle to flee. The roaring behemoth staggered out behind her holding his head, a bit of blood trickled over his hand.

Volt felt himself smile against his will, obviously the petite woman had managed to clobber the beast and knock him out long enough to make her escape. She was a damned tigress. Then the image of the furious goliath rushing at her with his meaty fist raised about to pummel the helpless, vulnerable female, hell, Volt didn't even have a thought but to slaughter the fucker. And he did. Bastard will fry in hell.

After seeing the savage destruction he'd wreaked on the girl, he wished he could butcher him all over again. And again, only very slowly.

He did not like the thorn of admiration he felt looking down at her. Well, he'd spent enough time with the bitch, he reminded himself of his hatred for her. Still, she shouldn't be left alone, she was too ill. He'd get Sadie to- He heard a whimper. Stepping closer, he saw her head thrash and more whimpers pour out of that pale pink mouth he'd spent too much time staring at the past days.

When she thrashed harder he hurried and sat down on the bed. Carefully grasping her thin shoulders, he held her to stop the thrashing. "Anastasia, calm down, you are going to hurt yourself. You're safe now." Undoubtedly she was fighting the demons that had abused her.

"No, please," she cried in raspy breaths, tears eked out the corners of her closed eyes. She struggled against his grip crying, "I can't take any more, please stop…" her head rolled back and forth with her pleadings.

She tried to bring her arms up to fight him off, Volt moved his hands to her arms and held her down. "I- I won't do it, I know you will kill me, but I won't, too many people to die…" her tormented voice diminished. Then she struggled harder. "Please, no more, no more, please!" she shrieked and tossed her chest to get him to release her.

Damn, she's going to hurt herself more, Volt gathered her up and he sat on the bed with his back against the headboard. He set her on his lap and restrained her with one arm, the other clutched her jaw to keep her head still. "Anastasia, I am not going to hurt you," *not yet*, "open your eyes, you are safe now."

He held her gently yet firmly as he told her, "Nero Lamontagne can't get to you, the big red-haired freak is dead, he can't hurt you anymore, shh," he soothed her as more tears streamed. Her chest heaved with frantic breaths of fear as she struggled to get free.

Holding her snugly but not too tight, Volt rocked her as he made soothing sounds. It was working, she stopped thrashing, writhing in his arms. Her lashes fluttered on way too pale, too thin cheeks. Then they slowly opened. Amazing green eyes dazed from being so ill gazed up at him in confusion. She whispered, "Please don't hit me anymore, please," the tears rolled.

"No, Anastasia, I am not going to hit you, no one is. You are safe now. You are no longer held prisoner in Lamontagne's estate, you have been rescued."

Long cinnamon colored lashes flickered at him, she carefully looked around. A frown of bewilderment flooded the pallid face as she didn't recognize her surroundings. "I- where am I?" The huge green eyes turned back to him.

"You are in my home."

Without moving, she glanced down and realized she was on his lap, in his arms, she was wearing only a thin white nightgown. With a yelp of fright, she started struggling again crying, "Let go of me!"

"Okay, okay, settle down." Volt gently lifted her and set her on the bed then moved to sit on the edge facing her with his palms up to show he meant her no harm. Which was difficult at best. He was a big muscled man, a stranger, and he was well aware of how tough and dangerous he looked. And she was small and delicate to begin with, and now severely injured and terribly fragile dressed only in a nightie, after all she'd been through it would be crazy to believe she wouldn't be frightened of him.

"Who, ah, who are you?" Her brows drew down in a confused, wary frown. "How- how did I get here?"

"I am-"

Her eyes widened in greater fear. "You- you're the one that was beating that man to death in that alley!" She moved to scramble across the opposite side of the bed to get away from him then she cried out in agony.

"Ah, shit," he groused, "sit the fuck still, you are exacerbating your wounds." He slid to his feet and backed away. "I am not going to hurt you, but you've been seriously injured, you must stay still." Even as he spoke he saw her eyelids lower as she grew dizzy, faint from her sudden exertions. Her body collapsed against the headboard, she slumped over.

"Dammit, Doc's gonna kill me," he muttered as he approached the bed. Rolling his arms under her, he lifted her and laid her back down flat on her back, tucked a pillow under her head and pulled the quilt over her. He tugged his phone out and called the doctor.

Chapter Twelve

She was in and out for the next several days. Volt continued to feed her protein shakes and water, tea, she was barely conscious when he ministered to her.

"Volt," Doctor Emerson Granger hailed him cheerfully as he entered the room. "How's my patient doing today?"

"Doc," Volt greeted Granger while he settled Anastasia back against stacked pillows and looked down at her critically. "She has brief moments of consciousness, but not for more than a few minutes or so at a time."

Moving towards the bed, the doctor remarked, "She looks stronger, she has better color. You're keeping her clean."

"Yeah, Sadie and some of her friends bathe her, help her use the bathroom. I'm able to get tea and shakes down her. But shouldn't she be up and around by now? Is she not going to recover?" His friend Kenan who asked him to rescue her is not going to be happy. He'd called every day checking on her progress.

Granger set his medical bag on the end of the bed. "She's had terrible trauma, Volt, her body has a lot to heal. She heals best while she's sleeping, and she'll experience less pain if she's out of it. I think she's sleeping more now than actually being unconscious. Her color is healthy. I'll examine her. I'm sure you have things to do, go ahead while I get busy."

"Yeah, sure." Volt stepped back but didn't leave.

Granger sat on the side of the bed and pulled the covers down to past the girl's feet and reached for the buttons on the nightgown. He had three undone and Volt cleared his throat.

"Ah, she have to be naked for you to…examine her?" His brows sunk down over displeased eyes.

Looking over his shoulder, Granger answered, "Yes, she has injuries over every part of her body. You need to leave, Volt. I can't have you hovering over me getting upset that I'm seeing her nude."

Crossing his arms, Volt's lips pushed out in denial. "It's not upsetting me, Doc, for cripe's sake. I don't even know her, why should I care what you do?"

The doctor undid all the buttons on the gown and was about to push the sides apart exposing her body when Volt blurted, "Doc, I don't think-"

Granger turned around with an exasperated glare. "Volt, get out."

Hesitating, mouth still pursed, Volt's gaze flipped from Anastasia to the doctor. "Yeah, okay. I have things to do. I'm too busy to hang around while you examine a woman I don't even know. And if I did know her, I sure wouldn't care who sees her naked, even if I didn't hate her for what she did-"

"Volt," Granger snapped, turning back to his patient, "out."

A few days later after the doctor left from doing his checkup, Volt strolled into the kitchen. Sadie was at the stove preparing dinner. It smelled of Hungarian goulash, spicy, meaty. He headed to the commercial fridge and removed a beer.

"How is she?" Sadie set a wooden spoon on a plate.

"Doc says she should be fine. Says she's on the mend."

"Oh, wonderful. I've noticed her moments of being awake are stretching. Jubal is in with her now."

Pausing the bottle at his mouth, Volt grunted, "Why?"

Sadie turned back to the goulash. "The bruises are clearing, she may be emaciated, but it's obvious how stunning the young woman is. Some of your other boys are in her room to see her as well. Rex just left, Greco was in earlier. They-"

Volt strode down the hall. His rented home was a palatial modern building sprawled on a mountain overlooking a pretty village that surrounded a sky blue lake. A man passed by one of the wide windows. One of the sentries. Volt had brought in dozens of his people to guard the mansion and the perimeter of his acres of lawns and forest. He had to be prepared if Lamontagne or someone else came after Anastasia and tried to take her from him like he took her from Lamontagne.

Of course, Volt's crew was ten times better trained than Lamontagne's. He had trained them himself, they were precise killing machines, like phantoms, no one saw them coming. No one was getting within miles of Anastasia.

When he reached the room, he saw besides Jubal, several of his mercenaries stood in a semi-circle around the bed. Anastasia was awake, she was propped up and...smiling. She was doing more than smiling, she was giggling at something Jubal said.

The men chuckled with her, they all grinned like loons at the girl. Hell, she was wide-awake and sitting up, talk about doing better. When he saw her last night she had taken one look at him and screamed like he was the damned boogeyman and then passed out.

Volt's face ground into harsh planes, he started to order them all out when Anastasia caught sight of him. Her eyes widened as her lips parted. Terror squeezed the bruises that still lingered on her face and she let out a wounded, frightened sound. Seeing her angst, the men quickly shifted, moving closer together to form a protective barrier around her. And that pissed Volt off.

He stepped towards them and Anastasia sobbed, "Please, he's going to kill me, please don't let him!" Volt's expression darkened when Jubal moved between him and Anastasia.

"Volt, you probably should back off for now," Jubal suggested, his grin crooked. "Let me explain to her what-"

"Get the fuck out, all of you, out," Volt commanded, his jaw gritting so hard his ears moved.

"Volt," Jubal's grin vanished, he said, "she's frightened of you. Let me-"

His mouth a hard line, Volt glared at Jubal. Jubal sighed. "Okay. Come on guys, we're outta here for now."

As his men traipsed past him, each frowned their concern for the way he was handling his terrified guest.

Last one out, Jubal said quietly to Volt, "She was being a good citizen, a Samaritan, that night, Volt, you can't hate her for being a courageous compassionate, brave woman. Be gentle." He patted Volt's shoulder as he exited the room.

Volt's attention wasn't on his men, it was on her. Anastasia's knees were up under the blanket, her arms wound tightly around them in self-protection. All Volt could see were enormous green eyes radiating panicked fear across the room.

Chapter Thirteen

Stassi couldn't believe those big tough men had left her alone with that- that murdering hoodlum.

He was slowly moving towards her, dark eyes glittering animosity under hooded lids. Confusion rolled over her in waves. He was the man she saw beating and stabbing that guy in the alley, but he was also the man who killed Rufus. He hadn't killed her. He had the opportunity then, and all the times she was unconscious in the bed. Confusion roiled through her brain. What on earth was she doing here with him?

Visions blossomed of being embraced in strong arms while a deep accented voice, a strong voice murmured gently over and over that she was safe, chasing away the nightmares of Rufus, the prison cell, the starvation, the terror.

Warm breath wisped in her ear while soothing sounds in some other language whispered while warm liquid trickled down her parched throat easing the dehydration, relieving the soreness. Held firmly, it had felt like she was nestled in a cocoon, a gentle yet hard cocoon.

She blinked, her body rigid as a pole as more images pressed into her tired brain. Those strong arms that had held her, were they his? Her brows lowered at the improbable thought. No. There was no way that bruiser could be so gentle with her.

Her forehead crimped, but he had that strange accent, it sounded as frightening as he looked. Muscled torso, lean hips, thick chest, she remembered it felt like granite but he'd held her so carefully it hadn't hurt her withered body.

Stassi eyed him warily as he approached, stricken with fight or flight, but she was still too injured to flee. She sank into the pillows, crushing them against the headboard as she shrank from him. "Please…" God, she was so tired of begging for her life, pleading for the torture to stop. "Please don't hurt me."

His steps slowed as he came up to the side of the bed. Sticking his hands in his pockets to show her he wasn't going to hit her, he grated, "Calm down, Anastasia, have I hurt you yet?"

Too afraid to talk, she shook her head. Then, she inhaled a trembled breath, her voice thin, quivering, she said, "No. But that day, that day in the alley, you swore you would…get me. You cursed me, and told me you would make me pay for calling the police on you."

His hands slid from his pockets and he crossed his arms over his chest. His short black hair waved slightly on his head, he wore a black sweater, black jeans, black boots. The black knight. "That is correct."

She blinked. "So, what are you going to do to me?" Stassi shifted, trying to squirm away from his intimidating presence. She shifted again and moaned, her hand to her ribs as they screamed at her for moving them.

"Shit, girl, stop moving. You have stitches you're gonna tear out, for cripe's sake." He took a step closer, his arms dropped.

She put a hand up. "Why didn't you just kill me when you killed Rufus instead of torturing me like this, waiting for you to – to beat me or stab me, or," her chest hitched with a sob of fear and pain firing in her head. Scrunching over, both hands went to her head as she bowed it, trying to stifle moans of suffering.

"Goddammit, I told you to stop moving. Just stay still, I said I'm not gonna hurt you."

When she raised her head, the horrendous pain streaked out her sodden eyes. One palm lowered to her ribs again, the other covered her forehead, she slumped as her body rolled over the bed.

"For fuck's sake," cursing, Volt went to her. "You will learn to listen to me, woman." Sliding his arms under her, he lifted her and resettled her lying against the pillows. "Here," he poured a glass of water from a carafe on the nightstand, handed it to her, shook out a pill from the bottle beside it into his palm, and held it out for her to take.

Aching lids scrunched over Stassi's eyes as she gingerly regarded the pill in his hand as if she thought he was going to grab her when she reached for it. His forearms looked like he pumped iron 8 hours a day, even his fingers looked strong.

A sigh of annoyance, he held his hand out further, carping, "Just take it, Anastasia, I don't need Doctor Granger, or Sadie for that matter on my back that I scared you into hurting yourself."

She did as he said then twisted to set the glass on the nightstand and cringed with pain.

"Damn," more curses and he snatched it out of her hand and set it down. "Okay, we need to talk. Sit back and try to stay the hell still."

Stassi's lips pushed out in a mutinous moue at his ordering her about. She sat back but her body stayed stiff, still in the flight mode.

Realizing he was scaring her by looming over her broken body, Volt moved a chair next to the bed and sat down. "First off," he said, settling back, crossing an ankle over a knee. "My name is Voltang Saldano. I am an international, ah, sort of agent. I get hired to find people. People that are either at risk or wanted by the authorities. That day in the alley, that man, he had snatched a child, a little boy. The police, FBI, no one could find him or the child. As in all those types of cases time was of the essence."

Could she have been so wrong? "But, you were hitting him, you cut him, I saw you."

Volt folded his hands and set them in his lap. "Yes. I hunted him, captured him. He wouldn't say where the child was. I was finding out where he'd stashed him."

"You were torturing him!"

"It was necessary to get him to talk."

"But, once you found the, uh, bad guy, shouldn't you have turned him over to the police? It's their job to interrogate-"

"Sweetheart," sarcasm laced his words, "the police have rules they have to follow. Civil rights, an attorney, patience. As I said, the boy's life was hanging in the balance. We needed to know right then where he was. The perp had a long record, he knew the system, he would have immediately lawyered up, he never would have told the police, he never would have admitted to taking the child. The boy would be dead and the perp would walk free to grab another child."

"But the police-"

"I don't give a damn about the fucking police!" he shouted. Stassi blanched.

Shaking his head in frustration, Volt's voice was tight with the patience he was trying to cling to. "Listen, Anastasia, they never would have gotten the guy to talk, the kid would be sold or dead. End of story. I get hired to do what the cops can't."

She stared thoughtfully at him. "Legally? Is what you do legal? Who hired you to find the child?"

He glared cryptically at her for a moment. "If it was your child, and you knew the bastard would never tell, and your baby, your son was dying or being sold as a sex slave in some foreign country, would you care if it was legal or not?"

Her lips parted to say something, then they closed. She silently shook her head. "The boy," she was scared to ask, what if her interference caused his death? "Is he…"

Volt lowered his leg, planted both feet on the floor. "He's fine. I got out of the filthy bastard where the boy was just as you were…interrupting us. I was arrested but quickly convinced the cops what I was doing. They raced to save the kid. The guy had stashed him in a cage in a cabin hidden deep in a forest." Suppressed rage rose, clenching Volt's jaw. "Anyway, they got the victim, he was fine, physically anyway. I verified who I was and who hired me, the cops let me go."

"Oh thank God." Stassi thought these things only happened in the movies. Her hand splayed over her rapidly beating heart. What if they had been too late to save the child due to her interference? She couldn't bear to think about it. "Who hired you?"

He considered how much to tell her. Leaning forward, he rested his forearms on his thighs, clasped his hands, and said, "Indirectly, the boy's father. He went through avenues to certain people that contacted me. There are some police that, well, walk the edge, they would have hinted to him who to contact to reach me. Don't ask who, I can't, won't tell you."

Her gaze flit back and forth over his face, should she believe him? He was not in custody, he must be telling the truth. Most of it anyway. She was there in his house, alive, recovering, he had brought her there. But why? The confusion only mounted. Nervous fingers clutched at the throat of her nightgown, she asked, "Were you hired to find me? I don't know anyone that would…could, find someone like you. Or anyone that would even try."

He shrugged. "If Francis Crick knew how to find someone like me he would have tried. You are quite valuable."

She pondered that. Then back to the little boy, she asked, "How are you paid? Was that child's father wealthy enough to hire, uh, whatever you are?"

The side of his mouth lifted. "No. The government paid me. The military actually, they have funds for special ops, crisis extractions, those sorts of things."

"How much did you receive for rescuing me?"

A wry arch to one brow he regarded her coolly, again discerning how much to tell her. "I wasn't actually hired to find you, I was…it was a favor." His expression stated he wasn't going to tell her who he did the favor for.

When he didn't thunder at her or seem to be about to pummel her with his fists, settling against the pillows she let her shoulders relax a little. Letting his answer go for now, she asked him, "How did you find me?"

Volt sat back again in the chair. "It wasn't that hard. I did the usual, starting with obtaining all surveillance tapes in the area, they replayed the vehicles present the day you were taken. Didn't show you being abducted, Vinca was careful to park out of sight of the cameras, but we got the plate of the van from a camera it passed down the street. Unfortunately it had been a stolen vehicle. However, once I knew the reason why you were taken, I narrowed down the people that could be involved."

"Weren't the people who grabbed me on camera somewhere?"

"No. Vinca Nivelli is a professional, too careful to be caught on film. He would have snatched you out of any camera view. He killed the security guard that was supposed to be escorting you to your car. One of the scientists saw him take you, but once the slain guard was found they assumed that he was the one who escorted you out and someone else murdered him and took you.

"It wasn't until I interviewed the scientist that I figured out what happened. Unfortunately, he doesn't remember what the guy looked like because he wore a uniform and a cap. Uniforms give people anonymity, people all look the same in a uniform, no one looks carefully at the person. But he did remember the guy was real big, brawny, well above average height. Perfect description of Vinca."

"Uh huh. So these people you narrowed down, how did you find out that it was Mr. Lamontagne or this Vinca person who was the one who abducted me?"

He informed her, "Vinca Nivelli works for Nero Lamontagne." Then he explained how he found her. "I sent my feelers out to five men, had them watched. Questioned people in the areas where these five men live, work, the people they know. Watched as supplies were delivered, and did a variety of other information gathering.

"There was unusual activity at one of the laboratories in question. We finally bribed the right person and he told us the rumor that a woman was being held in a dungeon at Nero Lamontagne's estate."

The pain pill was taking effect, her body felt lighter, she had so many questions she tried to sort in her mind. "So, you rescued me." The image of him fighting Rufus flashed in her head. "Is Rufus really dead?"

"Oh yeah, trust me. You saw me stab him." He appeared calm, almost laidback, but his body was coiled tightly, he watched her under low lids that hid his thoughts.

She looked away as she recalled the chaotic scene. It had been horrendous. Men running everywhere, screams, gunshots, she thought she was going to be raped by dozens of soldiers and killed. Rufus had almost gotten to her, his fist was raised to strike her the second he was within reach.

Then, apparently he saw Saldano approaching and he moved back to assess him and Saldano jumped between her and Rufus causing Rufus to stumble back further. Saldano effortlessly beat Rufus to a pulp, then he stabbed him- blood was just everywhere. It was terrible to say, but she was glad he was dead. He'd hurt her so gravely, and he can never touch her again. "Mr. Lamontagne," nerves struck her at the thought, her voice wobbled, "he might come after me again."

"No doubt he will. But you are safe here, no one can penetrate this compound, I have dozens of men patrolling. My soldiers are ten times the fighters he had. As long as I have a full crew on board he cannot get to you here. Even if they got on the land, they'd never breach the house."

Stassi peered up at him with a labored sigh. The man was the epitome of unfaltering strength. It wasn't just his strapping physique, his looming height, power and fortitude radiated from his arrogant bearing. His rough accent seethed with grit and determination, the formidable aura surrounding him was replete with dark mystery.

She felt a sense of security, that he would never allow anyone to take her from him. Finally, since the moment her apartment was ransacked and she was abducted, Stassi was able to fill her lungs with a full breath of calming air. She was safe. But, she narrowed her eyes in suspicion at him. "You swore you would get back at me, harm me for getting you arrested. Am I right in fearing you?"

His expression revealed nothing, no anger, no kindness, he leveled a hard look at her. "You jeopardized my mission. That little boy could have died because you got involved. As someone I was sent to extract, lady, you were low on my list of people I'd want to risk my life and my team to rescue. Unfortunately, I am not a forgiving man. I only did a favor for a friend."

She nodded in appreciation of his forthrightness. "I see. I...can understand you feeling the way you do. I'm sorry, however, if the same circumstances happened again, I would do the same as I did. I hear a person in need, in distress, I am not going to ignore it and look the other way. If only someone had helped me get away from Nero." Her shoulders twitched with a mirthless smile, she said, "I mean long before you came."

She glanced around at the large, comfortable room. "Why did you bring me here to your home if you...despise me so much?"

Volt stood up, pushed the knees of his jeans down straightening them. "As I said, you are not safe. Lamontagne will want you back and I'm sure there will be others after you. There is no point in my saving you just to toss you like a baby bird back out to the hawks. Doesn't mean I have to like it, or like you."

Stassi didn't know the man, but still his cruel words cut deep. She lowered her head so he couldn't see how much his words hurt her. Then, raising her head, she said stoically, "I understand. That man in the alley, is he dead?"

Volt was quiet, again deciding how much to tell her. "No. But he'll wish he was."

Her brows lifted. "What happened to him?"

He peered hard at her before answering. "Because of the way I got the information about the child's location out of him, he could not be tried for the abduction. Or for anything else from the poisonous tree, such as the child porn on his computer or the sex trafficking ring he stole the boy for in the first place."

"Oh, gosh, Mr. Saldano, that man, that animal is not out there harming more children because of me?" Her hand at her throat, the wretched guilt of what she might have been inadvertently complicit in climbed like bile, letting the man escape justice to continue his evil deeds.

His stare was harsh, punishing. "Thanks to you he could have been." Volt let that guilt stew for a moment. Seeing her battered face crumple in devastation, he informed her, "No, he's not out running free. Somehow," his dark tone lightened somewhat. "He managed to end up in Mongolia. There was evidence that he raped and butchered some young girls there. The police in a small village sent the evidence to their prosecutors and he was found guilty and sentenced to life. Prisons in Mongolia are not country clubs like they are here. He might not even last a week, who knows?" His shrug and tone said 'who cares?'

She inhaled sharply. "But if he was innocent of those charges, then another guilty murderer is still out there-"

Shaking his head with a cold smile, Volt said, "No. The beast that was guilty was executed long ago for other crimes. The evidence the police produced had been recycled to use against our offender."

It was so much to comprehend, to take in, all this horror, death, brutality, deceit in justice. Stassi rubbed her eyes, combed her hair back off her face with trembling fingers and sighed. "I don't know how you can live in that ugly world, Mr. Saldano."

He appraised her tunnel vision with a hard look, said blandly, "You think about where you'd be right now if it wasn't for men like me. It's a job."

He was right, he'd saved her life. She admitted it with a small, abashed smile, "Yes, you are quite right. I am sorry for judging you. Thank you for saving me, I am grateful with my whole heart." The sincerity warmed her pallid complexion.

His face stony, he said coolly, "You were just a job, like I said, I do my job."

The pair stared at each other for a few beats. Then she said, "Speaking of jobs, I need to go back to work."

"Of course. As soon as you are on your feet, I will take you there."

Her mouth quivered slightly, her bravery waning, she asked, "Will I be...safe there? My home?"

"Probably not."

"I see. Well…" she plucked at the blanket. As she rolled her eyes up at him, his gaze was on her chest. Red bloomed in her pale cheeks when she realized how sheer, how thin the nightgown she wore was. Pulling the blanket up to her neck, she asked, "Who…um, I wasn't wearing this when I…" Her dress had been filthy and in tatters, but she was still wearing it when Rufus was killed.

His gaze rose from her chest to her face. "Not me. My assistant, housekeeper, whatever you want to call her, Sadie, she and a nurse bathed you and dressed you. You know her, she's helped you with the bathroom and whatnot. When my men are around, you will put a sweater on over the gown, or stay under the blanket."

Her brows hopped at his stern instruction. "Excuse me?"

"You heard me. They are red-blooded males, they're going to check out the merchandise. They like what they see, they'll go after it."

Pink no longer colored her cheeks, they were pale again. "Are you saying they would assault me? I'm not safe here?" She pushed the blanket aside and slid her legs over the side of the bed. "I need to go." A wave of dizziness washed over her. Planting both hands on the mattress, fighting the dizziness she wriggled to get to the edge of the mattress, his hard hands came down on her shoulders holding her in place.

"Stop. You have nothing to fear from my men. They would never force themselves on a woman. But, they may desire to seduce one. You are fragile right now, injured, ill, they wouldn't realize how vulnerable you are. And, dressed like that," one brow arched as he indicated her gown, "you are waving a naked sheep in front of the wolves. Now," he did as before, lifted her and placed her back to reclining against the pillows. "You will do as I say. You are perfectly safe here. You will stay until you recover."

"My apartment-"

94

"Not safe. You're staying here."

"But-"

"I have work to do." He stepped away from the bed and headed for the door.

Chapter Fourteen

It was a few weeks before Stassi was able to walk for a distance without aching, tiring, gasping for breath. She weaned off the pain medication and used the gym Volt had shown her in the house. She hadn't seen much of him, of course the sight of her angered him so he obviously stayed away. Apparently his men grew bored with her because after a couple of visits they no longer came by.

She had worked out in the gym, jogged on the treadmill and worked with some light weights. After showering and dressing in faded jeans and a pearl colored sweater she found her way to the dining room. Volt had seen that a suitcase of her clothes and phone were retrieved and brought to her. Sadie was just setting a plate of eggs and pancakes on the table.

"There you are dear," the older woman welcomed her with a smile. "Jubal informed me that you had worked out in the gym and now showered and dressed. I assumed you'd head here next. You know I keep the food warm for stragglers."

Sadie and another woman cooked for Volt and his men. The other woman, Colleen kept the house clean and the household running while Sadie's job was to oversee the household and look after Volt and his business, whatever that entailed, Stassi had no idea.

Stassi took a seat as Sadie left and returned with a glass of orange juice and a cup of tea for her. Smiling her thanks, Stassi stuck a fork in the eggs. "You are so kind to me, Mrs. Durant. I know you take care of Mr. Saldano and the other men, you don't need to wait on me. I keep telling you I can take care of myself."

"Tsk tsk, dear, I've told you to call me Sadie, everyone does, or just Sade as Volt calls me. And it's my job to oversee that everything runs smoothly here, and part of that is taking care of Volt's guests."

"Hmm." Stassi poured maple syrup over her pancakes and added a dab of butter to them then dug in. "These are delicious, Mrs. Dur, ah, Sadie." She took a big bite, chewed vigorously and swallowed with a moan of pleasure.

"I wish I was staying here longer and maybe could help you cook, I could learn so much from you. And, I am not Mr. Saldano's guest. I am his…rescuee I guess you'd say. And a very reluctant one on his part. He doesn't like me or really want me here. I think it's time to get going, I'm pretty healed."

Sadie hovered, watching Stassi eat. "Oh honey, he doesn't not like you. He certainly wants you here, he's cracked the whip over his crew to ensure your complete safety. He's paid for your health care out of his own pocket. He's supervised your recovery from top to bottom."

Chewing a piece of bacon, Stassi disagreed. "He's barely spoken a few words to me, he's never present when I am at lunch or dinner. I know he and his team eat breakfast and are out and about before dawn. Other than you, I've been kind of lonely. His men don't seem to like me either, they've also stayed clear."

Sadie laughed. "Not for want of trying, dear. Pretty much most of Volt's men have attempted to spend some time with you, but Volt has ordered them to stay away from you."

Feeling sad at her words, Stassi said, "See, he hates me."

"Honey, I don't think it's due to hate that he orders his men to not hang with you, I think it's more in the line of-"

"Sadie," a gruff voice cut her off. Volt entered the room.

Although he'd deliberately broke in stopping her words, Sadie grinned at him. "Ah yes, I have things to do. I'll see you later, Stassi." With a saucy wink to Stassi, she left to attend to her tasks.

"Anastasia," he started.

"Can you call me Stassi, Mr. Saldano, Anastasia is too long to say." Besides, with his accent, it kind of gave her the creeps the way it rolled long and dark off his tongue. Then, a thought came to her, she narrowed her gaze at him, "Mongolia. Where that dreadful man ended up. You're from somewhere around there, aren't you?"

"You could say something like that, the land of the fierce pagan pirates," was his non-answer. His gaze traveled down her figure and up to her rosy cheeks, shining eyes. "You are looking much healthier, on the way to complete recovery it appears."

Her breakfast mostly gone, Stassi set her fork on the plate. "Yes. I believe it's time for me to return to work. Mr. Crick has had his secretary Karine Benton call me constantly to ask when I was coming back."

His mouth firmed with irritation. "I told them you were not to be harassed. I said you would return when you were completely well. You're still tiring too soon, you aren't-"

Stassi pushed her chair back to stand. "I will gain my energy back in time. But Mr. Crick is right, I need to get back to work." Picking up her plate she moved past him, careful to keep a distance between them. "In fact, I'll go pack now."

"Anastasia, I don't think you're ready to-"

She swung around with a forced smile. "May I have your address so I can call a taxi?"

"Anastasia, listen to me-"

She interrupted him again, "I am ready to leave. I need to call for a ride, Mr. Saldano, please."

His face stiffened in a frown of disapproval. He bowed his head slightly. "All right. I will drive you myself when you're ready."

"Oh, you don't have to put yourself out, I know you want me out of your hair as soon as possible, I'll call a taxi, I just need this address."

"I said I would drive you."

Chapter Fifteen

A day later, they rode in silence. At her insistence, Volt took her to her apartment. He carried her suitcase inside and set it in her bedroom and came back out. Glowering down at her, he said, "Anastasia, it isn't safe for you to stay here."

"I know, you've only said it a hundred times. I have nowhere else to go and I certainly can't afford to stay at a hotel until all this business is done." She pulled out her phone and swiped it on.

Boots planted shoulder width apart he crossed his arms over the black sweater he wore with black jeans. Rolling his thick shoulders as if annoyed, he said, "I've told you that I can provide protection for you at my home here in Nevada. You may remain there."

"You hate me, can't stand the sight of me, want to punish me for almost foiling your mission. Why would you invite me to stay at your home?"

"The favor is not complete. Your life is still in danger."

"The favor was to rescue me, not provide ongoing protection, and at your personal home no less. Thank you for the offer even though I know it killed you to feel you had to offer it."

Irritation flickered in his eyes. A disgruntled sigh rumbled in his chest, he gave in. "As you wish. I'll have men posted for your protection, here and at the lab."

She said with an awkward laugh, "Mr. Crick has security, and I can't afford to pay for bodyguards. I'll just be super careful and make sure everything is locked up tighter than a drum."

He regarded her as if she had two heads and was four-years-old. "Anastasia, people like Vinca Nivelli aren't stopped by locked doors. I myself could get in here in less than 10 seconds."

Eyes wide with astonished disbelief, she squawked, "How?"

"Never mind, the point is, you can't prevent these people from getting to you. You will have the security I mentioned, I don't want to talk about it anymore. You ready to go to the lab?"

"Uh…" seeing his face closed off, hooded lids and mouth firmly resolute, Stassi exhaled in consternated resignation. There was no point in trying to argue with him now, he was like a chunk of hard ice. He must have really owed someone something huge to go to this extent for a favor. It had to have been Mr. Crick but being modest, Mr. Crick didn't want her to know, so Volt had denied it was her boss.

"Do you need some time to settle in before we leave?" he asked with stiff politeness.

She shook her head. "No. There is nothing to do here except unpack my few things and check my mail. I can do that later."

The first five minutes in the car neither said a word. Volt rested one hand on the wheel, the other on the compartment between the seats. As usual, his face was set although his jaw seemed tight and a vein pulsed at his temple.

Stassi ran through in her mind the initial things she needed to do as soon as she arrived at the lab. She glanced at him a few times, his profile was as tough as face on. Her hands were clasped over her purse in her lap, she tried not to fiddle with the purse strap. Volt made her nervous like he always did when they were alone.

She didn't know exactly why she felt nervous. Yes he was a strong, secretive, dangerous man, and he made it clear he didn't like her. But, the entire time she had stayed at his place he had never once laid a hand on her or even threatened to. Her safety and recovery seemed to be his paramount concerns. Still, she couldn't put a finger on it why his close proximity made her tense.

Clearing her throat, she said, "Please text me an itemized list of what I owe you as soon as you can. I will need to know how to budget for it. If you require it right away I can probably get a cash advance on my credit card." She glanced at him when he didn't respond.

His brows were so low he squinted, his mouth tight, the vein twitched faster at his temple.

"Mr. Saldano? Did you hear me? I said you need to-"

He bit off, "There is nothing wrong with my hearing."

She turned to face him. His scowl so black he looked disturbingly furious. "Mr. Sal-"

"Not discussing it," he said with such finality Stassi knew he would not budge.

Turning again to face forward, she folded her hands primly in her lap, her fingers curled over the purse and said calmly, "Fine. We'll talk about it later. Just prepare the numbers for me." She could have sworn out of the corner of her eye she saw his eyes roll.

Brant met Stassi at the entrance to Exbiotics. She had called ahead so they knew she was returning to work. When she walked in past security, Brant's face lit up like the 4th of July. He hurried to her with open arms.

"Thank God, Stassi, you're all right! We were beside ourselves with worry when we learned you'd been abducted. It'd been so long, until Mr. Crick heard from some guy named Saldano that you had been rescued from some foreign country but that you were on your deathbed we-" he broke off swallowing a sob of relief and threw his arms around her.

"Brant, I'm fine, um…" Stassi tried to extricate herself from his embrace but he only hugged her more tightly, his face in her hair. One arm around her shoulders, the other stroked down until his hand was lower than the inner swell of her lower back.

"Brant, uh, you can let go now, I need air." Her pushing at him was ineffective as was trying to squirm out of his clinch. Suddenly she was jerked free. Or, actually Brant was yanked away from her.

"What the hell," Brant cursed, glaring at Volt.

"Voltang Saldano," Volt introduced himself through a locked jaw, eyes cold black stones, "the 'guy' who called Crick." He didn't hold out his hand to Brant. "Anastasia had been critically injured and has not yet fully recovered. Manhandling her roughly will set her back."

It took a beat before Brant got steady on his feet. Combing his fingers through his hair, he scowled rudely at Volt. "Who the hell are you?"

"I just told you, are you a bit thick?" Volt's accent making him sound arrogant and condescending. He was a few inches taller than Brant, dressed in all black as usual including leather jacket, he stood impassively with his hands on his hips.

Brant turned to Stassi. "Stas, what the heck is this guy-"

"I need to get to the lab, Brant, I have so much to catch up on." Stassi gave Volt an artificial smile. "Thank you for everything, Mr. Saldano, saving my life, housing me these past weeks, seeing to my healthy recovery, the ride here. I appreciate all you have done for me. As I said, please text me those figures, include the um, cost for the security you have here for me."

She held her hand out to him to shake, but he glanced at it then looked up to her heartfelt expression. Her smile was awkward but her gratitude was 150% real. When he didn't take her hand, she stood on tiptoes and kissed his cheek. Lowering to her heels, she tucked her hands behind her back, smiling with discomfort, she repeated, "Thanks again."

Wordless, Volt's eyes narrowed at her. She couldn't read his expression. He said, "I'll take a look around, set up my men."

"Stassi!" Valentina King rushed across the wide lobby and hurtled her body at Stassi grabbing her in a bear hug. She gushed with joy, "You're safe! You're home!" The brunette caught Stassi's arms and stood back to look at her. Smile beaming on her plump face, her round brown eyes like hockey pucks adrift with happy tears, she exclaimed, "You look better than I expected from the horrid stories we were told about your abduction. I missed you so much!" She hugged her again.

"Let her go, Val, let the rest of us have a moment," Charlie Shaw said, pulling her to him he wrapped his arms around Stassi for a long hug. Releasing her, his eyes damp, his voice warm he told her, "So glad you're safe and sound, Stas, we missed you like crazy. I was afraid Cody would have to grow up without knowing his Auntie Stassi," a catch in his voice, he coughed to clear the emotion clogging his throat.

"Oh, Charlie, I'm fine, I'm so happy to be home." The pair gazed at each other with affection.

"God, must we be subjected to such dreary drama?" Juliette Moore's sarcastic voice dampened the joviality. Then, "Who have we here?" her voice went from dry to coy in a blink. She strolled over to Volt and held out her hand, the back of it up and fingers limp as if she expected him to take it and kiss it. Tilting her head, long red hair swooped over one eye, her large lips in a practiced coquette's smile, she said, "Hi, I'm Juliette Moore, so incredibly pleased to meet you."

Volt's eyes lowered to her hand. He gave it one quick shake without introducing himself. Tugging his hand from her grip since she wasn't letting go, he said to Stassi, "I'll be in touch, Anastasia. My men will keep an eye on you. Anything untoward you notice, tell one of them immediately. I will text their photos and names to you." Without another word, he turned on his heel and strode away as if he owned the place and disappeared down a hall that led to the security department.

"How does he know his way around here?" Brant grumped at Volt's rude dismissal of him.

Stassi stared off to where Volt had gone, she replied with a shrug, "He probably had a blueprint of the place before he even came after me."

"Wow," Dixy Lee said with an enthralled voice as she joined the throng, "who was that? He kinda looked scary." She pulled a fuzzy blonde curl over her mouth and chewed on it. "He made me feel uneasy like he was a jungle cat on the prowl or something just as dangerous."

"Scary hot, with a crazy sexy accent," Juliette crooned, staring off to where he'd disappeared to.

"He...saved me," Stassi told them in a quiet voice. She was mortified to have been abducted and having had to be rescued. All she wanted was to forget the entire episode and get to work. Brant read her mind.

"Okay everybody, I need to take you to Mr. Crick, Stas. He wants a debriefing then get you to the lab." Brant slid his arm around Stassi's waist. He muttered, "That tough guy was kind of proprietary of you, honey, what is he to you?"

Smiling, she answered, "The black knight that rescued me."

"You need to hook me up with him, Stas," Juliette urged.

"But he's so scary looking, Juls." Dixy shivered with apprehension.

"Yeah, that's so hot. You have his number, right, Stassi?" Juliette traipsed after Brant and Stassi heading to the elevators.

After having to endure hugs and teary welcome backs, Stassi was ready to settle in and get back to work.

Chapter Sixteen

Putting away the last test tube, Stassi sighed tiredly. She had expected to be kept on edge worrying that around every corner someone would be looming to grab her and she'd be back in that nightmare cell with another vile monster like Rufus torturing her. But, a week passed with zero drama. Juliette still pestered her for Saldano's number, other than that life was peaceful and she worked every waking moment of every waking day.

The security team Volt had planted around the lab and her home were tremendously discrete. They were so invisible she thought Volt had pulled them from bodyguard duty and sent them home. Then there was a disturbance at the front of the lab one morning as she was entering. Every once in a while a lunatic would protest whatever Frankenstein antics they thought the lab was up to and try to storm the security desk to wreak havoc.

That morning as staff was arriving, a fanatic shrieking obscenities and throwing stones from a bag he carried at everyone forced his way inside. People screamed and ran blindly from the lobby. Before Stassi could take a step, two huge men swooped in, picked her up and in seconds she found herself outside locked in a Hummer with a third man as the other two raced back inside the lab to quell the upheaval.

Moments later, the two bodyguards hustled a bound man out the front doors and to one of the several police car that came roaring up to the entrance.

"Wow," her face pressed against the window, Stassi murmured in shock at how quickly Saldano's men reacted getting her out of the way and to safety, and capturing the fanatic quickly and without harming him.

She had sort of thought maybe Saldano would give her a call; just to check on her health, see how she was doing. But then again, she told her oddly disappointed self, as he had stated to her, more than once, she was just a job. A favor owed to someone.

When she asked Mr. Crick if he was the one who had hired Saldano to come to her rescue, he had responded in bafflement, and denied any knowledge of knowing people like Saldano even existed, and therefore had no part in her rescue.

It was so strange, she still wondered who would care enough about her to hire someone to come for her. She had no close friends, just the few she worked with and none of them would have any idea of how to find someone, a mercenary, or agent type as he had referred to himself.

Saldano wouldn't even tell her how the person who charged him with finding her had even learned of her kidnapping in the first place. She supposed there had been mention in the news. She didn't look into it though, didn't look up archival reports, it was such a devastating chapter in her life that she shoved it way, way down inside. She feared reprising nightmares if she pondered on it, read the horrible story of her abduction. She sure as heck did not need to relive it even in writing. Maybe it was a matter of misidentification. Perhaps whoever hired Saldano thought she was someone else. Well, either way, she was grateful for the rescue.

Yes, it was all so very strange. Well, she just wanted to put it all behind her and move on. Making a mental note to call Saldano and remind him to send her a bill for his services, he hadn't responded to the last three texts she sent him for a bill, maybe a phone call would work, Stassi reached for the door handle, but it wouldn't budge.

"Excuse me," she said to the man in the front seat. "I can't get the door open."

His eyes revolving unceasingly scanning the area, he grunted. "You stay here until we get the all clear."

"Oh, I'm sure everything is under control, and I need to get back to work, so," she tugged at the lock but it wouldn't move.

He ignored her, still scanning the area.

"For the love of," sighing, Stassi sat back. His men were just like Saldano. There was no arguing with them. They took control and that was that. She couldn't complain, they were only trying to protect her. Still, it wasn't pleasant being so controlled.

After the fanatic episode, another uneventful week passed. Getting ready to go to work in her tiny, plain apartment, Stassi took a bite of her peanut butter toast, and smiled wryly, a couple of weeks ago she was sitting in luxury eating like a queen. Before she could miss it, she recalled the harsh faced, cold man that had kept her under his iron thumb until he delivered her home. Well, she had learned, Saldano's men were as immovable as him. Thoughts of Saldano struck her.

Voltang Saldano. Enigmatic, dangerous, stubborn man, he annoyed the heck out of her, yet he stayed bouncing around in her mind. Well, she'd had a traumatic incident, it was no wonder. He did save her life, after all. Cleaning the knife and plate her toast was on, she took a last sip of coffee and put the cup in the sink. She just needed to complete the darn formula and get on with her life. Time to get to the lab.

She brushed her teeth and slipped her ankle boots on, after grabbing her jacket, she reached for her purse when her cell rang. Hitting 'accept' before she could even answer it a voice shouted from the phone.

"Stassi! Stassi!" Charlie Shaw was sobbing and shouting at the same time he was barely intelligible.

Her heart started beating fast she said, "Charlie, calm down, what's going on? Is Melinda-"

"Cody! They have my baby! Stassi, you have to do something, you have to do what they say or they said they would-" his voice broke off in guttural heaving sobs.

"What Charlie? Who? What's wrong with Cody?" She held the phone from her ear as he shrieked and cried and cursed. "Charlie, Charlie, you have to calm down, I don't know what you're saying, take a deep breath."

"My baby! My baby!" he screamed. His heavy racing breaths reverberated through the phone. "God, Stassi, you have to get him back! You have to!" She could hear Melinda wailing in the background just as distraught as Charlie.

"Charlie, is anyone else besides you and Melinda there that can talk to me?" She tried to speak as calmly as she could, but hell, he was scaring her.

"Unh, unh," he babbled incoherently. Then, someone said, "Hello? Is this Stassi?"

"Yes, who's this? What's going on?"

"Um, I'm Donna Purl, Lindy, uh, Melinda's sister-in-law. I was here when- when," she gasped when her words choked. A second to gather herself, her voice shaking, she said, "While Charlie and Melinda were asleep apparently someone came into their home and- and took Cody. Charlie was getting ready for work and Melinda was making his breakfast when they realized they hadn't heard a peep from the baby. When they went to check on him, they- they-" she broke off with a sob.

"Okay, Donna, it's okay, tell me what happened."

Sounds of weeping, then, "Cody was not in his crib and there was a note with a number to call. Charlie called and it was a man, he said he had Cody, and if you didn't go to him he'd-kill the baby." Screams and cries raged in the background. Donna cried, "They said we can't go to the police or he's- the baby is- dead!"

"I...don't understand. Me? Why would someone take Cody and want me to-" *oh God no.* It was Lamontagne, blackmailing Stassi into returning to him. She slapped her hand on her forehead, she couldn't think. Images of the cell and Rufus flooded her mind, no, please, no, she begged silently.

"Stassi," Donna cried," please, you have to do what they say, please!"

Stassi was good as dead if she went back, and they would probably terminate the baby as soon as she showed her face. She couldn't, she just couldn't go back there. Her heart felt like a steel bar was wrapping around it and squeezing, squeezing, she couldn't think. There was no way out. No, she was never going back to that torture, no, no, no!

"Stassi," Charlie grabbed the phone yelling, then he spoke slower, quieter, "please, Stas, he's my baby, my boy. Please, you have to help us, please."

"God, Charlie..." anguish for them pierced her words.

Charlie stopped begging, but his traumatic sobs were very audible as are Melinda's.

She never stood a chance. It was her life or a baby's. "Okay," her acquiescence a resigned exhale of dread.

His sobs rent louder before he could speak. "Sta- Stassi, thank you, thank you."

Stassi spoke around the fatalistic terror climbing up her throat, "What, uh, how am I to contact Mr. Lamontagne?"

In mid-sob Charlie said, "He's not the one who has my son."

"What?" Who else could it be? Surprised, she asked in tense confusion, "Who then, Charlie?"

"It's um, a guy said he was calling for Talis Falk."

Shock reverberated through her body, *Talis Falk*. "The man that invented the bacteria? That Talis Falk?" She was being stupid, how many Talis Falks can there be in the world?

Sniffing loudly Charlie replied, "Yeah, that Talis Falk. Although Mr. Crick told us it's an alias. He apparently has many aliases to keep people from finding him."

Oh goody, she's wanted by a man who doesn't exist. Stassi wiped her palm across her sweating forehead. Her life had gone into the crapper. What did she ever do to deserve this? All she ever wanted was to study science, environmental science. As far back as she could remember her dreams had always been about saving the world for future generations of people and animals.

When her professor had heard about the bacteria, and they had a sample in their hands, he gave her the challenge of finding an antidote. Now the professor was dead, and Stassi had been abducted and tortured, a baby has been kidnapped, and now Stassi has to sacrifice herself to yet another monstrous demon. Because anyone who would snatch a 6 month old baby and use him for blackmail is even above Satan.

Swallowing her brain-boggling fear of what she will have to deal with next, she asked, "How am I to get in touch with him?"

Sniffling, Charlie took a minute, then said softly, "He will call you at 7:30 to give you instructions.

"Okay," she replied even softer.

"Stassi…"

"Yeah?"

"Thank you. I know how terrified you must be, I would never ask this of you or anyone, but he has my boy. I offered myself in your place, and I was told if I balked again in any form he would," a sob cut off his breath, he paused to get a grip. "He- he said he would cut off Cody's, ah, his penis and FedEx it to us."

The thought of it sickened her. "I understand, Charlie, it's all right." Her stomach tumbled down to her feet and went splat on the floor with dire dread. If he'd do that to a baby, what is in store for Stassi?

Charlie started sobbing again. Stassi said, "I have to go, Charlie, it's almost 7:30 now."

"Stas," he wept, "k- keep in touch if you can, let me know how- what-"

"I will, Charlie, bye now." She hung up quickly before she could back out of the deal. She set her keys on the table, no point in going to the lab now. But she needed to call Mr. Crick and tell him- Her phone rang in her hand startling her.

She looked at it and read *unknown number*. Staring at it, she did not want to answer the call, no, never, never. It felt like snakes were twisting and snapping their fangs in her gut. She pictured Cody the last time she saw him. Chubby legs, gurgling with laughter, he was on the floor entertained with the faces Charlie was making at him. The phone stopped ringing.

"Oh no! No!" Grabbing the phone she quickly tried to reply to it. In the missed call section the words *unknown number* showed again. When she tapped on it in reply, instead of a dial tone a buzz- buzz sounded. The call wasn't going through.

"What have I done?" she wailed, panic slamming her. "God, please don't let that baby-"

Ring- the display showed *unknown number,* Stassi pushed the accept button so fast she almost pushed the cell right out of her hand.

Clearing her throat so she could get the words out, she willed her voice to be strong, brave, but it came out in a frightened whisper, "H- hello?" Silence. "Hello?" Nothing. *Please,* "Hello, Mr. Falk, I'm here?" The statement came out as a question. Silence. She was about to speak again when he responded.

"Ah, Anastasia Athens, about time."

And her heart froze. She knew that voice. It haunted her frequent nightmares. Old nightmares crashed into new nightmares.

"Anastasia? You need to talk to me or I'm hanging up and the baby will suffer. Badly."

Gulping down her torment, Stassi stammered, "M- Mr. Callen?" The chuckle on the other end of the phone was obscene. It brought that day back like a hammer to the head. That day, she'd been so helpless, violated, her childhood snatched away in one instant.

"Ah, I am delighted you remember me," he sounded very pleased.

Her head whirled with static thoughts, ears roared as blood rushed to her head, she couldn't think, she was going to puke, clutching the phone, she hurried to the sink.

"Anastasia, or, Stassi I recall your little friends called you. It appears the cat has caught your tongue. I hope when you arrive to my house you will have regained your tongue." There was a pause, then he spoke, "I know you're still there, I can hear your hysterical panting. You are scared. You should be."

"Y- you're supposed to be in jail, prison, how…" her voice failed her as she spoke with the last person she ever thought she'd ever have another conversation.

He no longer sounded humorous. "I got out, dear heart. Got tired of following rules and looking out at the world from behind bars. I…discharged myself. And," his chuckle ugly, he told her, "I left a few bodies behind. Corrections Officers, they should have been more vigilant, less careless and lazy.

"Anyway, just so you know, I hadn't forgotten about you. I would have reached out to you sooner but I needed to build my dynasty first. But now you have been brought to my attention and I find I cannot wait any longer for you."

"You…are you saying you escaped from prison?" she whispered, she had no strength to speak louder. "The police, they must be looking for you."

"Oh they are, my sweet. Hence the name change. Or, make that changes. I've had to travel incognito while I stole enough money, sold enough sex slaves, trafficked enough weapons and drugs to finance my dynasty."

"Dynasty? What do you-"

"You'll see. Two birds, one lovely stone. I get you because we have unfinished business, and I get you to give me your formula for the antidote to my bacteria. I was coming after you anyway so I get the winning points in that you are the chemist they're all talking about." The hard edge to his tone told he wasn't quite as amiable as he was pretending to be, he was holding back his rage.

When she didn't say anything, he went on sounding calmer, "You showed promise in the science fields when you were young, but, shit Stassi, I never thought it'd be you. It knocked me for a loop when I heard about the counteractive formula and that it was you who conceived it."

"It's not completed, Mr. Callen. I'm still-"

"I know!" he barked furiously. "You don't think I don't know what goes on in this world? Soon to be my world. Mine. I will own it. I need your antidote so no one else can create it. But, just in case they do, if I have the chemical makeup now I can develop a curative agent for the antidote and my bacteria will survive."

Stassi remained silent.

His sigh flung annoyed. "All right, enough of this one-sided conversation. As soon as you pack you will slip out the window on the east side of your apartment and go to that place, that fun place where you students went to for field trips. One of my men will meet you there. Go now. Pack as much as you can fit into a large backpack, you won't be coming back. Make sure you include a heavy jacket, gloves, hat, waterproof winter boots."

She choked out a perplexed, "Why?"

"Ah, she does still have her tongue. Well, my scared little rabbit, my bunny," he chuckled at his description of Stassi. He couldn't see her straighten her spine, clench her fists. "Where I live is secret and it's impregnable. Only way in is by helicopter but at the moment the oncoming winter winds are too rough for choppers. There is no way to get to my home by vehicle, motorbike, snowmobile or the like. Hiking in and up is the only way to reach it. It's snowing up here in the higher altitudes."

"I don't understand, Mr. Callen," she murmured.

"You will be hiking up my mountain, Stassi, dear. My man will guide you. My home is not on any map, no one can find their way there without a guide. It will take oh, a week or more. That's getting through the forest and then up the mountain."

Stassi was stunned. "A mountain? Where? What state?"

He laughed. "No state, darling, another country."

Blinking rapidly as his words sunk in, she parroted him, "Another country? Where?"

Laughing again, he said, "You'll find out when you get here. My man will get you on my private plane. Once you land, a jeep will ferry you to the beginning of the forest. From there you start hiking. I don't have to tell you, Stassi, you come alone, you tell no one about this. No police, FBI whatever. I find out you told anyone or you have someone with you, or are followed, the child will die and I will grab someone else you care about and start over. You understand me?"

"But, Mr. Callen-"

"I can't wait to see if you taste as sweet as you did so long ago. You were a child then with tiny budding breasts and tight as a bullet hole. But you are a woman now, my research tells me that you are…lush. I can't wait…I can't wait." There was no misinterpreting the torch of lust in his voice, the excited desire in the heavy breathing.

Oh God, not again, her brain railed at her to slam the phone down and run and hide. Silently gulping deep breaths, forcing dry swallows to ease her taut throat, her heart hammering against her ribs she schooled her voice to sound calm, cool, secure in her maturity. She stated definitively, "No, Mr. Callen, or Mr. Falk as you call yourself now. We will discuss my work when I arrive, anything else is off the books."

A yawn sounded through her phone. "I am growing bored with this conversation, Stassi. You will do what I say, all that I demand. Pack light, you'll be carrying it. Leave in ten minutes and slide out that window so those men that are guarding you don't see you leave." He disconnected.

She could not close her mouth, it hung open in shock, her phone went blank in her hand.

Chapter Seventeen

After she packed essentials and two changes of clothes in a backpack, Stassi called the lab and told the receptionist to tell Brant she wasn't coming in, that she was sick. Policy specified she was to speak directly to him when calling in, but she could barely string a few words together, she would be unable to lie to him.

He would find out soon enough when she reached her destination. She would call him then and explain. If he knew where she was going he would send the police to stop her.

She looked at the phone shaking in her trembling hand. Giving herself a pep talk, she muttered, "Okay, Stas buck up. It is what it is, no innocent baby should perish because I'm afraid." She'd stuff her fear, she'd go dammit, and she was getting Cody back. As far as the formula, she'd have to address that when Mr. Callen finally ran out of patience when she never provides it.

She'd already done this rodeo with Lamontagne. She didn't break then and she sure as hell was not going to give in now. She'd suffer through it; take her own life if the torture became too unbearable. What a thought. She swiped at the tears stinging the backs of her eyes as they seeped out.

A knock at her back kitchen door startled her, her heart raced again. Did he come to me? Shoring up her flagging courage, she muttered, "Okay, calm down, Stas, do what you have to do," and trod to the door and opened it.

The man standing with insolent conceit whistled when he saw her. His hands curled around his hips, his gaze like a lascivious hand stroked up and down her body settling on her breasts.

He wore a thick camel-hair coat, jeans, flannel shirt and sturdy boots. His brown hair was cut shorter on the sides than on top, he had a spot of beard in the center of his chin. Tall, muscled, if she was watching a movie then he would fit the mold of an enforcer for a mob boss. He was good looking in a sleazy, bullyish kind of way.

"Whoa, babe," he clucked, his pupils dilated over lurid brown eyes, "you are one smoking honeypot. Callen said you were hot when you were a kid, but shit, you are scorching my eyeballs. How am I gonna keep my paws off you? Callen said he'd have my head if I fucked you, he'd cut off my nuts if I put my hands on you in any sexual way."

Gaze still roaming all over her body like a thick wet tongue; he shook his head with a satirical smirk. "Gonna be a damned long journey."

Stassi stood aghast at the crude man's verbiage. "I was supposed to meet you somewhere, why are you here?"

She inched the door a little so it was almost closed.

"Falk don't want some hacker listening in on our plans, it was a red herring. Your guards will be watching your side window, and waiting to follow you somewhere. I waited until they positioned themselves in view of the window." He peered inside the apartment.

She sure did not want him inside her home alone with her. "I'll get my things and be right out." She went to shut the door but he stuck his boot in blocking her from closing it. She had to back up or he would have walked right into her as he pushed the door open and barged inside.

"Yeah," he grunted, glancing around her small brown and white apartment. Since she worked constantly, there was little of a lived-in look of the place. No mementos or photos of friends or family, just plain, serviceable furniture that came with the apartment. "Where's your shit?"

"My…?"

"Clothes, toothpaste, whatever, your shit?" He spotted the backpack near the archway of the kitchen and loped over and picked it up. "Got it," he said. "Anything else?"

"Um, no. Just my jacket." She hurried to the chair where she'd set it. Shrugging the jacket on, she moved quickly to the door. The way he was looking at her she feared he would have her naked on the floor and be on top of her in a flash if she didn't get out of the house.

Chuckling behind her, his eyes glued to her butt, he said, "Good you packed light, you're gonna have to carry it. I have a large duffle with necessities to carry when we get to hiking." He guided her to hurry behind a tall row of shrubs. They then moved from the shrubs and across the back of the next door neighbor's lawn and then down the side street. The crisp air bit a chill into their bare faces.

A black jeep was parked in the shadows. He opened a back door and tossed her pack inside then opened the front passenger door and gestured for her to get in.

This is it, she thought, once she climbs in that jeep there'd be no backing out. Belly feeling like mosquitos were torpedoing, zinging madly around inside, her feet didn't want to move. She was paralyzed.

"Babe." The man gestured to the door again. He stood behind her as if he planned on tackling her if she changed her mind and tried to make a run for it.

Heck, she didn't even know his name. Snapping out of her paralysis, Stassi sucked in a deep breath, and climbed into the jeep. The man shut her door with a smirk and wink.

He hopped in the driver's side and they were off. He kept glancing at her, his gaze raking down her body until they reached the expressway then he had to concentrate on the traffic.

"What's your name?" She was going to spend a lot of time with him, she might as well be friendly. But not too friendly, she figured he was the kind of guy if a girl looked in his direction he'd take that as an invitation and be all over her.

"Roger, babe, as in Roger over and out, get it?" Glancing at her he snickered and patted her knee.

Pushing his hand off her leg, Stassi said with a hint of anger, "Listen Roger, let's get things straight. First off, do not touch me, I don't appreciate being touched by a stranger. Second, my name is Stassi, not babe. Please do not call me babe." She hazarded a glimpse over at him. Her lips bunched, he was chuckling.

Thumbs tapping on the wheel, he shot her an amused grin. "Sexy as shit, and cute too, sweet little temper. I'm liking it. We won't be strangers long, babe." His attention back on the road he didn't see her roll her eyes.

She asked, "So, now that I can't tell anyone, where are we going?"

Glancing at her he grinned again. "Romania."

She knew they were going out of the country but she never dreamed of… "Romania?"

"Yup. Ain't nobody gonna find you there, huh?" and he laughed like it was all a fun joke.

He drove to a small private airport and led her onto the plane Marcus Callen owned. It was a never ending flight, they stopped several times to refuel. Roger sat up front with the pilot drinking straight from a whiskey bottle.

Stassi stretched out on one of the large comfortable seats and set her backpack next to her to discourage Roger from joining her. Fortunately, he passed out and didn't wake except when they landed to refuel. Then he'd start drinking again until he passed out. Stassi wasn't sure if he was a drunk or was afraid of flying. Whatever, it worked for her; it kept him away from her.

It was dark when they entered Romanian airspace. Flying beneath the clouds, Stassi could see twinkling lights and cars down below. After some time, the lights grew fewer and farther between. Even in the glooming darkness, she could just make out the silhouette of dark mountains, irregular black humps lurking in the twilight far away in the distance.

A tiny row of blue lights appeared to be the only things in the inky black moonless night that was guiding the pilot. Stassi couldn't even see ground until they were bouncing slightly on it.

Peering out the window as the jet slowed, she only saw a few hangars. It was another private airstrip. That was how they evaded Customs. Didn't they have to file flight plans and signal when they were in country's airspace? Of course, she thought, she was dealing with criminals, they had their ways.

"Okay, babe." Roger picked up a duffle bag and her backpack. His eyes were half-closed and bleary. A dark shadow covered his jaw now making him look even more treacherous than he had before, like a disreputable hoodlum who broke gamblers kneecaps that owed money.

No one approached them as they left the jet and walked across the small tarmac. Another jeep was waiting at the airstrip for them. Roger tossed their belongings in the back and opened the passenger side door. "Your chariot, princess," he mocked.

Stassi climbed in the seat aware he wasn't being a gentleman opening her door for her, no, it was an opportunity to ogle her butt. She ignored him knowing he would enjoy seeing her get ticked off.

They drove along a dark highway for hours. Eventually, Roger turned off onto a dirt road and he followed that until it curved into a forest shrouded in thick trees and dark shadows. The moon finally showed its face and was the only faint illumination slicing silver traces along tree tops. Stassi wondered how Roger could see the road, it blended into the hunkering darkness.

They didn't speak, Roger drank more whiskey and smoked one cigarette after another. She should have been worried that he was drinking and driving, but there weren't any other vehicles out there and he'd just snigger at her and do as he pleased anyway.

Miles into the woods, the dirt road grew thinner and thinner until Roger stopped the jeep, put it in park and shut it off. Stassi could see nothing. Peering into the darkness she asked, "Where are we?"

He laughed. "Middle of nowhere, babe. From here we hike." He popped his door open, and considering how much he'd had to drink, he moved agilely around the jeep and removed their bags.

Stassi hadn't noticed they had driven up to a higher elevation. There were small scattered drifts of snow. She could see halfway up the mountains jutting darkly against the horizon where the moonlight showed the peaks were completely draped in white. Green firs heavily dotted the glistening snow like a sprinkling of jade stars.

Slowly Stassi slid out of the jeep and into the cold, dark cloak of night and trees. "What about the jeep?"

Holding her backpack, he said, "Turn around." He waited while she did and then slung the pack on, the straps wrapping around her shoulders. Reaching into the back of the jeep, he removed a shotgun and hung it on a strap over his shoulder.

Then he hauled the big duffle over his other shoulder. Thin blankets were rolled up and tied to the duffle.

"You're just leaving the jeep here?" She hated to leave the warmth, comfort and safety of the vehicle.

"Yeah. When the weather is too rough for choppers we have to get up and down the mountain on foot. No one that shouldn't will come across it here. Come on, let's hit it." He lightly cupped her elbow to turn her in the right direction then he started walking.

He didn't stride as fast as he could, he would have left Stassi way behind. Since she was the treasure he was entrusted to bring to the fortress, he was very careful with her. He had told her that if anything happened to her, he wouldn't live to see the next sunrise. Marcus Callen was not a nice man and he didn't tolerate failure. She already knew he wasn't a nice man.

They hiked in the dark for miles until they reached a small clearing. Inside the clearing of smashed down grass was a small circle of rocks and inside the circle lay thick branches and kindling for a fire. Evidently Stassi and Roger weren't the only hikers that used the site.

Roger set the duffle down and removed the blankets. Inside the duffle were packets the size of a pack of cards. They opened into twin-size plastic sheets. He laid the sheets out and set the blankets over them. "You need to piss," he said and motioned to the side of the clearing, "go behind that tree, no further. There are animals out here that would see you as a treat on a silver platter. Here," he handed her a packet of disposable toilet paper.

She did as he said, quickly. She couldn't see a thing in the black night when she returned except the flame of a fire he had started.

"Here ya go," he said, passing her a power bar and bottle of water. "We'll eat better tomorrow when I can see to hunt. Eat that then go to sleep. Crack a' dawn we're on our feet."

She was exhausted, he didn't have to tell her twice. Gobbling down the bar, she finished the bottle and lay down on the plastic sheet and pulled the blanket over her, using the backpack as a pillow. Apparently Roger was tired too, in minutes she heard such loud snores she figured she didn't need to fear bears or wolves or whatever, they'd be frightened off with the sound of a jackhammer breaking up cement.

The sun wasn't even thinking of rising yet when Stassi felt a hand shake her shoulder.

"Wake up, babe, time to go."

Rubbing her eyes as she sat up, she watched Roger roll up his blanket, fold the sheet until it was back to the size of a pack of cards. After he stuffed the sheet inside the duffle, he strode off to the side, not very far and she could hear him peeing.

Stassi stretched and yawned, then got to rolling up her blanket and folding the sheet like he had. At least he moved a little bit away from her, on the hike he barely stepped off the path to urinate. It amused him how embarrassed Stassi got from his unabashed crass behavior. Again, it's not like she thought he was a gentleman. She used a bit of water to brush her teeth and wash her face.

They took breaks, but although she worked out and jogged fairly regularly, Stassi wasn't up to walking for an entire day.

Roger didn't hide his annoyance with her lack of stamina, they had to stop before sunset. He had planned on getting in several more miles before stopping. Stassi dropped to the ground with a groan while Roger made a fire.

"I'm gonna go find dinner," he tossed out blithely as he took off with the shotgun slung over his shoulder. He had the bloodthirsty gleeful expression of someone looking forward to killing something.

Hearing periodic gunshots, Stassi dozed on her blanket she'd laid out until he returned.

His face was crunched up in a scowl, his hands empty. "Gonna be fuckin' power bars again, toots. Tomorrow we can refill our canteens and leave the empty water bottles." He stomped to the duffle, pulled out a couple of bars and tossed one to her. It landed on her blanket. She was starving and the bar was gone in a few short minutes.

Roger laid out on his side on the blanket bracing on a forearm, his legs stretched out, he watched her eat while he sucked at a flask. "You look much better to eat than those fuckin' bars, babe," he leered with shiny eyes, licking booze off his lips.

Stuffing the empty wrapper in her bag, Stassi ignored him and settled back down snuggling under her blanket, his snickers irritating her ears. She also wasn't too happy picking up his trash after him. He thought nothing of negligently tossing candy bar wrappers, tissues, cigarette butts, empty water bottles as he traveled along. He left too much debris for her to completely pick up as he kept walking at a quick pace. She decided she could always find her way back out by following his trail of trash.

The sun was on the verge of rising when Stassi was startled awake. Something heavy was crushing her body- No! Rufus! She opened her mouth to scream, but, wait, Rufus was dead. No, it was Roger who was on top of her, his mouth sucking all over her face, her neck, he tore at her clothes, groping everywhere he could reach.

Hitting out at him she yelled, "What are you- stop it Roger!"

"Can't not fuck you, girl," he rumbled, fumbling at her jacket. It was freezing, they had slept in their clothes. "Don't worry 'bout the cold on your nekked body, hon, I'll keep you warm."

He roughly just jerked her jacket right off her then snatched her sweater off even more easily. Stassi fighting, slapping, clawing, screeching at him to stop didn't slow him down a bit. Grabbing her t-shirt he tried to tear it but couldn't and it was tighter and didn't slide off her shoulders like the sweater had so he went for her pants.

"Stop! Roger, dammit, stop!" Breathless from struggling, she tried to catch his wrists to hold his hands back shouting, "You said Mr. Callen would kill you if you do this, stop!"

"Naw, don't care, he ain't here right now and we are. Where's that button on your pants, oh, got it." He yanked the button open and jerked her zipper down. He climbed on top of her, shoved her legs apart to kneel between them.

Realizing he couldn't get her pants off that way, he rolled to the side. Grasping her hands in one of his, he lassoed one of her legs with his to hold her from kicking at him and tried to tug her pants down with his free hand.

Her piercing screams loud in the silent night, Stassi brought her free knee up and tried to slam it into his groin but he jerked out of the way. "None of that, babe, be a good girl, just give it up easy, I'll make it plenty good for you. All the ladies love me."

He had to let go of her hands to get her pants down, she rained blows to his head but he must have had a head made out of rock because it hurt her more than him.

After she punched him in the temple he slapped her, hard. "Now, quit it, girl, I'm takin' what I want. If I have to knock you the fuck out to get it, I will."

Stunned momentarily from his strike, Stassi shook it off and hit at him, but he wrapped his hands around her neck and squeezed. "I said stop, babe, you've really pissed me off now, I'm gonna throttle you until you pass out and I don't have to fight with you."

Stassi gacked, "*Stop*," gouging her nails in a frenzy over any skin she could reach. He squeezed harder, choking, she struggled to suck in air, dots started popping in her eyes, she was falling unconscious- then-

His hands ripped off her so hard her neck was wrenched along with them. Her hands went to her pained throat, she scrambled to sit up and couldn't believe her eyes.

Voltang Saldano, his big chest heaving with fury, as soon as Roger hit the ground where he threw him, Volt leaped at him and the two men commenced to brawling.

Two more men emerged from the dense woods, both wearing grins. They stopped near Stassi, folded their arms over their chests, boots akimbo, and cheerfully watched Volt beat the living shit out of Roger.

Stassi thought she must be dreaming, where had they come from? How on earth, in a foreign country, deep in the vast woods, before morning's twilight were they here? The only reason could be her. They were there to take her, hurt her for the formula. She inched back from the two men watching the fight, maybe she could run for the cover of the trees.

"Uh huh," one of the men shook his head at her said with a grin, "you stay there. Don't feel like chasing after you right now when I'm enjoying a good fight."

Stassi remembered him from when she was recovering at Volt's home. He was Jubal Cain, with dark auburn hair and dark blue eyes that had smiled friendly and spoke calmly to her when he realized she was so broken and afraid.

Sitting on her blanket, eyes rounded in disbelief, Stassi twisted her head from him to the men brawling, although now it was turning to a slaughter as Volt pummeled Roger into the dirt.

When Roger lay still, curled in a ball and crying, Volt wiped his bloody hands on Roger's jacket and stepped a few feet from him. He turned from the bloody whining heap that was Roger and aimed his fearsome gaze at Stassi.

Frozen in shock, she just stared wide-eyed at him, her gaze flicking from him to his men to Roger and back to Volt. Volt moved to her, hunched over and held out his hand. Her elbows bent, Stassi leaned back on her palms and looked at his hand like it was a wild grizzly's claw about to slash strips of skin off her, and didn't move.

With a huff of impatience, Volt stalked closer to Stassi then crouched down in front of her. He reached out and tugged her shirt down then picked up her sweater. "Lift your arms," he told her. She blinked at him but remained motionless. "Anastasia, you need to put the sweater on before you turn blue."

He shifted to his knees and held the sweater over her head, forcing her to raise her arms so he could pull it down over her. Then he reached for her jacket and held it out.

Stassi realized then that her teeth were chattering. Roger's assault and Volt's sudden appearance, the awful fight, the chilly air, set her teeth to clacking and her body to shivering. She let Volt help her on with her jacket and even stayed still as he zipped it up. He raised the collar to cover her neck. Then he wound his fingers around her biceps and helped her to stand on wobbly legs.

The entire time she just stared at him trying to grasp how he came to be there. In another country, in the dead of night, in middle of a jungle of thick dark forest.

Chapter Eighteen

Like she was a child, Volt tugged her pants up the few inches Roger had gotten them down, zipped them and closed the button. Not able to wrap her mind around what was happening, Stassi stood still and let him. At the same time, Volt's men rolled up the blankets, the plastic sheets and kicked dirt over the dying fire.

"How- I mean, how did you get- why are you here?" she stammered out through chattering teeth. Appalled that she stood still like a mannequin and let him practically dress her.

Volt pulled her sweater and jacket down neatly and asked, "Where are your gloves and hat?"

"Huh?"

"I said-"

"Volt, bro, fucker's gone," one of his men called out.

Volt and Stassi looked over to where Roger had been lying in his own blood, and the man was gone.

"You want us to go after him?" His breath a vapor, the man with fairer coloring than Volt motioned towards the thicket.

"Yeah, Greco. Can't have him announcing our presence," Volt said. "I want to get going. Jubal, check the duffle, see what he has in there. And grab the shotgun." Roger had fled without the bag or the weapon.

Volt grasped Stassi's arms again to steady her. He asked, "You okay?" Within the crisp clearing, their voices encased as if in swaddling from the thick vast forest surrounding them sounded oddly muffled. Grass damp with dew was sprinkled with dried leaves. Sections of fallen dead trees covered in springy moss sprawled like corpses on the cold earth.

Greco took off through the only opening in the crush of trees to find Roger. Jubal knelt to the duffle bag and started removing items from it.

Volt stroked his thumbs over her arms, she pulled away from his grasp and moved a step back. Voice husky from the cold and turmoil and hurt throat, she asked again, "Why are you here?"

He cocked his head scanning her face then her body, then asked, "Did he hurt you?"

Her lips pulled in with chagrin. "No. You got here in time. Again. Mr. Saldano, answer me, why are you here? How did you find us? I...were you looking for us?" She drew a knit hat from her jacket pocket and pulled it down over her mahogany braid then removed gloves and tugged them on. The chattering teeth slowly diminished as she grew warmer. She'd brought long-johns in her bag, she would need to slip them on soon.

"Anastasia, you know that I was asked to recover you from Lamontagne. As I told you, we expected Lamontagne as well as possibly others to come after you, thus, I had bodyguards watching you, which I had informed you. Along with them, I tapped your phones at work and home, as well as put a GPS on your cell and car."

"You what?" she croaked indignant. "How dare you! You should have told me this."

"You were apprised of any essential information you needed to know."

Her hands slapped on her hips. "Need to know? This is my life, I need to know everything! You can't just-"

He talked over her, "We picked up the call from Talis Falk and his demands that you trade yourself for Charles Shaw's child."

"But how did you find-"

"My men aren't that stupid, Stassi, unlike you. They didn't fall for the old 'we'll lure your bodyguards away and you sneak out the back door' trick." Face hardening in anger and incredulity, he callously chastised her, "I can't believe you were so foolhardy, so recklessly stupid to allow that bastard to blackmail you into going to him. You didn't contact me, you didn't call the police, the damned FB-fucking-I, at the very least tell your goddamned boss. What the hell were you thinking?"

Snapping out of the rest of her bewildered fog, her lips pushed back out, brows lowered in pique, Stassi retorted with a snap of her head, "I was thinking I need to save that baby." She glanced around the clearing and her shoulders slumped. Her arms rose in helpless capitulation, "Now that you've run Roger off how am I to do that? When we don't show up Mr. Callen said he would hurt Cody Shaw."

His head angled back in question. "Who is Mr. Callen?"

She watched Volt's man removing items from the duffle bag then swung her head back to him. "He is Talis Falk. Falk is an alias. He is a wanted man so apparently he's had many aliases. Mr. Callen is…was, uh, my…" she felt mortified heat rush to her cheeks.

"Your what, Anastasia? We've been behind you this whole way. We had planned to follow you and that asshole up to Falk's fortress, make sure you stayed out of the compound and we'd get the baby. Then we heard you screaming. Maybe I got carried away when I saw that bastard strangling you. Now, I need to know everything, if I'm kept in ignorance I can't protect you. Speak to me."

His arms crossed in a steel block of annoyance and anger over his chest, feet spread lodged on the ground. He wore a heavy black coat, and as usual, black jeans and what looked like combat boots. Contrary to his asking about her hat and gloves, his dark hair whisked around in the wind and his hands were bare.

She so did not want to tell him, after her parents, and that time she almost blurted it out at the bar, Stassi had never told anyone about the heinous episode, the worst time in her life. Worse than Glenn Dyke's betrayal with Juliette, or her father's beatings.

Volt lowered his head to maintain eye-contact with her. "Anastasia, I have to know everything to help you."

No, she could not speak about it, tell this virtual stranger. Sure, he'd rescued her, twice now, and nursed her back to health and continued to weave a wall of protection around her even after he'd done his duty extracting her from Lamontagne's clutches. But, he refused to tell her who hired him to retrieve her, and he was still a stranger to her. Why was it such a secret that he'd been sent to find her? She knew nothing about him. Not where he's from, not his family, his job, nothing.

"We will stand here until summertime, Anastasia, until you tell me about this person and what your involvement with him is. Judging by the tapes of your phone call there is more going on than just the damned antidote. This guy is part of your past, and the way you sounded while talking to him it was a very unpleasant part." Volt stood between her and Jubal Cain rummaging through Roger's duffle, he wanted her full, undistracted attention on him.

Seeing his jaw jut up, the way he stood like an unwavering barricade, giving in, she sighed miserably then drew a weighty breath as all the old pain of memories flooded her like crashing waves.

Turning her head slightly from him, her eyes lowered, with resignation she said, "All right. He," the air sunk out of her chest before she took a deep breath and went on. "Marcus Callen was my 6th grade science teacher. I was…not quite twelve years old. He, uh, was always touching me, not quite inappropriately, not that at that age I was totally aware of what that meant.

"Then," she began, moving her head to face Volt. Her gaze banked with such horror and pain told she had floated from the present moment in the dark, chilly forest, to somewhere else long ago. "One day he made me stay after school let out. Said I was talking out of turn or something and I needed to be detained and punished. Said I was to write 'I am a bad girl' on the board a hundred times. I started to write, then…"

"Then," he prompted her when she trailed off.

"He, suddenly dragged me into a closet and he-" her voice broke, eyes immediately welled with distraught tears at the memory of her teacher with his huge hands pinching her tiny breasts, then lifting her skirt, pulling her underwear down and…

"He fucking assaulted you?" Volt shouted in a confounded whisper.

She turned her head to the side and lowered it as old shame painted her face dark red. "He… hurt me, so badly, I…bled. Bruises on my thighs from his brutal assault had appeared later. He cleaned me up and threatened me if I told anyone, my parents, friends, anyone at all, that he would kill my parents and I would get kicked out of school. He told me I would have no one, nowhere to live, nothing."

Volt slid his hand under her chin lifting it so she had to look at him. "You believed him?"

Her snort bitter, she replied, "I wasn't even twelve, Mr. Saldano, of course I believed him. He was not only an adult, he was my teacher. They were gods to us in those days. Then, the next day he told me I would have to…let him do that all the time, whenever he wanted. I...couldn't. So, I broke down and told my parents.

"At first they didn't believe me. Then, they forbade me to speak of it ever again. My father was running for office. He wanted to be governor of our state. He said if this got out, there would be a terrible, sordid scandal, all the attention would go to my- my assault and not to him. It would blow his chances of winning the election."

Volt's mouth clamped into a hard line, his eyes narrowed to fierce slits. Shock and horrified amazement that her parents would act like nothing had happened to her thundered in his eyes. "They didn't help you, and you never told anyone else? You've lived with this all this time?" His thumb brushed along her jawline, neither seemed to be aware of it.

"For a while. Then, he came after me again but he wasn't as careful as the first time. The first time he locked the classroom door and took me into the closet, knowing what he'd planned to do in advance. The second time he was just, swept away with desire, or so he told me. He had shoved me over his desk so hard my head banged on it almost knocking me out.

"He was ripping at my pants, when, we didn't hear the door open. I was shrieking, and he was intent on what he was doing, until, we heard a shout. He froze, we both looked over. A teacher had walked in. Her face was white as a sheet, her expression," Stassi's mouth curled in dour mirth. "Well, to say shocked would be an understatement."

When she didn't go on, Volt said, "Then what happened?"

One shoulder bumped, she moved her chin from his grasp. "Mr. Callen swore up and down and backwards that I came on to him, that I wanted it, that it was consensual, that I seduced him."

Volt spat in revulsion. "You were eleven, Anastasia, what the fuck? Did anyone believe him?"

135

"It didn't matter if they did. I was a minor. At first my parents tried to squash the uproar. They knew I still had class with him every day, they were...unconcerned if he assaulted me again. They were willing to let him rape me whenever he wanted to, even to the point of agreeing it was consensual to keep the scandal from going public. I was...just something that could get in the way of my father's political career. They were also afraid that the brutality my father unleashed on me behind closed doors might get out."

Volt started, frowned. He spoke carefully, "Brutality?" When she didn't speak, he said, "You've told me the worst, Anastasia, get it all out."

Stassi wrapped her arms around herself trying to pen in the full-body shudder. "My father had beaten me ever since I could remember, but after this happened he was unrelenting. He would beat me until I was broken and unmoving."

His expression blanked into grim rock, erasing any emotions he may have been feeling, he asked coolly, "What about the hospitals? They had to report the violent beating of a child."

"Huh. When they took me they said they were all accidents, childhood accidents. They hit different hospitals so as not to arise suspicion."

"Your ma, didn't she try to interfere?"

Emitting a snort of disgust, she said, "She never opened her mouth. Ever. He would order her to their room when he was about to 'discipline' me."

"Siblings?"

"My brother was older. I remember he tried to stop Dad once, but never again. Whenever Dad started on me he ordered my brother to leave the house. One time he stayed and there was a huge...oh, I don't know, I was sent to my room. I only heard the shouting. The next day my dad signed for my underage brother to enlist in the Army."

Volt peered down at her. Stassi's voice stayed modulated, no emotion, but her face was a map of grief and resignation. "Do you see him? Your brother?"

A twist of distaste then her mouth pulled in, she shook her head. "No. Not since he left. He tried to call me, I refused his calls. Even as an adult I blocked his number. I have no time for a coward. The police were called once. My dad lied, said my brother had hit me. After that, the beatings worsened.

"Then, my dad died in a car accident when I was fifteen and my mother fell ill so I was sent to an aunt I never knew existed until I left for college. I never spoke to my mother again after I was sent away. She did nothing to protect me, help me. I want nothing to do with either of them. Ever." Bitter spite rolled out with her angry, unforgiving words.

"Why did your da beat you and not your mother or brother?"

"Ah, they said once that my father had a little sister that forever lied to their parents with stories about him. She made up that he hit her, killed neighbors' pets, shoplifted, set the shed on fire. He took his own lickings I understand on a regular basis. Apparently I looked just like her, so I was his little sister in his mind I suppose. He was getting back at her through me."

Volt glanced over at Jubal who had the contents of the duffle spread around him. It was so quiet in the enclosed clearing Jubal could hear every word Stassi said, but he pretended he was busy and wasn't listening. However, the rigid line of his wide shoulders indicated he caught every devastating word.

Back to Stassi, Volt asked, "The teacher? Callen? How did that all sort out? Please tell me he was arrested." He frowned with a wrinkled brow. "If he was arrested, how can he be out here, sending someone to bring you to him?"

Still looking at the ground, her head tilted, she wiped at her eyes. She'd thought she had no more tears for the wreck of her childhood. Stiffening her spine, she pulled her shoulders back, told him, "The teacher who caught us had gone to the principal who called the police. The police went to my folks. As I said, they tried to hush it all up, sweep it under the carpet. But I was a juvenile, the teacher was horrified at what she'd seen, she heard my screams, the principal was beside himself with rage. Mr. Callen was arrested. With the teacher's witnessing along with my deposition, he didn't want to take his chance at trial. He took a plea and was pronounced guilty of sexual assault of a minor and sent to prison."

"How long was his sentence?"

"It was supposed to be 14 years. I Googled him and found out he served 2. According to Callen, when he escaped he set upon creating his, as he called it, his dynasty. He claimed that when he was satisfied with his completed kingdom, he was coming…for me."

Volt looked over at Jubal. "J," he said and waited until Jubal turned to him. "I want everything on Marcus Callen and all his aliases. I want to know how he amassed his fortune. All his known addresses, relatives, friends, everyone who ever had contact with him, and his prison records."

Jubal nodded and pulled a satellite phone from his own large back pack.

Stassi said, "He told me that he dealt in weapons, sex slavery, drugs. Apparently no pie was too dirty or immoral for him to stick his fingers in."

"You hear that, J?"

Jubal held a hand up, he was speaking into the phone.

"Mr. Saldano-"

"Anastasia, you know my name is Volt."

She blinked at him. Was he being friendly? Squinting her eyes, trying to read his impassive expression, his cold, cold eyes, she decided no, he just preferred to be called by his first name. "I need to find some way to contact Mr. Callen. I need to tell him," she paused, "no, I can't tell him what happened. He has to think I came alone with Roger. He can't know about you. I'll tell him…that an animal, a- a crocodile or something grabbed Roger and ran off with him."

The edge of Volt's full lip lifted. "There are no crocodiles in the Romanian mountains."

Frowning at this, she asked, "What is here then?"

Volt smiled. "Lynx, bear, wolves."

"Okay, it was a lynx. They're like a lion aren't they? My head was always embroiled in science, I paid zero attention to anything else unless it had to do with science, and the environment."

That brought a little chuckle from both Volt and Jubal. "Ah, not exactly. That guy, Roger, he was a big man, a lynx isn't as huge or ferocious as a lion or a tiger. Roger would likely have been able to fight the creature off. His pants were torn in our scuffle, I saw a huge knife strapped to his leg."

"You were able to pulverize him, Mr. Saldano, surely a wild jungle cat could take him down."

"Hmm, maybe if it attacked him from behind. Better off with a pack of wolves or a bear to be sure." Watching her ponder this, the coldness in his dark eyes twinkled for an instant.

"Okay. Whatever. The main thing is how on earth am I going to contact Mr. Callen? I certainly don't have his number, Roger took my phone from me. Maybe there's a map in his duffle bag?" she said hopefully looking over at Jubal.

"Anastasia, did you see the man once reviewing a map since you left the airstrip?"

Forehead crimping, she mumbled, "No." Her shoulders drooped with bleak defeat.

"Doesn't matter, you are going back home. We will figure out what to do about the baby."

"What!" She got in Volt's face. "No way. I am going up that mountain, with or without a map. Mr. Callen won't hesitate to hurt Cody. I have to do it."

"No, Anastasia, I will not allow you to-"

"Not allow me! You can't stop me, get out of my way," she started stomping away from him and Volt snagged her arm halting her. "Let go of me," she demanded.

"I can stop you, Anastasia. Tie you up, toss you over my shoulder, and carry you out."

"Please, Mr. Saldano, you have to believe that Callen will harm Cody if I don't show. I swear, for God's sake, he raped me when I was a child. He went to prison, he has a grudge and he wants my formula. He will hurt that baby, and he'll hurt him badly to make me pay. I *must* go."

Volt glared at her shaking his head. "No, he's going to want to hurt you too. It's too dangerous, you are returning home."

"I don't give a damn how dangerous it is, Saldano, I have to do it. If you stop me and that baby loses an arm or an eye, or his life, can you live with that?"

Growing infuriated, Volt shouted at her, "What about *your* life, Anastasia, is your life any less important than the child's?"

Her body drooped. Then she lifted her shoulders, straightened her back, raised her chin, "Yes. That's the point. I have lived a life, Cody has not. He must have his own opportunity to have a full life. He has…good parents that love him so much, they all deserve for him to have a happy childhood, grow up safe and loved. My…disappearing will only affect me. If the baby dies," a shudder ripped through her almost like a stinging pain.

"If Cody, well, it will affect his entire family." She pleaded, "You must understand, he will torture Cody."

Angry impatience blasted at her, "Yeah, and Callen will do the same to you. Lamontagne didn't even have the history with you, and look what he did to you. Anastasia, you can't-"

"If you take me home, I will wait until he contacts me and then I will do this all over again, except this time I will know how to keep you out of the loop. Let me go."

They glared at each other. Volt could see the blind determination in every rigid bone in her body, the bolt of steel in her pretty eyes, she meant what she was saying. He gave it one more shot, "You have no map, no way to contact him."

"Maybe if I just continue on in the direction we were going, one of Mr. Callen's men may appear. Roger said they all have traversed this mountain; this clearing, the fire pit, someone made it so people would have it at the ready."

"Sure," he laughed humorlessly, "you'll just blunder along and hope that you go in the right direction with no way to take care of yourself in the wilderness and pray that by some sheer chance before an animal gets you, or you run out of water or starve to death, someone will stumble onto you. Yeah. Good plan."

"It's all I have. It will have to make do."

"Right," Volt said loaded with sarcasm. Shaking his head at the stubborn idiocy of the young woman, he left her to stride over to where Jubal was putting items back into the duffle. He bent and picked up a satellite phone. "This will work."

Puzzled, Stassi reminded him, "But I don't know Mr. Callen's number."

"Don't need to, honey," Jubal offered. "It should show in the phone's records. Roger would have been calling him and vice versa. Even if there is no number imprinted, we can still trace it easily enough."

Volt tapped on the phone for a few minutes. He smiled. "There's one number called out."

He sobered quickly and trod back to where Stassi stood. "All right. You call Callen, tell him a bear attacked Roger and tell Callen to direct you to his compound by phone. If he mentions hibernation, tell him maybe up on the mountain but it's still warm enough down here for the bears to be roaming. Of course you want to discourage him from trying to send someone to collect you."

She stared at the phone reluctantly. Things were already complicated, now they'd grown twice as bad.

"You can do it, Anastasia," Volt encouraged her gently. "It's better than you wandering aimlessly in the snow on a treacherous mountainside," he held the phone out to her to take. Not that he ever would let her wander off alone.

Chapter Nineteen

"Roger, you're calling early, what's happening?" A staticy voice answered Stassi's call.

"Ah, this isn't Roger, this is Anastasia Athens calling for Marcus Callen." Dead silence.

Then, "Where the hell is Roger? He would never let anyone get their mitts on his satphone much less a broad. Who the hell is this?"

"I told you, Anastasia Athens. Mr. Roger had a bit of a...an accident with a bear. Now, I must speak with Mr. Callen. Tell him Stassi is calling."

It took grumbling and a bunch of questions about Roger that the man repeated again and again in a huffing voice indicating he was angry and walking. Finally, he must have gone to Callen. Stassi could hear male rumblings, the man on the phone and Callen's.

Then the familiar male voice said, "Yes, this is Marcus Callen. Is this Stassi Athens?"

The familiar voice stabbed nausea into her gullet. She slapped her palm over her mouth afraid she was going to vomit right then and there. Over her hand she saw Volt and Jubal watching her. Seeing her sudden distress and putrid green tinge her fair skin, Volt took a step to her. She held her hand up to stop him. The phone to her ear, she lowered her head, sucked in a heavy breath and said, "Yes, Mr. Callen, this is Stassi."

"Well, well. What's this I hear about Roger and a bear?" His tone signifying he thought it was a joke, humorous rubbish. "I am not in the mood for fooling around, Stassi, put him on the phone," he demanded.

It took Stassi some time to convince Callen of Roger's demise. She spun the story they had concocted of a bear rushing out of the woods and taking Roger screaming to the ground. He yelled at her to run. She tried shooting the shotgun at the bear, but she didn't know how it worked. She threw stones and screamed at the bear, but it was biting and goring and roaring, it was horrible, so horrible and he kept yelling at her to run. So she did.

She told him after a while she backtracked, however when she returned, the bear and Roger were gone, but his duffle was there and the satphone.

Suspicion threading his tone, Callen said, "You couldn't work a gun but you managed to call me on the satphone?"

Her eyes flicked to Volt, his mouth pinned. They hadn't thought about that. Stassi said quickly, "Oh yes. Professor Chandler used to go out in the field on you know, environmental experiments and studies and we stayed in contact that way. He was often out in a desert in Arizona, or a mountain top in a foreign country." She hoped Callen didn't think to contact the university and verify what she said.

Before he could consider it, she spoke quickly, "So, I am stuck out here alone, Mr. Callen. I need you to give me directions or talk me up to your...place." There was a stretch of silence again.

"It's too dangerous, Stassi for you to make your way here alone. I will send men to find you. Stay where you are, I should be able to get a satellite lock on your phone." He made a grunting sound. "Or maybe not. We're enveloped in thick clouds at the moment, they will block the links. We're lucky we can talk right now. Still, stay where you-"

"I don't want to waste time, Mr. Callen. I want to come there now. I only have so much food and water. Just tell me which direction, I have a compass from Roger's bag, I can follow it. There must be trails you can guide me to."

More silence. Stassi could hear Callen speaking with the man that had answered the phone. Then he came back to her.

"All right. We'll try it your way. But, you have several days on the relatively level land then it's a grueling uphill hike when you reach the foothills then the mountain. Once you reach a certain point I will need to give you more information."

"What do you mean more info-"

"Tell me where you are, where did you two spend the night?"

She didn't want him to know her exact location, he could send men to get her. "Um, we spent the night in a clearing. Before dawn broke we started walking, heading west. There are a few trails out here, made by animals maybe?"

"How long have you been hiking?"

"Oh, um, an hour then the bear attacked," her words broke on a gasp. There was an attack, actually, two of them. First when Roger assaulted her and then when Volt pummeled Roger. At least she sounded properly upset at Roger's attack from the pretend bear, it would keep Callen believing she was alone. "When I ran I lost the trail Roger was following."

"Which way are you headed?"

She paused as if reading the compass. "Um, I think I'm going northwest."

Callen was quiet. Then he said, "Okay, Stassi. Continue heading in that direction. Follow the trail you are on. In due course you should reach a trail that crosses it, it'll be going north and south. Move to that trail and head north. You'll eventually come upon a cabin you can sleep in for the night, at least you'll be out of the elements, and can relax vigilance against a possible animal attack like poor Roger. Now, get the shotgun I'm going to walk you through how to shoot it."

She looked to Volt. Volt picked it up and brought it to her with a nod. "It's heavy," she muttered, "I don't like guns."

"Yes well," Callen said, "you're alone in the woods you need some sort of protection." He told her how to release the safety, put it to her shoulder, aim, and gently squeeze the trigger. "If you shoot at an animal you will undoubtedly miss it, but the loud bang may run it off, and you will be deaf for quite a while. Now, call me in four hours or if you run into trouble. Goodbye, Stassi, be careful. I want you alive and well when I get my hands on you. Won't be any fun to play with a maimed or half-dead toy."

"Okay. Wait!" she said before he could disconnect. "I need to hear the baby."

"You don't need shit, Stassi, just get your ass here."

"Mr. Callen, if you don't prove that you have Cody Shaw or he's not...dead, I won't take another step in your direction." She heard mumbling again.

Then she heard Callen's muffled voice, "Don't argue with me, Ini, get the fucking baby." Then he said, "Hold on, sweetness, I have to retrieve the child. It won't take but a moment. Doesn't really affect anything, no matter where you are or run to, my people are expert trackers, they will find you. But I'd rather you didn't take off willy nilly into such a perilous wilderness. Anyway, tell me, how did you and Roger get on? Did he dare take what is mine?"

The gall of the man, Stassi fumed. Seeing Volt's hands roll into fists, he looked like he was going to snatch the phone from her, she turned her back to him. "Mr. Callen, I belong to no one, especially deviant vermin like you." She heard a delighted chortle.

"You are no longer the terrified little pubescent girl are you, my sweetness? I am so excited. I thought about nothing else whilst I rotted away in prison but you, how tender you were then and how juicy you would be now. Well, building my kingdom too of course, that took a lot of plotting and scheming and networking.

"Now, you, I knew when I was ready I could nab you up with no trouble. You may be all grown up, but you are still a defenseless young woman. This antidote you've come up with is only icing on the cake, you, my sweetness, are the cherry on top. Get it? Cherry? You remember, I took your cherry, I-"

Stassi slammed the phone against her hip, her face darkening with outrage.

Volt touched her arm, whispered, "He's doing it on purpose, he's trying to get your goat. It's fun for him. Don't let him get any enjoyment out of getting under your skin."

She grimaced her rage and humiliation at him, then nodded sharply. Lifting the phone, she said calmly, "When you are tired of playing pervy childish games, Callen, put the baby on the phone and let me get on my way."

He laughed roughly. "Oh, good, Stassi, you are going to give me a fight. That excites me even more, I can't wait to-" A baby's crying sounded in the background.

Her palm splayed over her heart as it contracted with the cross of worry that he was there and in danger, and relief that little Cody was still alive. She had to assume it was him, the baby couldn't speak and it was a gamble Callen didn't have any other babies in his home.

She spoke loudly, "I will call in four hours, Callen, and I will want to hear the baby. Don't try to make a recording of his cries, I will know." She didn't say goodbye, just shut the phone off. Her complexion paled, she wiped the back of her hand across her brow.

"You did great, Anastasia," Volt praised her quietly. He unclenched his fists, but his fingers stretched out straight then curled into rigid talons as if he wanted to grab something, or someone, and rip it apart.

"He's just a baby, Saldano, an innocent in all of this." Against her will tears welled. She turned her head so he couldn't see them. Wasn't quick enough.

"We'll get him," Volt swore. He moved a hand to her, then dropped it. He ordered, "Let's pack up this shit and get going. Jubal, call Greco, see what's happening with that Roger scumbag." Volt helped him repack the duffle as Jubal contacted Greco. The men spoke so quietly, Stassi couldn't hear a word they said.

Standing up, Volt slid the duffle bag over his shoulder, he already had a backpack strapped to his back as well as a shotgun. Jubal picked up Stassi's pack and tossed it over his own on his shoulders and strapped Roger's shotgun with his.

"I can carry it," Stassi spoke out, but they ignored her and Volt said with a small wave to her, "Let's go," and started walking. She hurried to walk beside him. He stopped.

"No, you stay between us," Volt told her giving her a little push back and started hiking again. Jubal stayed close to her back.

After an hour or so they came to the trail that Callen had indicated crossed the one they were on. They moved to the secondary trail and continued heading straight north. They took periodic breaks. At four hours, around noontime, as they left the woods they came upon a grouping of boulders in an open field.

A rustling in the bushes behind them drew their attention. Stassi stiffened preparing to run from some wild beast, but Volt and Jubal remained calm. A few seconds and a figure emerged from the scrub. It was the man they called Greco.

All three men had the same height with broad shoulders and thick biceps and chests. Sharp cheeks and square jaws, strong noses, except for their different coloring, Stassi thought they could be brothers. Greco had lighter hair and complexion with tawny eyes. Jubal's hair was dark auburn, and he had dark blue eyes. Volt was just dark. Black hair, eyes, aura.

Stassi sat on a small boulder, Volt and Jubal moved apart from her and spoke quietly with Greco. Greco said a few words, the male trio glanced over at her in tandem then huddled another minute.

Breaking from the other two, Volt ambled towards Stassi. The drying chilled grass crackling from his boots crushing it sounded eerie in the open field. With a brief shiver, she rubbed her arms, brushing away the spooky thought.

"Here, you want to call Callen." He held the phone out to her.

Accepting the phone, she said, "That man, Roger, did Mr. Greco say what happened? Did he find him? He probably needs medical care," her tone carried accusation of the terrible beating Volt had given him.

"He was going to choke you until you passed out, Anastasia and then rape you without mercy. And likely not just once, or even twice. You needn't feel sorry for him."

"But, I could have fought him off-" She stopped at his arched brow. "Anyway, we should see that he can get to a doctor. Where is he?"

"Make your call," Volt ordered then stomped away to join the other men and turned his back to her.

Stassi glared crossly at him. "Bossy jerk," she muttered. He wasn't going to tell her what happened with Roger. She had a sudden queasy feeling. Had that man Greco…killed Roger? The thought struck her with panic. Was she traveling with stone cold killers? Tearing her gaze away from the men she stared at the phone in her hand. Of course she was.

Recalling the way Volt's men had dispatched Lamontagne's soldiers, the way Volt himself had pounded Rufus to death with his bare hands then stabbed him without hesitation. And the guy he'd beaten and stabbed in the alley. Now Roger. Volt had pummeled him so badly Stassi had been amazed he had been able to get to his feet and flee. Another severe shiver rippled through her. She was heading to danger with danger as her escort.

Then she pondered, perhaps Volt wanted to get his hands on her formula and Callen's bacteria and was using her as the conduit to get to Callen. There was really nothing she could do to prevent Volt and his men from staying with her. But, she couldn't worry about that now. She started dialing, her only mission was to get to Cody Shaw and get him out of there to safety, to his parents.

The conversation went as before. Stassi spoke briefly with Callen, hearing the baby gurgling, at least he wasn't crying now. There was much static and their voices went in and out finally losing connection. She looked up to the sky as she disconnected. Thick dark clouds clotted the sky obscuring much of the dimming blue.

They had MRE's and water for lunch. Greco found a stream for them to replenish their water with added chlorine drops. When they ascended the mountain they could melt snow to drink. Hiking for hours with infrequent breaks, the group came upon a small cabin off to the side of the trail. The wood had been painted brown and green to blend in with the forest, knee-high grass surrounded it like a balding old man's sparse fringe.

"Mr. Callen said we might reach this place and we could stay the night here." Thank goodness, she sighed with weary welcome. No hard cold ground tonight. She was so exhausted as soon as she laid her blanket down she was going to quickly pass out.

"Jubal and I will go inside first, you stay here with Greco," Volt told her.

"Okay, Bossy," she muttered with cheek.

He swung around so abruptly she faltered back a step. "What did you say?" He glowered down at her.

She held her ground. "Well, you are very bossy, always giving orders. I don't have to do what you say. I can do this on my own, I don't need you and your," she looked over at the other two men who were grinning at their squabbling, "posse."

Volt's gaze slid to his grinning friends and back to her. "I am giving the orders because I have the experience. My men do as well, but I am in charge and they know it. You need to learn that, Anastasia."

Rolling her eyes with a huff, Stassi went to stalk past him to the cabin and he snatched her arm halting her. Leaning into her he spoke harshly, "You will do as I say, Anastasia, for your safety. You cannot, will not do this alone. Don't make me force you to do as I tell you."

Her mouth fell open in affront. "Force me? What the hell does that mean?" She jerked at her arm but he had a grip of iron.

"Disobey my instructions and find out." The side of his mouth nicked up in a sly threat. They glared at each other for a few seconds.

Stassi could read his intimidating dark eyes, he wasn't making empty threats. Her own eyes narrowed at him, she told him, "Just because you are bigger, stronger than me doesn't make you my boss." She tugged futilely at her arm. He held her so easily, so taut she wasn't even able to move his arm with her jerks much less break hers free.

"That is exactly what makes me your boss, as well as my experience. Have you ever spent a week in the woods? Ever climb the side of a mountain in the snow? Fight off a cougar, a bear, a wolf? Renegade soldiers? Killed, cleaned and cooked your dinner over a fire you made yourself?"

At her silence, he said, "I have. Now, you stay here with Greco while Jubal and I make sure the cabin is clear." Bending his head, his mouth at her ear he whispered, "I can bind and haul you wherever we go if you don't do as I say, try me."

She said nothing, just glared back at him. But when he and Jubal moved to the cabin, she stayed where she was. Beside her, Greco stifled his grin. Apparently her and Volt's tug-o-war fighting was amusing to the pair.

Several minutes passed before Volt and Jubal exited the unlocked cabin. Jubal held something by the tail.

"Is that-" She broke off with a gasp, her hand to her mouth.

"Yep," Jubal acknowledged, grinning at her, "it's a rat. Big one. Too bad they don't make good eating." As big as a cat, the huge rat was dead, one of the men had killed it. Jubal trod around the side of the cabin and threw the rodent into the woods.

"It's safe now to go in, we cleaned out the largest of the spiders." Volt set a hand on the small of her back giving her a nudge towards the building. She didn't move.

"Spiders?" she repeated meekly. Giant rats, humongous spiders, oh Lord.

"It's fine, Anastasia, we cleared them and a few other things out. I promise." His grin widening, Volt gave her a gentle push to the cabin. Greco held the door open and Jubal went in first, then Stassi with Volt at her back.

The structure at a quick glance was three rooms. A living room, tiny kitchen and down a hall a bathroom. It was dim and dingy as would be expected. There were a few dusty windows. Floor was wood planks scuffed and pitted from wear and time.

Jubal said, "No electric of course, but there is a fireplace and a pump for running water. There are no beds, we can sleep here where the fireplace is," he gestured to the large living room. Several plain chairs and small wooden tables filled the space. Volt and Greco were pushing them to the side walls to make room for their sleeping bags.

Jubal detached Stassi's pack from his back and handed it to Volt. Volt removed the rolled blanket. "That won't be warm enough for you, what the hell were Callen and Roger thinking? You will freeze to death on the damned trail." As he was speaking, using the pile of wood and kindling stacked beside the large stone fireplace, Jubal and Greco started building a fire.

Stassi didn't know what to say to him so she said nothing. Her job was to do as Callen told her so she could get to that baby. Her comfort wasn't important, getting the baby safely home was. It would be nice if she made it safely home too, but she knew better than to count on that. Callen had proven himself to be as vicious, cold-blooded and ruthless as Lamontagne.

She took the blanket from Volt along with Roger's blanket and set them on the floor. She rolled one out and lay down on it then pulled the other to cover her. Her lids felt like they had stones on them weighing them down she was so tired.

"Anastasia," Volt said. She didn't move.

His voice was closer, he crouched down beside her. "Anastasia, you have to eat."

Mumbling, "Lea' me 'lone, tired," she burrowed deeper under the blanket.

"You can't sleep with your jacket and boots on."

"Cold." Her body shivered under the blanket.

"Stubborn woman," Volt sighed. He unrolled his sleeping bag and opened it. Then he pulled up the bottom of her blanket and removed her boots. "Sit up, Ana," he told her.

She didn't move. Volt shuffled behind her and lifted her so she was sitting with her back resting against his chest. She mumbled, "You warm, Saldano," and snuggled against him. She couldn't see his smile.

"Okay, off with the jacket." He tugged it off her. Scowling with her eyes closed she complained, "Mean. Cold, Saldano," she rubbed her arms.

"Yeah, that's me, mean." He gripped her upper arms turning her to face him. Her hair flopped in her face, he smoothed the locks back. "Ana, you eat, wash your face, then you can sleep in my sleeping bag. You will be warm in it."

Her lids cracked a hair, green eyes peeped haughtily at him she announced, "I would rather freeze than sleep with you, Saldano." Dual snickering came from near the fireplace.

Volt stood and brought her up with him. "I'm not going to share the bag with you, your virtue is safe from me. But you are going to wash up and eat before you sleep. And you have to call Callen."

That pushed her lids up. Her eyes were red with exhaustion, she nodded. "You're right."

"Here ya go." Jubal handed her, her toiletry bag he'd taken from her pack. "There's running water with the pump. Be prepared, it's cold. Bathroom's that way," he pointed to a door.

"First," Volt said, "you eat. Sit on the stone bench of the fireplace. You'll be warm and you can eat while you call Callen."

"Humph," she sniffed. "Bossy." But she was too tired and hungry to argue with him. Besides, he was right. She stumbled to the stone bench and plopped down, then looked confused as to why she was there.

Jubal followed her with a grin. "Here, honey," he gave her an MRE and the phone. "It's all set to dial, just push that button," he pointed at the satphone.

"'K, thanks." She gave the handsome man with the auburn hair and mischievous eyes a weary smile.

While she made the call, the men laid out the blankets and sleeping bags, stoked the fire, carried on quiet conversation. The phone call went on as before. Callen answered like they were lovers, "Hi sweetness, I am so excited you're coming, I can't wait to see you."

She didn't respond to his foolishness, just demanded, "The baby, Callen. I'm tired and I don't want to play games."

"Huh," he grunted. "It appears you are doing fine traveling on your own. Kind of surprises me. Do you-"

"The baby, Callen or I'm hanging up."

He groused some more then she heard Cody's baby cries through the phone and her heart tensed. "You better not be hurting him, Callen," she threatened.

"Just get here, Stassi, I'm waiting. Follow the trail you came in on heading north tomorrow, call me when you take your first break. We can-" Stassi hung up and tossed the satphone on a table then headed for the bathroom.

When she returned, she dropped her toiletry bag on a chair and plodded to her blanket. As she was sinking down on it, Volt grabbed her arm holding her up. "Nope, I told you, sleep in my bag." He maneuvered her to his sleeping bag and pressed her shoulders to kneel down on it.

Shifting to sit, blinking through strands of hair, she cocked her head and asked, "But where are you sleeping? You'll be cold."

He bent over, one hand braced on his knee, he tapped the end of her nose lightly. "Don't worry about me, beautiful. We're taking turns patrolling, we can share bags."

Lips pushing out, her forehead creased. "Patrolling? For what? The animals can't get in here now, you closed all the windows and the door."

"Not the four-legged animals we're concerned about. Now, lie down." He pushed her shoulder gently forcing her to lie on her back. Then he pulled the bag over her and zipped it up. It was big, big enough for two or three people.

She muttered, "Four-legged, how can..." and she drifted off.

Chapter Twenty

Her bed felt oddly hard. Stassi moved her arms to stretch and found she was bundled in something, and couldn't push her arms up. She remembered. *Oh, the cabin.* Peeping one eye open she saw four faded wooden walls lit only by the orange flames still sparking in the fireplace. Furniture, only shadows of dark lumps shoved off to the side made space for the sleeping bags and blankets laid out on the floor.

Her one side felt warm, she rolled over- and halted.

Volt Saldano lay on a blanket and another covered his strapping body. He was positioned only inches from her. They had found linen and pillows in one closet, Stassi thought gratefully, it was not pleasant using a backpack as a pillow. Someone had kindly slid one under her head last night as she slept, because it wasn't there when Volt had been pressing her down on the bag to sleep.

Stassi unzipped the bag expecting a rush of cold air to hit her, but with the men and the fire it was warm inside the cabin. She glanced over, on the other side of where she lay but several feet away, Jubal was asleep in his bag.

Greco was in the tiny kitchen zipping up his jacket and looking out the little window. It must be his turn to patrol. Stassi didn't want any special treatment because she was a female, but still, she was glad they hadn't put her to service. It had been cold enough inside when she'd fallen asleep, the last thing she wanted to do was wander around the building outside in the icy air in the dark.

No worries there, no doubt Volt would put the kibosh on her being outside alone anyway. For someone who made it clear he despised her, he was contrarily protective of her health and safety. Of course, he may want her formula and the oil bacteria and he needed to get her safely to Callen to obtain both.

Since he couldn't see her, Stassi took the opportunity to study Volt. The harshness of his features were less razor sharp in his sleep. He still looked formidable, terribly so, that aura of dark danger ever present. She couldn't actually see it, but she could…feel it? Sense it?

Shaking her head with a silly smile, she was being fanciful. He had thick and long lashes that curled on his sharp cheeks, black stubble covered his strong jaw, he had full lips carved so hard they probably hurt whomever he was kissing. *That's it.*

Stassi sat up swiftly. Last thing she needed was to picture Voltang Saldano kissing her, uh, she meant kissing someone. Not her. Certainly not her. But, she found the image of Saldano kissing another woman vaguely, unnerving. *Jeez,* she silently scolded herself. It was highly improbable the man ever even kissed a woman. No, he was the type to just…do it. Just like he fought. Fast. Rough. Brutal even. Take what he wanted then walk away without a word.

Okay, enough of that crap. She got to her feet and stared down at him. A lock of inky hair waved over one black brow. Stassi had the urge to push it back. Good heavens, she let out a rushed breath, what was the matter with her today? She needed to use the bathroom. Yes, a shower, she felt grubby. Jubal had told her they had running water but it would be cold. Really cold.

She started to walk away, then, she knelt down, lifted the sleeping bag and lowered it over Volt. Then she looked for her backpack, finding it, she headed for the bathroom.

Greco turned around as soon as she stood up. He nodded unsmiling at her then turned back to look out the window as he pulled gloves on. A knit hat covered his head now, he was obviously going out to do a perimeter check.

None of them would put it past Marcus Callen to send men to seek her out. Her experience with Roger was enough to quell any desire to be alone with anymore of Callen's men. And, she couldn't let Callen know about Volt, he had threatened the baby if she didn't come alone. Originally she would have preferred to go it alone, but now, Stassi realized that such a foolhardy move could result in her injury or death. She really did need Volt's experience to safely traverse the forest and the mountain.

The bathroom was actually off a small chamber. She had to walk through the chamber to reach the bathroom. Which was fine, she could dress in the compartment instead of the bathroom which was quite small.

Washing as fast as she could, the water was *freezing*! Stassi wrapped her hair in a towel and slung another around her body. Another closet in the chamber had revealed towels and a few other things, a medical kit, shampoo, soap. She wondered who supplied the necessities and washed the towels. She brushed her teeth then plodded out of the bathroom to the connecting chamber.

The only furniture in the room was a table, otherwise the space carried only a few empty boxes and crates. Her backpack was on the table. She was pulling out some clean clothes when she realized her legs were still damp and it was freezing in the room with no fireplace to warm it.

Mumbling in a ragged breath, "I hope to hell there's a faster, easier way out of Callen's compound, I hate to have to do this all over again in the reverse." She lifted her leg and set her foot on one of the crates to dry it.

Removing the towel, she bent to dry her leg- and she heard a sound- a sharp inhale, she swung her head around with a yelp.

Volt was standing inside the doorway to the room, his eyes raking up and down and over her naked body.

"Oh!" she yelped again and pulled the towel in front of her. But he had to have seen the naked profile of her body, thankfully her leg had been up to hide her privates, hopefully her arm blocked his view of her breasts!

"Get out!" she shrieked. He just stood there, a small smile playing around those carved lips, and his gaze floated over her body again. "Saldano," she exclaimed, "a gentleman would close his eyes and remove himself!"

He prowled towards her, growling, "Never been accused of being a gentleman, Anastasia." He was a few feet away, his gaze on the top swells of her breasts not hidden by the towel. Dark eyes dilating with heat, he whispered a thick rumbled, "*Ana*."

"What are you doing? Get back, get out, Mr. Saldano!" She tried for formality but he wasn't leaving and he was still moving towards her. Six inches or so away he stopped, and reached out and slid his hand around the back of her neck and jerked her towards him hard enough her body banged into his.

His hand cradling her neck, forcing her face up, he slammed his mouth onto hers and seized her lips. Slanting his head, he pushed her lips apart and shoved his tongue inside her tender mouth, and stormed into a rampage of tasting, nipping, sucking. Voracious growls reverberated against her mouth as he fervently devoured her.

Stassi's head went spinning like a top with heat and utter oblivion under the assault of his mouth. He shoved his tongue halfway down her throat as he tasted her lips, her teeth, then besieged her captive tongue.

His hand stroked around her body to her lower back and he drew her body tight against his, and she could feel the thick heaviness of his arousal as he nudged one of his legs between her thighs. The rough texture of his jeans on her bare thighs ratcheted the intense sensation, Stassi melted into his hard body with an abandoned frenzy of passion.

All thought vacated her brain, until she felt his hand on the towel she held in front of her and he was pulling it away- she put her hand on his chest and pushed. He didn't budge, she tore her mouth from his and gushed, "Stop, *stop*."

His body stiffened. He didn't let go of her, his head drew back to peer down at her. His cheeks were flushed, dark eyes glittered dangerously at Stassi from under lusted lids, his big chest rose rapidly in and out with fast breaths. Equally, her cheeks blushed dark rose, under half-closed lids her eyes glazed green, her breaths rushed, chest heaving.

"Anastasia," his murmur guttural, husky, his accent drawing her name out exotic and rough. His fist was wrapped around the top of the towel, his other hand still pressing against the inner swell of her lower back. The strength and heat of his hand permeating through the towel.

"No, I don't want-" her words cut off and her breath thrust out when he yanked her back against his body and his mouth captured hers again and he sucked at her lips to get her to open them. He pulled at the towel, and Stassi shoved him as hard as she could.

Caught off-balance, not enough to send him back a step, just enough there was space between them, and she hauled her hand back and slapped him. His head didn't even flinch from the hit.

Now he did step back with a slight bow. Voice a gruff rasp, his gaze poured over her half exposed body before settling on her eyes that were part angry, affronted, and part aroused. "I deserved that. I…apologize, Anastasia for taking liberties. You were so stunning, so innocent, yet so terribly sultry in that pose. You are beautiful as it is, but, nude," his gaze again strolled down her half-covered body, it rose as the side of his mouth lifted.

He said, "I fear I lost my mind for the first time in my life. My only wish is that I'd been a second earlier, or later, whichever would have lent me the perfect view of that spectacular body wholly naked."

"Mister-" Her face blew up scarlet, she lifted her hand threatening to slap him again. Instead, she pointed at the door and ordered, "Get out before I start screaming."

The side of his mouth now cut up into a curve. "No doubt my men would rush in to rescue the ravished damsel." His face turned serious. "Again, I apologize, it won't happen again." Spinning on his heel he strode out, carefully closing the door behind him.

Her lungs expelled the taut breath she'd held and she slumped down to sit on the crate. She sighed out loud, "It's going to be a long, awkward journey." How imprudent to not have locked the door. While she sat to catch her shuddering breath, waves of aroused heat roiled off her body, her mind was still feeling his mouth, his hands on her.

"Well," Stassi laughed drily, "that will teach me to conjure up ideas of him kissing me. I must have telepathed my thoughts straight to his caveman brain and he assumed he could just swoop in and take what he pleased."

She came out brushing her hair, dressed in jeans and a soft pink sweater. Not making eye-contact with Volt, she trod to the kitchen where Jubal had set out food and water for their breakfast.

Volt knelt beside the duffle repacking items. He looked up at her. "We'll have to leave the duffle at some point, Callen will know you couldn't carry it yourself." At her nod, he went back to what he was doing.

Greco must have come back inside, he still wore his jacket, he stood near Jubal with a mug that steam poured out of. Someone had made coffee in the fireplace. Clearly the two men knew something had happened between her and Volt. They knew she'd been in taking a shower, and that Volt had been inside for a few minutes before quickly, and with some sort of tell-tale expression, exited the room.

Her face was red as a beet. Jubal and Greco were careful to not look at her, their mouths tight from holding back grins like silly schoolboys.

Jubal leaned against the kitchen counter eating. Well, she needed to get things back to normal, she said with a small laugh, "Gosh, I'd kill for a cup of coffee."

"Or hot chocolate with marshmallows." Greco grinned at her as he reached for another mug from the cupboard above the counter. And that broke the ice, the men started chatting about the weather they were expecting to meet when they started up the mountain.

Chapter Twenty-One

Four days of bone-wearying travel, each day blended into the next. The only excitement was when a leopard charged from the brush right at Stassi. They had been walking single-file with Volt first then Stassi, Jubal and then Greco. The cat went after Stassi because she was the smallest of the group.

They heard it scrape in a run from the scrub and snarl before it lunged at her. In a blur of movement, Volt threw his body into the wild cat knocking it on its side and Jubal was beside him with a dagger raised. Greco fired off a gunshot into the air, and the animal sprang to its feet and disappeared into the brush.

It happened so fast Stassi couldn't even get off a scream. Greco and Jubal raced to where the cat disappeared and followed it to make sure it was gone. Volt got up and hurried to Stassi. He grasped her arms, holding her out to examine. "You okay? Did it hurt you?"

Skin white as bone, she just stood blinking at him, her body trembling now that what had almost happened set it. "Uh," she mumbled, staring up at him, fright blaring from her green eyes. Then those eyes narrowed at him. "Saldano, what were you thinking jumping that- that creature? He could have bit your head off or clawed you in half!"

"Seriously?" He rolled his eyes at her inanity. "You were the cat's planned meal, sweetheart. If I hadn't knocked him down you would have incurred some serious damage before we would have been able to stop his attack. Geesh, woman," he forked unsteady fingers through his hair, pushing it off his forehead. He remained steely but clearly the near-attack on her had unnerved him. Glaring at her like it was her fault, he said, "That is why you are not traveling alone."

Breathing hard from the anxious exertion of the moment, Jubal pushed through the thick brush and said, "It's starting to snow. It's gonna be real hard going now, all uphill, we need to hit it."

They had already felt the steady incline since starting up the face of the mountain. Greco emerged right behind Jubal. He slid the strap of the shotgun he'd fired back over his shoulder and started walking. The others fell in step behind him.

Volt arranged for Jubal to lead the trail. He positioned himself and Stassi to walk next to each other behind Jubal, keeping his body between Stassi and the brush, and then had Greco at the rear. Volt took long, slow breaths to calm the adrenalin, and, he had to admit it, the panicked fear that slammed into his body when he saw the wild cat come running from the scrub heading straight for Stassi.

He told her the truth, if he hadn't knocked it back so quickly, those huge sharp teeth would have stabbed right into her neck and then the three men would have been chasing it through the woods as it ran off with its dinner in its lethal mouth.

Damn, he should have tied her up, tossed her over his shoulder and into the car and taken her right back home like he'd initially threatened. She had no business being out here in the savage raw wilderness hiking up a snow covered mountain to trade her life for a baby's.

The leopard was bad enough, at least Volt and his friends could fight it off, he dreaded what would face her once she reached the fortress at the top of the mountain. A place where he might not be able to keep her safe by his side. He hated the unknown. Hard to plan for what you didn't know awaited you.

He glanced to his side as she trudged next to him. The long mahogany mane bouncing on her back in the thick braid. Damned stubborn woman, he silently berated her. Damned brave, stubborn, foolish woman.

Hell, if it were him, he'd do the same thing, barter his life for a child's. But at least he could reconnoiter, have a plan in place. And he had warrior experience, he could take care of himself. Stassi had set out so quickly before he'd been able to gather the information he needed on Marcus Callen. Or Talis Falk, whoever he was. In this case, Stassi was walking straight into the lion's den and Volt would have to figure out how to keep her from entering the fortress and getting himself inside instead.

The hiking grew more and more laborious. They trudged at a sharp incline now through inches of snow. Thankfully the wind wasn't harsh, just strong enough to pelt them with ever thickening snowflakes. But it made seeing difficult through lashes damp with snow-blurred sight, the air had turned icy, chilling exposed skin. They had bundled up tight with scarves covering as much of their faces as they could.

At her last phone conversation with Callen, he advised Stassi she would be spending one night on the side of the mountain, then she would reach his home later on the next day. He told her to wait, that he would send men to make a shelter for her protection from the elements but clouds packing in heavy cut the connection again. Thank goodness, Callen wouldn't be able to have his soldiers track her.

The night on the mountain was rough. The men rigged an improvised lean-to and they packed their sleeping bags almost on top of one another for the body heat.

Volt had Stassi zipped up inside his bag with him. Her blankets weren't going to cut the winter air. It was a long, awkward, uncomfortable night for Volt. And Stassi probably wasn't faring too well either being pressed up tight against him. Even in the bag she had been shivering. He slid his arms around her and she immediately stiffened then pushed to move away from him.

Tightening his arms, he whispered gruffly, "Just warming you, Anastasia, that's all." He needed to have a firm chat with his lower body and convince it of that. Spooning a luscious woman curled tight against him was going to be tough keeping his arousal from touching her. Last thing he needed was for her to get freaked and try to leave the bag. He could hear his friends' sniggers now as he fought her, forcing her to stay wrapped in his arms and her agitated protests.

It took a long time before he felt her body soften against his. Finally she slept, now he could perhaps end his torture and follow her into dreamland. Yeah, he prayed his dreams were bereft of images of him and Anastasia naked, entwined, and not to keep warm. Great, he needed to really stop thinking.

As the sun rose dim in the grey skies the next morning, the group tromped uphill. The going was slower as the angle grew steeper. The men were practiced with hiking mountains in all kinds of weather in all kinds of circumstances but they had to move slowly because Stassi hadn't the experience or stamina to forge through like they did.

"There, there it is," Jubal said suddenly and stopped. "You can see the stronghold, but…"

Volt asked, "But what?" Then they all stopped and looked up. "For the love of-"

"Shit," Greco grumbled curses.

"Everybody step back into the cover of the trees, we don't want some eagle eye sentinel to spot us," Volt ordered. Boots crunching virgin snow, they quickly ambled into the nest of firs that speckled all up and down the mountain like a handful of green jacks tossed over the snow.

Stassi blinked wide-eyed. "How on earth are we going to get up to it?"

Marcus Callen's fortress, a sprawling mass of stone and brick topped the mountain. Numerous windows glinted in the morning light, grey smoke hailed skyward from several chimneys.

"Looks like a colossal, jumbled square castle," Greco muttered. He held his hand above his eyes to block out the brightening sunlight breaking through spaces between clouds and glaring off the pristine carpet of snow spread around the compound and the mountainside.

"Kinda like a modern castle without turrets and shit," Jubal agreed.

Greco said with curiosity, "Odd how a tiny section of the what, fourth story? Juts way out over the-"

"Fucking gorge," Jubal finished for him. "The conspicuous issue is the damned gorge the freakin' castle overlooks. He couldn't have a moat like any other normal crazed king?" He scuttled quickly ahead darting from tree to tree so fast he was nothing but a brown dot blending in with the trees. He was gone several minutes, was huffing white vapor as he rejoined the group.

"What's the verdict?" Volt asked him

Jubal didn't look optimistic. "There is no way in hell to traverse the chasm. It's perfectly sleek like flat ice, straight down to the very deep bottom and the same back up to the compound."

They stood and took in the mighty fortress that instead of a moat to keep enemies out, a steep, deep crevasse was carved around the entire front and sides of the mountain.

Greco craned his neck, commented, "Judging by our topographical map, the backside of the mountain is also fairly straight up and down but without the damned gorge. The gorge is not on any of our maps. It's not real wide, but wide enough there's no crossing over it. No wonder Callen said the compound was impassible and impenetrable. It can only be accessed by helicopter, and he likely has the roof sabotaged as well."

"Okay, call him, Anastasia," Volt told her.

Her gaze stuck on the square stone castle in the air, Stassi pulled out the satphone and punched in the numbers.

Callen answered. "Stassi, my love, how close are you?" His voice silky menace, he practically cooed into the phone.

"I can see the fortress, Callen," she replied. "But I don't see how I'm supposed to get around the ravine. There's no way-"

"That is correct, love, there is no way around it. The fissure is too steep and sheer to navigate down or up it."

"But how then-"

Laughter trickled from the phone. "Why, we send a basket down for you."

She glanced at Volt who was staring at the fortress. "A basket?"

There was silence…then, a sound from far above, up the fortress. Their heads all tilted back as they gazed up.

Greco murmured in awe, "There is a crane, like an iron arm emerging from a hole in the building that's jutting from the fourth or fifth story."

They watched the rust colored iron arm stretch over the gorge, clear over it near to the side where the group hid. "Something's attached to it, it's lowering," Greco described what they were watching. As it descended lower, they could see it was indeed a basket. An iron basket large enough to hold a person. One person.

Callen's voice crackled from the phone Stassi held. Her arm had dropped in the shock of seeing the crane thing.

Volt touched her arm and nodded to the phone. Slapping her lips together to keep the nerves locked inside, she blinked, clearing the dazedness from her stunned eyes and raised the phone to her ear. Callen was talking.

"It's easy as pie, my lovely Stassi," he was saying. "When it lands, you just open the little gate and step inside. Close the gate, it'll click closed. Inside there's a harness you clip onto your belt or something on you. It's to ensure if a gust of wind suddenly shakes the basket that you don't accidentally tip out of it. It's a long way down," he chuckled.

The roses fled from her cheeks leaving pale fright behind. She looked up at Volt, his mouth was set in a hard grim line.

He put his hand over the phone and whispered, "You don't have to do this, Anastasia. I'll take you back home and my team and I will return here and get the child. I swear we will do it."

When Stassi didn't reply, Callen chuckled again, then his voice turned stern. "I am not a patient man, Stassi, do I need to lop off an arm or leg from little Cody and send it down in the basket to help you make up your mind? Quickly!" he snapped.

Shaking his head, his hand closed on her arm, Volt whispered, "We'll get the baby, Anastasia, you go home-"

She lifted the phone and said into it, "Okay. Give me a second to...to wrap my head around the whole gondola thing." She shut the phone off and shoved it into her backpack. She removed her gloves and hat and slipped those in as well.

"Ana-"

Stassi started towards the basket but Volt held her back. He said, "We'll wait here."

"But I have no idea what's going to happen, how long I-"

"Two days, Anastasia," he warned, "if I don't hear from you in two days we will come for you."

"Saldano, I can't-"

"Two days," he said, bent and slapped his lips over hers to stifle any objection. She stiffened for a heartbeat, then her lips parted to invite him in.

He had promised himself he wouldn't do it again, but damn, she was honeycomb and he was one hungry bear. Someone cleared their throat, then a slight snicker broke them apart. God he hated this, his stomach twisted with dread. "Okay, call me, Ana. Tell me what's going on. Call me if you need me-"

She broke from his grasp and stated sharply, "You will not come near the building until I have the baby safely out," and she strode purposefully to the waiting basket, boots crunching the brittle snow.

The men couldn't follow her. They had to stay in the copse of firs and watch her reach the basket then pause. She looked out over the gorge and the quiver that ran through her body was blatantly visible. Volt's stomach twisted in a knot.

Gingerly, Stassi unlatched the metal gate, opened it, and cautiously stepped into the basket. She hesitated again. Then, with a deep breath, she closed and latched the gate. The satphone rang in her hand.

She answered it. Callen said, "Put the harness on."

She looked up and squinted. She couldn't see into the castle, and there were no visible people outside it, but obviously Callen could see her. With an absent nod, Stassi stuffed the phone in her backpack then found the harness and lifted her jacket to clip it to her belt. What would she have done if she wasn't wearing a belt? Lasso it around her neck?

She shook her head with a wry smile. Frivolous thoughts she didn't need. She needed to concentrate on what was happening. To be alert to any way to grab the baby, flee the building and get down the mountain without the basket. Her shoulders lowered with her exhale, it didn't look feasible.

The basket moved and Stassi stumbled against the side. Her hands flew out and she gripped the railing. The bottom of the basket was rounded steel, steel slates curled up from the bottom to the railing with at least a foot of distance between them, then there was nothing else. No roof, nothing but an enormous chain that hooked the basket to the giant arm that was rising with her in it.

The contraption made a humming sound. As the arm moved, rising higher and higher then moving over the gorge, she gazed out to where she'd left the men, and she could see no evidence they were there. Of course as Volt had told her, he was an experienced soldier, hunter, warrior, he could hide in the hole of a needle.

Every time she looked down her belly pivoted, she raised her eyes to view the castle. The crevasse was so deep and steep, narrow, she couldn't see the bottom. It was like someone had taken a cleaver and chopped, taking a slice of earth, like a piece of pie, and threw it away somewhere.

In five minutes, the arm was withdrawing into the building and soon the basket slipped through an opening in the stone wall.

Chapter Twenty-Two

Stassi's fingers wound tightly around the railing, her heartrate skyrocketed when she saw him standing there, grinning like a wolf at her as if she was dressed in yellow feathers. It has been almost twelve years since she'd seen her ex-teacher.

Her last sight of him was when he had slammed her over the desk and was ripping her pants off and the teacher came in and screamed. Callen had frozen, his face bled white at the scream. He stepped back from Stassi. Seeing the horrified teacher, he ran past her and out of the room like his hair was on fire. Stassi recalled that when she had been at the police station an officer mentioned to another officer that the degraded pervert was around twenty-eight, so he was about forty presently.

She studied him with the eyes of an adult now. When he was her teacher he would have been considered handsome with his boy-next-door features, except he was grown up now and the obscene things he'd done in his life had hacked and sawed and chiseled the once soft features. Yet the narcissistic cynicism, depravity, sadistic sociopathy, were all masked beneath his still boyish, familiar face. No one would see the monster until it was too late.

Callen was tall, well-built with dark sandy hair he styled modern with the sides clipped shorter than the top, and fashionably trimmed scruff that was slightly darker than his hair. Faint lines arced his aggressive sapphire eyes and full mouth that crooked with a cruel bent. Surprisingly he sported a tan even living way up in the snowy clouds.

Yes, she was an adult now, yet her insides quaked as if she was still experiencing the agonizing pain and terror of that young girl he'd brutally raped. He had stolen her childhood, and also her adulthood because the trauma he inflicted on her deformed how she viewed herself as polluted, damaged goods.

A broken person, she hated the warped woman she had grown to be, and she profoundly feared men. And, she hated them too. All the men who left their imprint on her; her abusive father, absent cowardly brother, rapist teacher, Rufus, Lamontagne, betraying Glenn, none were great examples of the male side of humanity. Last thing she wanted was to be tied to a man, at his mercy. No, marriage, babies, family, those were not for her.

Because of Callen, Stassi would never live a normal life. She couldn't bear to have a male touch her, except for benign hugs from her friend Charlie. But that's because he's safe, like a brother. But not like her natural brother who had cowered and ran away while their father beat her.

She'd tried to have a normal relationship with Glenn Dyke, but she knew he felt her stiffening, her repulsion, always on the edge of running and screaming from him every time he attempted to do more than kiss her.

Even the kisses made her skin crawl. No wonder he'd fallen into Juliette's slutty web. Yet, Stassi pondered, she hadn't been afraid while Volt had been kissing her, unfamiliar tingles vibrated in her lower body at the memory. No, she hadn't felt fear, she had felt safe, desired...aroused. Her breath caught in her throat, no, that had to be a mista-

"Love, no hello for your favorite teacher?" Callen asked as he moved forward and unlatched the gate. "Your beautiful eyes are all wide and fearful, but your pretty lips are sealed tight. We'll have to work on that, eh? I had so many plans for you those many years ago, for us, for what I could teach you to do with that mouth. But that fucking interfering teacher-" His mouth twisted as if he tasted a rotten lemon.

He shrugged off the disturbing memory and pulled the gate open then held his hand out for her to take. She glared down at it like it was a scorpion about to sting.

Frowning at her reluctance to touch him, Callen said, "From this point on, you will do as I say. Failure to obey me, or resist my…attentions, will result in the child being harmed. Maybe even irrevocably." One sandy brow arched, his hand still out.

There was no choice, she had already jumped into the wolf's lair, and his teeth were white and sharpened, ready for her. She placed her hand, so much smaller into his large palm. He instantly squeezed hard, crushingly hard, she cried out, tried to withdraw her hand but he squeezed harder, bones crunched under his punishing grip.

He jerked her hand hard, her whole body wrenched forward. He pulled her close, his hand still so crushing tears of pain erupted. Callen lowered his face within inches of hers, lids slid down over fierce blazing eyes. "Your first lesson, love, do as I say or suffer the consequences. I can hurt you just as easily as the child." His soft, full mouth curved in a malicious grin. "It'll be a hundred times more satisfying and…titillating to harm you than the baby."

He brushed his thumb under her eyes, wiping away the tears that had sprouted from his vicious grip, then he drew her out of the basket. Loosening his grip, he said, "Let's get that backpack and jacket off you, shall we?"

Without waiting for her response, Callen grasped the pack, tugged it off her shoulders and dropped it on the floor. Then he took the zipper to her jacket, pulled it down then pushed the jacket off her shoulders. Tugging it down her arms, he removed it and handed it to a man that had been standing with him. He said, "Yannic, put this where she can't get to it."

Then he smiled at Stassi. "That should keep you from any escape attempts. You would freeze to death before you got a half a mile from here. The babe wouldn't last five minutes."

Stassi didn't reply. As he'd surmised, her mind had been busy with plans of fleeing with Cody.

"Okay, Stassi, let's have a look at you." Callen clasped her hand again, loosely this time, and held her out to view her body. She wore powder-blue jeans, and he noticed with a leer, a pink sweater that went just past her belt. If he tied her hands above her head, or bent her over, her bare midriff would be exposed. His pupils enlarged as his gaze heated while it trolled in approval down her figure.

"Oh yes, you have grown up, haven't you, love." Releasing her hand, he made a revolving motion with his hand. "Let's see the back, can it compare to your exquisite front?"

Stassi hesitated, his brows lowered, she slowly turned. Facing away from Callen she saw a man pushing a button on a panel on the wall then shifted a lever. The basket rose, then the arm folded, the entire contraption moved all the way to the side of the room then it lowered to the floor where it stilled. The man at the controls flipped a switch and the humming shut off.

Callen's voice came thick and husky from behind her. "Yes, yes, I have caught me a delightfully delicious treat." He tugged the band on the bottom of her braid off then stroked his fingers through the thick locks, combing them, fluffing the wavy strands down her back. "Turn around, love," he told her.

Stassi obliged and swiveled to face him. Callen wore a dark brown sweater over a collared shirt, brown slacks, polished brown dress boots. With his neat sandy hair and the academic outfit, Stassi felt swept back in time and he was once again her fated teacher.

All those feelings of terror, mortification she'd tried so hard to repress, the memory of the piercing pain in her tender privates burst in her, the pain suddenly present and palpable smothered her with a rush. A dizzying tormented rush of anguish socked right into her.

Her legs turned to rubber, her breath hastened, lashes flapped up and down. A panic attack was overtaking her, Stassi thought her heart would explode with the devastating toll of it all. *No.*

Forcing herself to take a long deep breath, her hands clenched. She can, she will fight it, she won't let him make her that frightened hurting, helpless little girl again. With a blink and a shake of her head the distress slowly disbursed, and a calm rolled over her, steadying her racing pulse and pivoting gut.

"Where's the gun?" he asked.

Uh oh, she'd forgotten about the shotgun that Jubal had carried for her. "It was heavy, I had a hard enough time walking. I left it where I spent last night."

The men had spent considerable time whenever they left a place they had stayed the night making sure all traces of them were gone. No footprints or matting down of grass from anybody but hers. Fortunately the steady slow snowfall covered their footprints. Volt said they couldn't leave any evidence for Callen to find that she hadn't come alone.

Callen's lips pushed out with his frown. He took in her delicate stature, her slenderness and the backpack she had to carry and nodded. "I see. I'll have one of the men retrieve it when the weather clears more." Giving her body another considering look he said, "I'm amazed you made it. You are one tough cookie, eh?"

Stassi glanced around. The room they were in didn't look like it was part of the castle, fortress, whatever it was. The walls weren't stone, they were plain white, the floor beige tile. There was nothing else in the room but the basket, and the equipment used to operate it. Hearing a whirring sound, she turned her head.

The man at the steel arm and basket controls had his finger pressed on a button. A pocket door slid across the opening she'd been brought through. It closed with a thud and a click. She tried to watch him surreptitiously, there was her only route of escape. But, they surely kept the room and equipment secured.

Maybe Callen was so arrogant thinking no one would try to flee from him that he didn't bother locking up the room. She hoped and prayed this was so, there was no other way out and down the mountain.

A man entered the area catching her attention. His gaze went first to Callen then it centered on her, and a suffocating breathlessness engulfed Stassi so powerfully she fought to stay conscious and not fade into a puddle of terror on the floor at Callen's feet.

Rufus, Nero Lamontagne, Vinca Nivelli, Marcus Callen were all ruthless violent men, but this man, Stassi rubbed her arms against the flow of pure evil emanating from the man, a lethality so potent it wrapped insidiously around and around her until she could barely drag in a breath.

To save herself, she tore her gaze from him. Unclenching her teeth, she was being ridiculously fanciful again. He was just a man.

"Ah, Ini, come meet my...mistress." Callen grinned and rolled an arm around Stassi's waist.

It took everything Stassi had to not shove away from his touch, the feel of his body pressed against hers made her physically ill, she kept her gaze on the knot of Ini's silk tie at his throat. He wore a suit, actually he looked...dapper. Degenerate dirtbag in a suit.

"Anastasia Athens, meet Ini Madarov, my...assistant." He smirked at the raised brow Madarov issued him.

"Ah." Madarov moved a few steps closer to the pair. "The little virgin student." At Stassi's gasp, an ice-cold cunning grin cut his face. At Callen's callous chuckle, Madarov shrugged negligently, said spitefully, "Oh, that's right, not a virgin, my buddy Marcus took care of that for you."

Stassi moved from Callen's encircling arm and said calmly, "That is correct, Mr. Madarov. Your despicable criminal friend can't get a grown woman to be with him so he has to resort to forcing his vile self on defenseless children."

She glanced snidely at Callen then turned her full gaze directly into Madarov's deadly eyes. "Your *buddy* is quite a *man*, isn't he? I bet the other men in prison gave him a taste of what he had done to me, hmm."

She turned to Callen and smiled coldly. "Did you enjoy their attention Mr. Callen?" She was tired of being a squashed bug with no spine, a helpless victim. Let's see how these morally corrupt men like it.

At the shock that suddenly raged on Callen's face, Madarov burst into laughter.

Callen smoothed the rage from his face, glared at Madarov. Bending to pick up her backpack he said coolly to Stassi, "Come, I was involved in an intense business development when you arrived. It will take a considerable amount of time to remedy, I must tend to it. I will take you to the room you will stay in until I complete my business and then we can...get together. Shall we?" He extended his arm.

Avoiding Callen's hand reaching to cup her elbow, Stassi insisted, "Take me to Cody." Keeping several feet away from him, Stassi allowed him to lead her from the room. Madarov's laughter followed them down the hall like a cackling jackal.

Annoyance at her dodging his hand, and aggravated at her offensive barking back at him, Callen replied crossly, "Fine. I'll show you the boy, you'll see he's being well cared for." Anger in his stalking stride, he said, "Today is yours. Tomorrow we will pick up our relationship where we left off. There will be time enough after I've fucked you my fill for you to hit the lab."

At the paling of Stassi's skin and her faltered step, a slight curl to his mouth showed he'd regained his smug upper hand.

Stassi held her head high and firmed her stride. "I see all the money and education in the world can't transform the vulgar, belly-dragging serpent into a nobleman."

Callen's head fell back with a hooted laugh. Snapping his hand out, he grabbed her arm before she could deflect, stopped and pulled her up short. A satisfied gleam lit his eyes when he saw the sudden fear flash before she schooled her expression into a smooth creamy, flawless sculpture. "Yeah, we're gonna have a lot of fun together, my baby student."

Snatching her arm out of his grip she started forward. "I am no longer a baby, Marcus Callen. Nor your student. We are nothing to each other, nothing."

He watching her hips flick back and forth in an angry sashay before he grinned and hurried after her.

As they entered the room Stassi could hear the baby gurgling and cooing. She approached the makeshift crib someone had put together for Cody. A stack of boxes encircled a small bed and lining the inside of the boxes were pillows. Cody lay on his back, his pudgy legs kicking, chubby arms waving. When she leaned over and peered at him he gave her a big toothless smile. Her heart melted.

"Hey, Cody," she whispered softly, "so good to see you, your mama and papa miss you so much." She bent to pick him up. Callen's arm blocked her.

"No," he said. "You show me some goodwill and I'll let you hold him."

Her head twisted up at Callen, cinnamon brows inverted in puzzlement. "Goodwill? Why can't I hold him, see if he's okay? That was our deal."

Callen crossed his arms over his chest, and lowered his chin that had become squarer over the years hardening those boyish looks. Scruff darker than his sandy hair layering his jaw added to the toughening of his features. Looking down his nose at her he said, "Our deal is whatever I say it is. I used the baby to get you here, and now I'm going to use him to force you to do everything I say. Bow to my every whim."

She stepped back from the bed and put space between her and Callen. "What do you want from me so that I can cuddle Cody?"

His mouth would have been pretty if not for the intrinsic cruel sneer, it lifted in a crafty smile. "We'll start with a kiss."

Stassi's lip wrinkled in disgust. "I would rather kiss a snake."

Her backpack slung over his shoulder, Callen grabbed her arm and pulled her towards the door. "Fine. We're done here."

She dug her heels into the brown carpet, said quickly, "No, wait."

Callen paused, he didn't bother hiding his smirk.

Stassi had to be able to tell Charlie that she not only saw his son, but held him and that he was not injured in any way. "All right, Callen. One kiss and I can hold the baby." Her plush mouth pulled in as she tilted her head back and closed her eyes, prepared for his quick buss.

She didn't see him drop her backpack or his smirk broaden or his hands come at her. But she felt the jerk of her body smacking into his and his hand fisting in her hair. His other hand splayed across her back. He pulled her hair so hard to tilt her head, her neck bent sharply with a crack, she cried out, and taking advantage of her open mouth he rammed his mouth over hers. Her hands went to his shoulders to push him away but he was an immovable brick wall.

Callen yanked her head to the side and angled his opposite to seal their mouths and forced her lips to stay apart. His gorging attack was ruthless and carnivorous, he held her body so tightly against his the breath was smashed out of her.

His hand twisted mercilessly in her hair, his painful grip keeping her helplessly immobile as he bit at her, savagely gnawed her soft lips, harshly chewed and sucked her tender tongue. It was grotesque and it hurt and she was completely unable to stop him or escape his fiendish seizure.

The kiss, or more accurately, brutal feeding, seemed to go on forever. Stassi thought she was about to pass out, could a person die from a violent kiss?

Grinding his mouth over hers harder and harder he moved his hand from her back to grasp her breast, his strong fingers squeezing it possessively in a hellish clench. Mauling it viciously, he gave it a rough twist before releasing it, and groaned in pleasure at Stassi's pained whimper.

Finally he broke from her, huffing and puffing, he gazed in bestial delirium down at her. His own mouth damp and red from his roughness, he still gripped her hair in his fist forcing her head back, making her look up at him, see his mastery over her. He sneered, "Now you may hold the baby," and he let her go so abruptly Stassi staggered backwards.

The back of her hand over her punished mouth, she caught her balance and glowered at him in angry humiliation. Quickly, before he changed his mind, Stassi hurried to the baby. Bending over, she slid her hands under his plump body and lifted him carefully, then gently cradled him in her arms.

Smiling at him, she whispered, "How're you doing, little one? Soon you'll be home with your mama and daddy. They said to tell you that they love you. They-" Callen suddenly snatched the child out of her hands and callously dropped him back on the bed.

"Wait! What are you doing?" she protested, reaching for the baby who started crying. "You said I could hold him!"

Callen snatched up her arm, grabbed her pack with his other hand and marched her to the door. Smiling wickedly, he told her, "I said you could hold him, I didn't say how long."

He stopped at the door and turned her to face him. "I am in control here, Stassi, I decide everything. You fight me, and as I told you on the phone, little Cody will suffer. I had no qualms about hurting you when you were just a child, I certainly am unconcerned about harming a sniveling baby. Now, we're going to your room," and he tugged her out the door.

Cody's cries turned into aggrieved wails as Callen forced Stassi to leave him behind.

Callen ushered a sullen Stassi down a rose-hued carpeted hallway, passing gilded paintings that hung in a row on blush walls. He led her down a flight of stairs and along another corridor. All the doors they passed looked the same, but eventually he stopped at one. He fished a set of keys out of his pocket and unlocked the door and opened it.

He pulled her into the room then dropped his hand from her arm. "Okay, love, this is where you will stay until I conclude my pressing business and have time for you. Someone will bring you a tray of food and drink, try to entertain yourself, it'll be the last time you are alone, and free of restraints, for a long great while." Tossing the backpack on the bed, he curved his fingers around his lean hips and watched her glance around the room.

"As you see," he pointed out, "there are no windows. No way for you to leave here unless I fetch you. Even if you could get out of the room and then the mansion, the only way down the mountain is to cross over the gorge, which is impossible, or go down the other side. Trust me, there is no way to traverse that side either. The incline is quite sheer, it would be certain death to even attempt it. It would be like sliding down a towering icicle."

Her bleak expression told him he'd hit home with the futility of her leaving the castle.

"So, changing the subject from perilous escape attempts," nodding to an armoire of gleaming cherry wood nestled in a corner, he said, "there is a peignoir inside. When I come for you tomorrow, you will be wearing it."

His mouth crooked in a provoking smile. "It won't be for long of course, but I still want to see you in it. I was in Paris and when I saw it in a shop window, an image of you attired in it flashed into my mind." He laughed. "That was a frequent happenstance, love, images of you, and me, nakedly entangled quite often popped into my mind. So, now that I finally have you, I plan to drown in all the fantasies of you that have fueled me these past years."

While he taunted her, Stassi put distance between them, inching towards a door in the side of the chamber. That brought a mocking grin to his pleased face. "You may attempt to lock yourself in the bathroom, love, but you must realize it won't stop me for a second. It would be a pity for me to destroy that lovely door, but alas," he elegantly shrugged his broad shoulders, "I will never let anything come between us again. Nothing."

His gaze speared Stassi with indomitable commitment to his promise. "By the way, just so you know, you went through a metal detector and screening system when you left the room with the basket. I know you have no weapons or GPS trackers on you. Just clothes, toiletries and my satphone." He glanced at the backpack. "Right, I need to collect the phone-"

Regardless that he could knock the door down, Stassi still moved towards the bathroom, at least for now there would be something between them. The door opened out, he might be able to break in but it would take some time. The look of him, his very presence made her sick. Her head ached from stuffing old horrid memories, and the dread of what was going to happen to her, and little Cody if she failed to free him. His dark voice swatted the thoughts away.

His attention hopped from the pack to her. "You know, I have a wee bit of time. I believe I'll take myself a small appetizer to hold me over. Come." He started towards her while pulling his sweater over his head. Tossing the sweater on the bed, his fingers opening the top button of his shirt, he walked faster grinning at Stassi's sudden look of panic.

His phone rang bringing him to a halt. He slipped it out and glanced at it before answering. "Yes?"

Stassi had almost reached the bathroom when she saw Callen scowl.

"I'll be right there," he stated into the cell then dropped it in his pocket. "Sorry love, our first tryst will have to wait." At the door, he said, "Remember my instructions, love, be ready for me tomorrow, in the peignoir. You don't want to anger me right off the bat, right my dear Anastasia?"

Grinning at the defiant lift of her chin, he remarked, "Ah, good, you want to fight. That will make it all so much more stimulating for me, but painful for you. Later, love."

Swiping the sweater off the bed, he was sliding it over his head as he strode out the door, closing it behind him. The lock clicked and she heard his footsteps muffled on the carpet head down the hall.

The breath Stassi held poured out deflating her tense stance. She flopped wearily onto the nearest chair. The room was utilitarian. Pale blue walls with white trim and chair rails, the carpet cobalt, a queen-sized bed centered in the room draped in a blue and white coverlet. Besides the armoire anchoring one corner, a table and two chairs in matching cherry wood were placed in front of the bed.

In curiosity, Stassi rose and walked to the armoire and swung it open. A single garment hung inside. "Oh, sure, why bother?" she murmured wryly, and lifted a corner of the scanty peignoir. The material was transparent but slightly shimmered when she moved it.

"This won't even hit me mid-thigh, and the front," she pulled at the lingerie to get a better look. "Uh huh, the scoop neck will cover my nipples and that's about it. Wonderful."

Closing the armoire, she started for the bathroom talking to herself. "I'll get cleaned up, take a nap, and hopefully in my dreams I'll figure out a way for Cody and me to safely escape. At least there's a real bed here, and heating."

Chapter Twenty-Three

A snick of a latch broke through Stassi's slumber. Rubbing an eye, she sat up with a stretch. A woman elbowed the door open then came through holding a tray in both hands. She started at Stassi's movement.

The woman said with quiet apology, "Oh, I'm sorry, I didn't mean to wake you." She scurried over and set the tray on the small table.

"It's okay, you chased away my dream." Stassi had been dreaming that Callen had Cody splayed out on a butcher block, his tiny arms and legs flailing, his chubby cheeks scarlet from crying hysterically. Callen was standing over him with a small hatchet in his hand, poised to chop off the baby's head. Laughing maniacally, goading Stassi, Callen grinned over at her.

Stassi was bound to a chair. She was struggling to break free and screaming for Callen to not harm Cody. A huge ugly grin at odds with his handsome face, Callen said, "I told you what would happen if you didn't obey my commands. The child's death is on you, my love," and his arm was swinging the blade down at Cody- Thank God the woman had woken her.

Perspiration dampening her brow, Stassi moistened her lips and asked politely, "What's your name?" Her gaze followed the woman's path to the table as she set the tray down, laid her ring of keys on the table then lifted a lid off a plate. The aroma of garlic and parmesan scented the air.

The woman turned a cheerful face to Stassi. Curls of brown tinseled with grey wisped against ruddy cheeks rounded in a friendly smile. Fortyish, plain as a schoolmarm with wire-rimmed glasses, a black and white striped dress wrapped around her short, plump figure to past her thick knees. "Myrtle, dear, Myrtle French. You are Stassi, Mr. Falk told me. He said to take good care of you."

Not correcting her on Callen's true name, walking towards her, Stassi replied, "Oh, nice to meet you, Mrs. French."

"Just Myrtle, dear. I've brought you some supper. There's a bottle of wine over there in the cupboard if you prefer rather than the tea on the tray," she motioned to a built-in double-door small cabinet. "The lid is the screw on kind and glasses are inside as well."

Of course. Callen would have considered a corkscrew to be a weapon. She'd noticed the cutlery on the tray was one of those foldable plastic spoon/fork all in one. The tines on the fork weren't even a quarter of an inch long, no way could it be used as a weapon.

Her hands clasped behind her back, Stassi nodded. "Okay, thank you." She leaned in and sniffed. "My, that smells delicious. Did you prepare it?"

The salt and pepper curls bobbed around her round face as she shook her head. "Oh heavens no, child. Mr. Falk employs several full time chefs for his men. There are at least forty people stationed in the mansion at most times. But don't fear, dear, they are on the lower floors, you shan't come in contact with them."

"I see. What floor are we on now?"

"The fifth. There are seven floors and four wings."

"Hmm." Stassi smiled her friendliest smile. "Listen, Mrs...ah, Myrtle, I'd like to step outside for a breath of air. I'll be right back." She swiftly strode to the door and twisted the knob. It was locked. She swung around with a silent curse. Then smiled again. "I suppose you have the key? May I borrow it for just a second?" She held her palm out.

Myrtle looked unhappy. "I'm sorry, child. Mr. Falk was quite clear you are to stay locked in this room until he comes for you."

"Mrs. French," twining her fingers together in front of her in a plea, she said, "Mr. Cal- uh, Falk is holding me here against my will. I'm being held hostage. Please, you must help me. He's going to harm an innocent baby if I don't rescue him."

"Oh dear." Myrtle's face crumpled, troubled that Stassi was upset. "I'm truly sorry, Miss Stassi, Mr. Falk has my son and my husband in his employ. He...well, my family would be in grave danger if I were to disregard his instructions. I am so, so sorry." She bowed her head then made for the door.

Stassi knew she couldn't overpower the woman. Myrtle was short but still taller than Stassi and she was stout and sturdy as a fireplug. Stassi considered bashing her over the head with something. Maybe the wine bottle- No, goodness no. She was here to save a body, not cause more harm.

But, she just had to get out of the room, her head turned towards the bathroom and she said quickly, "Oh, before you go, Mrs...um Myrtle, there is...uh," she thought fast, "a washcloth up on a high shelf in the closet in the bathroom. I would like to use it, but, I can't reach it. I was wondering if, well, if you wouldn't mind..."

Myrtle was happy again. "Oh yes of course dear, I would love to help you," and she scurried to the bathroom, unaware Stassi hurried and grasped one of the chairs and dragged it with her. As soon as Myrtle stepped inside the bathroom, Stassi slammed the door closed and shoved the back of the chair under the doorknob. Myrtle immediately started yelling for Stassi to open the door.

Ignoring her shouting, Stassi raced to the table, grabbed the ring of keys and then the satphone from her backpack and ran to the door. The second key she tried unlocked the door. She peered out. The corridor was empty.

She stepped outside and glanced down the hall. They had only traipsed down two hallways and one set of stairs. She was sure she could find her way to where Cody was being held.

Jogging down the first hall she then ran up the flight of stairs and jogged down the second hallway. Counting the doors, she remembered Cody's was the fifth one on the right. She stood in front of the door, panting, but she couldn't take the time to catch her breath.

She tried to turn the knob but it was locked. Lifting the ring of keys, Stassi tried one after another. Her heart throbbing in her throat, what if the key wasn't on the ring? What if- The last key turned and the lock snicked open.

Blowing out a held breath in relief, she opened the door and peeked inside in case there was someone with the baby. The room was dark, she felt for a light switch and flipped it up. A standing lamp turned on illuminating the small room. Besides the lamp there was only a table and the makeshift bed.

Diapers and other items to care for a baby were on the table. It appeared the room was previously unoccupied as there was nothing else in it. She hurried to the bed, her hand pressed over her heart, what if he wasn't there? Would she get another chance to get to him? Then she heard a tiny faint sound.

Peering over the stacked boxes, she saw Cody sound asleep with a small blanket laid over the bottom part of him. "Oh, thank God," she gushed and bent over the bed. He wore a long-sleeved t-shirt, pants that clearly covered a diaper, and socks. She took the blanket and rolled the baby in it, wrapping him snuggly and lifted him in her arms. He stirred, but his eyes remained closed.

"Okay, Cody," she whispered, the anxiety crawling up her throat made the words come out gravelly, "this is it, we have to do it." She made for the door, stuck her head out glancing in both directions. The coast was clear, and she stepped out and walked as fast as she could, hurrying down two set of stairs and following the way back to where the room with the basket was located.

Grinning in relieved delight when she pushed open the unlocked door, Stassi couldn't believe it. The room was vacant, the basket on the floor against the wall folded up as it was when they'd left it. Holding Cody in the crook of her arm, "Darn, kid, you weigh a ton," she said to him with affection moving to the control panel. It hadn't looked complicated when she'd watched the man work it earlier.

She pushed a large red button, and the whirring humming started. Glancing at the basket, she saw a light come on that was between the basket and the attached arm. Gingerly, she pushed the lever up, and held her breath again. The arm slowly rose. "Yes!" she crowed quietly. "I can do this!" She hugged the still sleeping baby, whispered, "This is it, Cody, we are out of here!"

With glee shooting off like firework sparklers all through her body, Stassi strode quickly to the basket, then she stopped dead. How was she to work the mechanics and be in the basket at the same time?

Thank goodness Callen had forgotten about the phone in her backpack. Unclipping the satphone from her belt, she pushed the buttons to dial Volt. He answered instantly.

"Anastasia, damn, are you okay? What's going on?" He was a cold harsh man yet his concern came through the wires.

"Yes, we're fine. I'm alone in the room that the basket is kept. Are you nearby? I'm going to lower the baby in the basket down to the ground."

Short silence on his end, then, "Yes, I'm here in the woods. You will be in the basket with him?"

"Um, sure," she lied. There was no time to argue with him. Once Cody was down safe, she'd raise the basket and figure out how she could maneuver the arm while in the basket. Maybe she could start the steel arm in action, get it out of the window then run and hop into it as it starts descending. But she wasn't taking that chance with the baby.

She bundled Cody up tighter and laid him on the floor of the basket. She grabbed the harness then groaned when she saw there was nothing to hook it to.

"Damn," she swore, he needed to be secured. She wrapped the harness around Cody and tied the loose end in a knot. Praying it would keep him safe, she ran back to the control panel. The panel was on the wall near the opening she had come through. First thing she did was find the switch that opened the access window in the wall. Flicking the switch she watched the wall.

"Thank you God," she rejoiced as the pocket door slid open with an unlatching click and then a slow hiss. The perspiration was tumbling down her forehead to her eyes. She dashed her hand across it and grabbed the lever, the steel arm easily maneuvered in whatever direction she moved the lever.

She pushed it up and the basket rose, then she pushed the lever to the side and the crane straightened and the basket headed towards the opening in the wall.

Slowly the arm moved the basket out the window. She stood and looked out the window. It was pitch black, she could only see the snow on the ground, the forest was completely solid blackness. Moving the lever, she watched the basket descend. Then, "Yes!" she cried seeing a flash of light in the darkness, blinking through the trees. Volt was signaling her that he was there.

Her tongue clamped between her teeth, Stassi kept moving the arm slowly, she was worried Cody could slide right out through the metal bars if she moved it too quickly. The basket only had to descend four stories and Cody would be safe with Volt. Then it would be her turn to-

The door slammed open and the man Ini charged inside straight at her. Panic struck her like a hammer. She had to get the baby down-

Wham! "You bitch!" Ini smacked her so hard she flew into the wall her head slamming into the plaster. The hit stunned her, she sank to the floor with stars twirling in her eyes.

Ini ran to the lever and shoved it hard to the side and then up, and the arm jerked violently back and forth.

Stassi crawled to the window and looked down. The ratcheting movement of the arm tipped the basket crazily side-to-side, and in horror, Stassi screamed as the precious bundle she'd placed on the floor rolled through the metal bars and flung out into open air, the harness held for a second before slipping off and Cody plunged like a bag of stones.

Ini snatched the satphone off her belt, tearing the belt loop, and threw the phone out the window. Before she could see what happened to Cody, Ini dug his fingers into her shoulders and lifted her and shoved her all in one motion towards the door.

"No! Please wait, I need to see what-"

"Shut up, bitch." His huge hand in the center of her back, he gave her a vicious shove and she stumbled out the door.

Ini wrapped his big calloused paw around the back of Stassi's neck and dragged her down the corridor. She knew it was useless to try to fight him, he was twice her size and looked as strong and mean as a raging bull.

She tripped he was moving so fast. Ini held her up by her neck and snarled, "Keep up bitch or I'll drop you on the floor

and drag you by your hair." He strode rapidly, long legs eating up the rose carpeting.

He didn't stop until he reached an open door. As he hauled her inside, she saw it was a bathroom. It was large, marble and gold flooring glimmered under their shadows. Infuriated at what she'd done, Ini hit her again and slammed her entire body against the tiled wall.

"Get the fuck down," he ordered her while shoving her shoulder. Stassi slammed hard to her knees, a sharp jab shunted pain into her knees. She swallowed her cry, damned if she would let him know how much he'd hurt her. The room was spinning from the whacks to her head.

Crouching beside her, the big blond grabbed her hands and pulled them up to a bar attached to the radiator. She heard a click, and felt cold metal snap on her wrist, then again on her other wrist. He had handcuffed her to the bar. Ini moved to his knees and got in her face. She didn't want to, but she recoiled from him. There was nowhere to go though, the cool tiled wall was at her back and she was restrained.

"There ya go, woman, how d'ya like that?" He tugged meanly on her arm so the cuff gouged into her skin. Grinning at her wince, he said, "You could have stayed snug and warm with food in your belly and sleeping on a soft bed while waiting for Marcus, but no. You had to try it. Well, you mighta got the kid out, but he has you still, now doesn't he?"

He had traded his dapper suit for a cream-colored cashmere sweater that hugged his massive chest and burly arms, and jeans that looked like they'd been starched. He dressed pretty finely for a thug.

"W- where is Callen?" she dared ask.

Like a bully, he tugged sharply on her cuffs again snickering at the pain he caused. "Weather cleared, he took the chopper to conduct his business. But don't get any ideas, woman, when the chopper lifts, spikes pop up like needles of grass, too many to get around so no one can access the mansion by the roof. Marcus loves his mechanical creations like the basket and steel arm." He leaned in close to her, his huge body obstructing her view of the doorway, her only escape route.

Stassi turned her head away from him. He was frightening with his face all hard jagged juts and hallows, scars and a rugged jaw like a brick, and he was missing the tip of one ear. Apparently he hadn't ducked a knife fast enough. Strange yin and yang, so debonair, polished with his apparel yet had the intellect and body of a mindless killing brute.

Some men, like Volt, although harsh and violent appearing, still managed to be handsome albeit in a tough way. Not this man. Ini Madarov was the colossal deadly villain straight out of a comic book, like a malevolent Thor that had survived many a lethal fight and desired more. There was nothing in his chilling blue eyes and the curl of his ax-hewn mouth but pure savage cruelty. It was like staring into the blind eyes and empty soul of a killer shark.

He sat back on his heels with his knees spread and reached out and stroked the side of Stassi's face. She made herself glare boldly back at him although terror quivered in every bone in her body. She felt his breath on her face, the heat of his body coating her, he smelled of cigar and cologne.

"Yeah, what a babe," he said, his gaze wandering over her body. Moving his hand to circle the front of her neck, he set his thumb on her pulse, he admired the bruise forming on her cheek from one of his smacks. Enjoying seeing her mouth pressed tight, her teeth clenched so she wouldn't whimper, he lowered his hand to her waist, and slid it just under the short pink sweater, his cold fingers splayed over her bare skin and she couldn't stop the quiver and gasp at his touch.

He lightly squeezed his fingers, grinning when she attempted to elude his grasp, twisting and turning to no avail. A sardonic laugh cut from his deep chest and he tightened his fingers so hard he likely bruised her ribs, any harder and he'd snap them.

Stassi stopped struggling. She readied herself for his hands to start groping before he assaulted her.

With that cruel mouth lifting at one end, he said, "If you were mine, you would be slithering on your broken belly all bloody, beaten and torn up, and you would be crying to me that you'd do anything I say, anything I want just to stop the torture. Then I would fuck you raw into next year." His smile widened completely aware of her struggle to not show her fear. A tiny scar on his mouth stretched with the harrowing smile.

"But," his thick shoulders shifted in an easy-going shrug. "Marcus will see to your punishment when he returns. I will have to wait for my turn at you. It'll be a while until he gets the shine off you, but," he shrugged again with a mild smirk, "I'll get you eventually. Until then," he patted her cheek, hard, her head flung to the right, and hoisted his huge body to his feet with a grunt.

"You will stay here until your owner comes for you. You ain't escaping this, honey. It was fortunate I'd come to check on you and realized you'd grabbed the kid and was trying to make a run for it." He bent over with his hands on his knees, sneered, "From now on, you'll remain restrained...forever. 'Cause that's how Marcus likes his women. Held immobile while he plays with them. See how you like that, bitch."

Knowing better than to kick the tiger, nevertheless Stassi instinctually half-rose to throw her leg out- His arm flung blocking her kick and she yelped at the jarring sting of her foot connecting with his rocky forearm and fell backwards on her butt, and she earned her own vicious kick but he wore steel-toed boots.

Laughing vindictively at her squeal of pain, Ini grinned at her. "Hell, you're feisty, I can't wait for my shot at you. I hope there's still some fire in you after Marcus gets done. Later, babe," he gave her a two-finger salute off his broad forehead and left her alone.

Stassi tugged, and lurched and wrenched at the cuffs, pulled on the bar, but everything was solid. She sat down with her legs curled to the side, her hands cuffed near her shoulders. Her knees ached, her cheek throbbed from where he'd hit her, the back of her head pounded in pain from slamming into the walls.

A cool draft brushed against the few inches of bare skin where her sweater was raised. She had planned on wearing a long-sleeved t-shirt under it but had dressed this morning in too much of a hurry eager to get to the mansion.

Tears bunched, she wiped them on the sleeve of her upper arm. Crying wasn't going to get her out of her predicament. She could do nothing but wait until Callen came for her then maybe while he's distracted unlocking the cuffs she can, what, blitz-attack him? Her head fell back with a groan at her hopeless dilemma.

"God help me, God help Cody," her voice trailed off as tears clogged her throat.

There was no way Cody survived. The fall was too high. Volt was a dozen yards away in the woods, even if he could have reached him in time the baby was so small and he'd drop like a tiny missile, Cody would have been way too hard to catch.

Chapter Twenty-Four

It was Stassi's scream that drew Volt out of the dark cover of forest and move towards the building. He cursed as he saw the basket swing violently and a small bundle shoot out of it. He only saw a flash of the baby's head to realize what it was. Dropping the flashlight he raced to the building with his arms out-

"*Oof-*" The baby landed in his arms as hard and fast as a plummeting anvil. Immediately, Volt snapped his arms around him like a wide receiver catching a football. His breath sprinting in his chest, Volt looked up at the basket to see if Stassi was okay. Cody bawled his pique at being hurled around in the cold air. Stassi's phone landed a few feet away in the snow with a crunch.

Seeing the basket was empty and was hauling back up to the window, Volt bit off a slew of curses.

"Where's the girl?" Jubal asked as he and Greco joined him. The three men looked at the wailing baby in Volt's arms then up to the basket that was disappearing into the opening in the building. A pocket door closed sealing the window.

"I don't know," Volt said, ire and panic gripped him, stalling his mind. Staring up at the closed hole, he heaved, "She didn't make it." *Goddammit*, was she too injured to have climbed into the gondola? "Here." He handed the baby to Jubal. Cody was hiccupping tears between cries. "You two get him to safety." He pulled his satellite phone from inside his jacket and started pressing buttons.

Carefully taking the baby, Jubal asked, "What the hell are you gonna do?" He tried to hand the baby to Greco but Greco held his hands up and stepped back shaking his head.

Scowling at Greco, Jubal settled Cody with the baby's belly against his chest and his tiny head over his shoulder. Rocking him gently and patting his blanket bound butt, he said to Volt, "I don't know about carrying a baby down this treacherous mountainside, man. What if I drop him or crush him or- or- you or Greco need to take him."

"You'll be fine, Jube, just hurry. Tuck him inside your jacket and wrap your scarf around his head." Volt started walking into the forest, the phone at his ear. Jubal and Greco followed him. Their boots made a cacophony of crunching sounds as they stomped through the snow, there was no way to tread silently.

"You aren't going with us?" Greco asked as Volt lengthened his stride. It was still snowing, the snow as high as their shins was going to slow them down.

Volt shook his head. "Partway. I'm stopping at the open field we passed before we started up the mountain. You guys are going to the chopper and getting the baby the hell out of here."

The trio trudged through the dark dense woods, vapor pouring harshly from their mouths from the strenuous trek. Whistling wind whipped through the trees slapping exposed skin crimson and tore tears from their eyes. They used their flashlights sparingly to keep someone from spotting them.

Looking down at the now sleeping child nestled warmly inside his jacket, Jubal said quietly, "Volt, what are you going to do about-"

"Yeah," Volt said into the phone. "I need you and your expertise. Get your gear and hop on the chopper, you already have the coordinates. I'll meet you at 80 longitude west by 30 latitude north. It'll be- yeah, there," he nodded at what the person on the other end of the phone was saying. "You see it on the rough map I drew of the mountain?" He nodded again. "It'll take me four hours to get there. Jubal and Greco will take the chopper. Later." He hung up the phone.

As the three men threaded their way downhill dodging tree trunks and ducking low limbs, the wind continued wailing through the thicket slicing at them and clacking bare branches together. Ignoring the cold and the icy wind, they talked about Volt's plans.

Greco said, "Volt, you know there's no way up the steep backside of the mountain. Besides the snow and ice like white glass, the gradient is almost seamlessly vertical. And we already know the front is inaccessible due to the steep gorge."

Jubal glanced at an iPad Greco was scanning. He said, "The graph diagram we got from the satellite reflects that when the choppers lift off the roof of the building spikes raise." Patting the baby's back while he walked, Cody gurgled and babbled inside the warm comfort of his jacket. "There is no way to get inside that fortress."

Volt didn't respond, just trudged as fast as the wintered terrain would allow.

Chapter Twenty-Five

Stassi's arms ached and tingled from being chained to the bar. The bathroom floor tile was cold and hard like sitting on a refrigerator. Since he'd bound her to the radiator, Ini had shut it off so she wouldn't get fried. She shifted to sit on her other side and give half her hip a break. At least she could now stand, originally Ini had chained her so she could only sit or kneel.

He had come in and hooked her up to a longer chain. Yeah, she could get some relief standing, but she was restrained too close to the bar so she still couldn't walk or stretch, and she could only stand for so long. Her ribs ached, head pounded and she was dizzy, even her face hurt.

"Creep did it on purpose," she groused to the wall, "he wanted me restrained but be uncomfortable and to suffer as well. Jerk." Ini had come in twice and released her and let her pee, roughly manhandled her then cuffed her right away again.

He had stood there the first time, hands in his pockets leering at her, waiting for her to go to the bathroom in front of him. She had sat back down by the radiator. No way would she pee in front of him, she'd burst first. He gave in and reluctantly left the room but kept the door open a couple of inches. It had been hours since Ini had been back to see her, and he had not brought her a bite to eat or even water.

Yawning, she wondered how long she had been stuck there. Judging by the loss of light in the small window up by the shower stall most of the day had passed. It's been at least 12 hours. Maybe they forgot about her and years from now someone would come across her skeleton- "Damn, Stas," she scolded herself, "don't do that to yourself. The trouble Callen went to, to get me here he will certainly remember to come for me." She awkwardly rose, using the wall for balance.

A loud hideous, snapping crack rent the air making Stassi jump and her heart launch into a speeding thump-thump. She looked to the door, and her pulse galloped into high gear. Marcus Callen had remembered her. He was standing in the doorway…holding a…bullwhip.

His feet braced in a wide stance, he slapped the leather handle end of the whip against his hand while he smiled at her. It was not a nice smile, it rapidly lifted pricks of fear over her skin.

"So," he said calmly, "I hear you had an active day." He took a few steps inside the large, glossy white and gold room. Slapping the end of the whip against his palm he said, "You know that your attempt to escape and free that baby was going to anger me, right?" His head cocked and a brow lifted in a droll arch. When she didn't respond to him, he suddenly raised his arm and slammed it down and the whip lashed in a sharp wave and snapped and cracked when the tip slapped the floor only inches from her feet.

Stassi flinched and plastered her body against the wall, the bullwhip was huge, the kind a cowboy would use on the thick hide of cattle.

Flinging his arm sharply the whip whizzed snapping in the air and cracking. Stassi thought she was going to wet her pants. Was he going to use that on-

"Answer me, Stassi." All semblance of pleasantry was gone, his face darkened in fury, he moved further inside the room.

"Move away from the wall. When I ask you a question, you answer it, you understand?" Another foot closer to her he raised the hand holding the whip.

"Y- yes, I knew I was taking a chance inciting your anger, but, I mean, if it was you wouldn't you have done the same thing?" Her brain pounded painfully so much she could scarcely think.

"I said move away from the wall." His arm lowered and a nod of agreement came with a crooked smile. "Yes, of course I would. But, since I am in charge, and I warned you not to try it, and because you let the baby get away-"

"He did?" Her face lit up with relief, she moved as far from the wall as the handcuffs would allow. "Cody survived the fall? Oh I've been so worried-" she broke off at seeing him shake his head. Her joy deflated.

"The infant could not have survived that high of a fall onto the frozen ground. The corpse is gone, either the people that were with you took it, or the animals did."

Observing her face stricken with devastation at that, he said, "It's your fault. You caused his death. Speaking of, I told you to come alone. You wouldn't have lowered the child to the ground if you didn't have someone placed there to get him. My men reported to me there were several sets of footprints in the snow in the woods. A set led almost all the way up to the building. I'm surmising that person was to retrieve the child. Well, a four-story drop, the kid would have plunged like an anchor to the bottom of the sea."

He chuckled. "Only faster and harder, my pet."

She wasn't listening, her thoughts were on Cody, her heart broke. How was she going to tell Charlie that his baby…tears slid down her bruised face.

A loud whizzing crack and what felt like a sharp cord snapped at her neck and wrapped around it like a lasso, she screamed at the sudden stinging pain. She had to get it off! Her hands flew to the coiled lash biting into her neck, the braided thong was too thin, too tight, she couldn't get her fingers between it and her skin. All she could do was wrap her fingers around the loose strip of the tail and pray it didn't cut her fingers.

"Now," Callen said, tugging lightly on the end of the whip, "I have your attention. Geesh, Stassi, what lengths I have to go to, to keep your attention on me." He tugged the whip slightly harder and watched her wince. "Let go of it before your hands are sliced to ribbons."

She let go of the loose part and again pried at the part wound around her neck. "Callen-"

He jerked the handle and Stassi lurched forward with a choke and bulging eyes. "Shut up," he told her. "I'm doing the talking from now on. You don't speak. You just do as I say. Now, get down on your knees," he jerked the whip down hard forcing Stassi to hit her knees. "Very good." He grinned cheerfully. "I have some good times planned for us, love, but first," he drew out a long knife-

He's going to stab me! Stassi thought, panic whooshed like smoke from a burning house, she was going to die right now, right here. Sitting back on her heels, she was pinned like a fly about to get its wings pulled off, she couldn't fight or run. His hand lashed out and he sliced the knife down the front of her sweater splitting it wide open. She gasped and quickly bunched the split sides together in her hand.

Callen yanked sharply on the handle again forcing her to bend over and bow her head. "Yes, nice, very nice. That is how I expect you to greet me every time we meet. On your knees."

"Sc-screw you," she choked out. One hand moved to curl around the tail twined around her neck, the other clutched the torn sweater.

"Ah, wonderful." He snapped the whip, her shriek of pain cut off. "You're gonna fight me, you have guts. I so admire that in a person. However, in my woman, I want strict obedience. I told you not to speak," and he yanked the whip again so hard she fell forward onto her palms. He tugged on the whip forcing her to crawl to him or be choked or decapitated.

Strangling, she was strangling, he'd lashed a garrote around her neck! He was going to choke her, the air was cutting off in her windpipe, she fought against the panic, tears of pain and terror streamed down her face, she was helpless to stop them. She wanted to rain curses down on his head but he held the whip down so she had no movement in her neck and the cord closed off most of her breath.

"Okay, sweetie, now for our fun. You are going to take off your clothes, accept the quite vicious whipping you're going to receive as punishment for your crimes, and then the rest of the games will begin. Got it?"

She didn't answer, couldn't cough a word out. He yanked on the whip. "You want to breathe Stassi, you'll start removing your clothes. Pants first, I can already see the top part of your glorious bounty." His heated gaze ogled her breasts mounding out of the silken bra.

Her body trembling with fright and the pain of the noose, Stassi couldn't get to her feet, she couldn't pull the damned cord off her neck, and she had no chance of fighting Callen. Again he wrenched the whip so hard he almost broke her neck. The cry of pain stuck in her throat, on her knees, bracing with one palm on the tile, she plucked with shaking fingers at the button on her jeans.

"Faster, love, I'm growing impatient, I want to start your strapping. I want to see scarlet welts and lacerations stripe that beautiful body, then I'm gonna take you right there on the floor rolling in your blood." He yanked the whip roughly, commanded, "Faster."

Lacking air, Stassi was growing lightheaded, tremors churned throughout her body, she lowered further to her forearm and reached for her zipper. There was a sound behind Callen, she rolled her eyes up expecting to see Ini there ready to join in the fun, and they widened in astonishment.

Callen turned around with a curse on his lips, Volt punched it off his mouth.

Disbelief flared in Callen's eyes before he reeled backwards, releasing the whip. Volt was on him in a beat, his fists flying so fast Stassi barely saw them move. Callen's head flung backwards then side-to-side, he raised his arms to fight back, but Volt relentlessly pounded him into the ground, and kept at it.

Stassi squeaked hoarsely, "Volt- the door-"

Ini charged in with a gun cocked and aimed at Volt, his finger tightened on the trigger with curses of outrage- "You're dead you motherfucker!"

Stassi's head clunked on the floor at the sound of the gunshot. "Nooo..." she cried, her lids fell over dizzy eyes.

"Stassi." A familiar voice jolted her lids back up. A man stood in the doorway holding a gun, and Ini was lying on the floor, blood pouring from his shoulder.

Peering through the fog dragging her under at the man who shot Ini Madarov, blackness closing in, she croaked, "Kenan?"

She must be dreaming. Her chest was cold, she realized her sweater was spread wide open exposing her skimpily covered breasts for everyone's viewing pleasure, but she couldn't lift a finger to cover herself.

Jubal Cain poked his head inside with a weapon clutched in his hand. Glancing around, he grinned. "Okay, I see everything is under control in here, I have to go back out and assist Liam and the team making sure all the mercs are on vaca, lights out if you know what I mean. See ya." He winked at Stassi and disappeared amidst a flurry of gunfire.

Last thing Stassi was aware of was Volt kneeling beside her, unwinding the whip's tail from around her neck, and she passed out.

They found the controls that worked the roof. Jubal maneuvered Callen's helicopter off the roof and Greco landed his chopper as soon as he was out of the way. Greco and several men jumped out, climbed down to enter into the mansion and quickly swarmed the building clearing it of Callen's people. Callen was clinging to life as Jubal flew him and Ini Madarov to the nearest hospital.

A third chopper landed and Volt carried Stassi up and out onto the roof. The whizzing propellers rotated in a blur kicking up a wind flaying their clothes and hair into a whirlwind medley. Volt bent under the propellers and handed the unconscious Stassi up to his man piloting the chopper. The pilot carefully laid her down on the small back seat.

Volt climbed in joining her. He closed her sweater and wrapped his jacket around her. Pulling her onto his lap, he strapped them in, and the machine lifted off the roof and soared away.

Chapter Twenty-Six

Her aching throat felt as grainy and dry as an ancient riverbed, Stassi lifted a hand to it.

"About time you woke, indolent woman. You've slept for almost two days."

Her lids pushed up. She was lying on a bed. She looked over and saw Volt lounging in a chair next to the bed. He was slumped comfortably, knees spread, a glass of amber liquid in his hand. Stassi glanced around recognizing her surroundings, her gaze flit back to him in confusion. "We are at your place?" Déjà vu all over again.

He nodded, said drily, "Where else would we be with deadly, rapacious headhunters chasing after you?" Stassi shifted to sit up, Volt leaned to her, said, "Easy, as usual you've had a bad time of it. Hell, I've never known a woman who attracted so much menace."

He got up, set his drink on the nightstand and helped her to settle back against the pillows behind her and he sat back down. "If anything, Anastasia, you certainly don't give a guy a boring time."

"I..." What could she say, it was true. Ever since the professor had given her the challenge of creating the antidote formula for the bacteria her life had turned dangerous, terrorizing. Even her past had blundered in.

But first, bending forward she asked, "Cody? Did anyone tell Charlie what happened to him? Did you, God I hope so," she uttered disjointed, "did you get his body?" Her face strained, wrought with grief, her body drooped with the heavy weight of sorrow.

"Sit back," he told her, nudging her against the pillows and rested back in his chair. "The baby is fine. Reunited with his mom and dad."

"He what? How-"

"I caught him, Ana, you thought I wouldn't?" He gave her a look of censure.

"Oh my gosh, Saldano, thank you, my goodness, I can't believe-" her hand over her mouth she couldn't believe Cody was alive! "You, you saved him, you saved me, again. You are...a remarkable man." Tears of gratitude slipped out.

"If I'm so remarkable, do you think you can be a bit less formal and call me Volt?"

"Hmm." She cocked her head at this brawny, tough man that kept pulling her fat out of the fire, and wondered why. Instead of asking him that she said, "That is an unusual name, is it short for something?"

He considered whether or not to tell her. "Ah, my full name is Voltang. I don't use it. Along with my accent it tends to put people off...makes them nervous. Like I'm Vladimir the Impaler, or something equally ghastly."

Her smile weak, she rasped, "I like it. It's unique. And it fits you."

A smirk played at his lips, he said, "I don't think I'll ask you what that means. How are you feeling? At least you're in better shape than when I snatched you from Lamontagne. Here," he picked up a cup of water with a bent straw poking out of it.

Holding it so she could sip, he commented, "Your voice is scratchy."

"I'm not an invalid, Volt, I can hold a glass of water," she protested. "I think I slept so much because I was afraid of where I was and what would happen to me. I was afraid I was going to wake to another nightmare. I mean, is there anyone else out there that's going to kidnap, imprison and torture me?" She reached for the water.

Volt held it out of her reach. "I'm sure there are more that want you, including Lamontagne, but no one is getting their grimy hands on you again. You'll do as I say and I will keep you safe." Ignoring her objection to his help he lightly batted her hand out of the way and brought the glass to her mouth and pushed the straw at her lips.

Stassi's cheeks tinted pink him treating her like she was a child, but she accepted the straw hovering at her lips knowing it was a waste of time trying to argue with Volt about anything.

He set the cup down when she indicated she'd had enough. His gaze focused on the marks around her neck and wrists from the handcuffs bringing a glower to his already harsh face. "That bastard, I want to get my hands on Callen again."

Swallowing roughly, Stassi croaked out, "From what I recall, there wasn't much left for you to damage further." She gently prodded at her tender neck, swallowing hurt.

Volt grunted. "If I'd had another couple of seconds with the depraved bastard it would be a moot point. Here, suck on these." He picked up another cup that had a spoon in it. He spooned an ice cube out and held it to her lips. She gratefully took it and moaned with bliss as she sucked on it.

His eyes on her mouth, Volt shifted uncomfortably in his chair and set the cup back down. "Tell me what you remember when we were there those last minutes with Callen."

Thinking back, Stassi spoke huskily around the cube, "I remember him strangling me with that whip, then suddenly you were there and you beat him." Closing her eyes at the image of Volt battering the life out of Callen, she sucked on the ice cube and took a deep breath. "Why do you want me to relive it? I thought I was going to die, it was almost as agonizing as my time with Rufus. Why would you want me to suffer through it again?"

"Humor me," Volt said, "there is a method to my madness. For one thing it will make you think twice if you disobey any instructions I give you." Disregarding her huff and irate look at his dictatorial statement, he said, "Tell me what you remember."

Her lips pursed, then she sighed. "All right. Um, after you beat Callen nearly to death," a shiver tickled her shoulders at the picture brought to her mind of Volt bashing at bloody Callen even after he was clearly no longer conscious.

"I remember you were unwinding that horrid thing from around my neck and," she paused, her face twitched in a rough wince recalling the feeling of the whip wrapped around her throat cutting off her air.

She crunched the ice cube in agitation, her fingers went to her throat as if to wrench the cord from her neck. "He…he told me he was going to whip me with it then he was going to-" A sob stole her words and her composure.

"Okay, take it easy, Ana, it's gone, he's gone, you're safe." Volt set his hand on her arm to pull her from the palpable memory. He slipped another cube into her mouth. When she'd settled back and calmed down, he asked, "What else do you remember?"

A terrible quiver shot through her core as Stassi fought the feeling of the whip tightening in a noose, squeezing until she couldn't breathe.

Volt patted her arm softly, anchoring her in the present. Calming herself with slow inhales, her head tilted as she fluttered eyes shimmering green with a mist of tears at him.

Something flickered in his eyes before they went back to their normal inscrutable harshness.

Rolling her head back against the pillow she looked up to the ceiling. "Um, oh, I remember Jubal shooting that nasty man, Ini Madarov. The blood, the shock on his face as he crumpled-" the rasp in her voice broke off her words at the visual image of that harrowing moment in the mansion. She was strangling, Volt was beating Callen, blood was gushing from Ini- it was horrifying- her breathing amped fast and shallow as panic overwhelmed her.

"That's enough, honey," Volt's guttural voice actually soothed her. "Forget about it, we'll talk about it later. You-"

Her lashes dashed up, she blinked hard then turned her head to him. "Volt," she gasped sitting up, her palm spread over her heart. "My…Kenan, my brother was there. It wasn't Jubal who shot Ini, it was Kenan? I didn't imagine him, did I? He was really there! Oh my goodness, what on earth, why was he there? Was he in cahoots with Callen? Oh no, oh no," she cried in bewilderment.

Volt quickly pressed her back against the pillows, curled his hands around her wrists holding them and said, "No, Ana, no, your brother was there with me."

Confusion mottled her pale face, her brow wrinkled not understanding.

He told her, "I've known Kenan, your brother for a long time. We've fought together over…ah, overseas. We've saved each other's lives too many times to count. The damned fortress was impossible to get to. I needed his expertise to bring me and Jubal and a couple other guys up the mountain."

Her brows arched as her bafflement amplified. "Expertise?" His thumbs were stroking her wrists, she found it oddly comforting.

Sitting back in his chair, still holding one of her wrists, Volt nodded. "Yes. He is a master mountain climber. Jubal and I are quite skilled in climbing, but the icy mountainside, the extreme steep vertical, we hadn't had much experience in that type of ice climbing so it would have been too slow going.

"So, I contacted Kenan, as he is an expert in scaling that sort of entity. He brought his special equipment and got us safely, and relatively quickly up there. He also fought beside Jubal and me as we worked our way through Callen's mercenary guards to get to you. A second chopper met us and the pilot took the baby home while we came for you."

Blinking incomprehensively at him, Stassi shook her head. "But, Kenan, no," she denied, shook her head again, long cherry brown curls ruffled across the front of the white nightgown. Her lips pressed tightly and drew down, eyes narrowed at him. Tugging her wrist from his grasp she claimed, "He hates me, he's a coward, he abandoned me to my father!"

Dropping his hands in his lap Volt folded his fingers together. "Yes, Ana, your brother. He's the one I did the favor for. He called me and asked me to extract you from Lamontagne's hold."

Grinning, his head shook. "And, boy I sure didn't want to. I knew your name, I read the police report from that day you saw me in that alley, but I didn't know you were Kenan's sister. I didn't connect your last name Athens. Last person I wanted to save was the woman who tossed me under the bus with the cops and almost messed with my mission."

Stassi sat up and leaned forward. "Volt, you know that I-"

"I know," he said and put his hand on her shoulder and gently pushed her to lie back. "I would have gone anyway. I never would have left a defenseless female in that situation, didn't matter how angry I was at her gorgeous ass."

She did a double-take. "My what?"

He chuckled. "Yeah. Even as angry as I was, I couldn't deny the instant attraction I felt for you. So intense, mindboggling, never experienced that before, Ana." Grinning at her blinking in bewilderment at him he then sobered. "The reason why I made you go through that wretched scenario was because I wanted you to realize it was your brother, that you saw him saving you with your own eyes."

She still looked at him in disbelief. "But why? After all these years? He left home, he left me with…my father knowing what he was doing to me."

"That's next on the agenda. I wanted to prepare you before he shows up."

"Shows up?" she parroted, then squawked, "Here? He's coming here? No, no, Volt, I am not seeing him. I told you how it was growing up. I want nothing to do with him. Send him away," and she flipped over to lie on her side facing away from him.

That lasted half a second before she felt her body being lifted up and sat back down reclining against the pillows. Fuming she complained, "Stop that. Do not reposition me." With that she went to roll over again but she felt strong arms encircle her and then she was lifted right off the bed and set down in Volt's lap.

"What are you, what do you think you're doing?" she sputtered and made to climb off but he dropped an iron arm down around her torso holding her in place.

In his deep accented voice, Volt admonished her, "This is the part where I said you will do as I tell you."

Her mouth parted but he tightened his hold. "Kenan is coming here, should arrive by the end of the week, he had business to finish up before he could come. You and he will talk. Without turning your back on him or arguing with him, you will listen to what he has to say."

"Are you out of your mind?" Her words burst out just shy of a belligerent screech, Stassi sucked in a deep angry breath. "First of all, you do not tell me what to do. Second, I will not see him. I refuse. If you insist I will leave."

"We're pretty far out from any neighbors, miles. A bit of a walk."

He was laughing at her! Struggling to break from his embrace, to no avail, she said, "I don't care. You can't make me do anything I don't want to do. Let me up, I'm getting dressed and then I'm outta here." She pushed at the big arms that encircled her, still to no avail.

His laughter left, his harsh face turned cold and imposing, he said sternly, "He saved your ass, Anastasia, twice. You owe him to at least hear him out. You have no idea what a bitch it was to climb up that goddamned mountain. He dropped everything to go out there and get us up it. And," he cupped her chin holding her from speaking or turning away from him, "you will do as I tell you and you will not be leaving this house."

Stassi started to sputter, tried to shake her head, but he held her immobile. "Yes, I can keep you here, you know you can't fight me. And, if you refuse to see your brother, I will toss you over my shoulder and dump you on your ass in front of him and hold you down. Do you want to incur that embarrassment? Or do you want to give your brother a minute of your time? He asked me to go find you, Ana, take you from Lamontagne. You would have died a hideous death if he hadn't."

Furious, Stassi growled her aggravation at his bullying, but he meant what he said. She twisted her head so he dropped his hand from her chin. "Fine. One minute. Sixty seconds and I'm out of there. I mean it. You can do your worst, you can hold me down, but you can't make me listen." The pair glared at each other.

Then Volt slid his hand under her jaw, cradling it, he murmured softly, "Okay. That's all I ask. Give him a minute then you can do as you please, except-" he said quickly, "leave this house. You are not an idiot, you know the danger that is lurking out there waiting to scoop you up. If I have to lock you down, I will, Anastasia, don't doubt it."

Her mouth in a crooked smile, Stassi said wryly, "Oh, so it's not okay for Lamontagne or Callen to keep me prisoner, but it's all right for you to do it?"

He replied firmly, "They didn't have your best interests at heart. They wanted to use you, hurt you, fuck you against your will. My only intent is to keep you safe, even from your own willfulness."

Turning her head, her large green eyes linking with his she said softly, "That's all you want from me?"

The tips of his ears reddened. "Ah, uh…" His Adam's apple bobbed with a thick swallow.

"Are you sure you don't want my formula for yourself? Are you forcing me to stay here because you want it?"

He blinked rapidly at her, her naïveté was…endearing, and, he was given a reprieve. Then he grew irritated. "Of course not, Ana. You are staying here simply because it's the safest place for you until all this formula shit is over. Callen is no longer a worry. Once they are recuperated and leave the hospital, he and Ini Madarov will be incarcerated and will serve long, long prison sentences. If they survive, that is. There's a lot of furious people out there that Callen tricked that want to get their hands on him. And those people would make him and Lamontagne look like Sunday school teachers."

He stood up and set her gently on her feet. "When Kenan comes we'll have lunch out on the deck overlooking the water. It's glass-enclosed so we'll be warm." He started for the door.

Stassi said, "I don't think I will join you two for lunch. I'm sure I won't have an appetite."

Volt sent her a weary glance then left her alone.

The room seemed to suck in like a vacuum without his presence. So big, masculine, dangerous, he filled the room and Stassi felt the very air vibrating with his vigor, his energy. The room now felt strangely empty, cold. She headed for the bathroom to take her shower.

Chapter Twenty-Seven

Dragging the brush through her hair each time harder than the last but nothing distracted her from her fretfulness. Stassi couldn't believe she was nervous to see her own brother. It has been well over a decade since she last saw him, and nine years since she spoke with her mother. Good riddance she'd thought when Kenan left at sixteen and joined the service. Leaving her behind. She was twelve when he left her under the brutal fist of their father.

Tossing the brush on top of the dresser, she muttered through clenched teeth, "I will stare at the clock while he talks, make sure he gets his damned sixty seconds." Then she would sail out of the room and there would be nothing Volt could do, she'd followed his order. His order. How dare he order her around, give her commands!

Well, she needed to nip that behavior right in the bud. Right after she shows Kenan the door she and Volt were having a discussion. Volt may have saved her life a few times. And originally at the behest of her brother, although heaven knows why Kenan even asked him to, regardless, Volt was not her boss.

Her heart fluttered, she would never admit it out loud, but she had missed Kenan over the years. Other than his looking the other way and leaving her with their lousy excuse of a father, they had loved one another. He didn't protect her from their father, but he did against other bullies that accosted her. Over long winters they played games together, he taught her so much, how to ride a bike, play baseball, built snowmen with her. Stassi sighed and hardened her heart and her spine. Nothing negates that he left her.

Checking her reflection in the mirror, she patted her hair and pushed it back off her shoulders. Volt had a suitcase of her clothes brought to the house. On one hand it was comforting to have someone take care of her, it was a unique experience. He fed her, ensured she had the best medical care, set up security at his home to keep her safe.

The past week he spent time sitting with her just chatting or playing cards or teaching her to play chess. He had a seriously dry wit and although he barely smiled, he often had her in stitches. He was brilliant she found out when he creamed her at Scrabble.

He had her favorite meals served, how he found out what she liked who knows, and she only had to mention something in passing to anyone, she needed a blow-dryer for her thick hair, lip gloss ran out, she loved bear claws, and the new things just appeared. She had to learn to bite her tongue, she didn't want to accept anything more from him. He'd given her enough, and what kinds of strings had he attached to them? She had asked him that at one point. He merely stared at her blankly, his jaw working but he said nothing.

On the other hand, it would be so easy to fall into becoming dependent on his largesse, his company, and when the danger in her life was gone, so would he be. Stassi felt her heart constrict at the thought. Banishing the feeling before she could dwell on it, she buttoned the pale blue thin sweater then tugged it down neatening it. It landed just at the top of her hips. She wore jeans a shade darker than the sweater, and her ankle boots.

Stassi hadn't heard a knock or the doorbell, but suddenly there were distinctive male rumblings. *God he's here*, nerves struck again. She couldn't do it. She could not bear to see him, all the pain, loneliness, the abuse of her childhood rushed back, her eyes closed against the barrage of desolate feelings that threatened to overwhelm her.

"Anastasia." Volt's deep voice broke through the heartrending thoughts swirling in her head.

She opened her eyes to see him coming towards her, his gaze took her in head to toe. He stopped in front of her, set his large hands gently on her shoulders. He spoke softly, "Baby, he's your brother, not a monster. You'll see, things aren't as you thought. Let him explain."

Confused at the endearment, anxious and angry that he was making her meet with Kenan, Stassi turned her head from him.

At her silence, he curled a finger under her chin lifting it so she was looking at him. "Take a few long, slow, deep breaths, gather your composure."

Breathing in his familiar male scent and his strong presence reassured her. The weight of his hand on her shoulder, supportive finger under her chin, and his strong body curled over her made Stassi feel safe.

Staring into his dark, fathomless eyes, Stassi realized he was going to stand there until she did as he said. Her shoulders rose with a deep breath, she let it out slowly. He dropped his hands. She pushed her shoulders back, tossed her hair behind her back and sighed as if she was going to the guillotine. "I'm ready."

"Good girl. Come on, he's waiting in the morning room." Volt took her hand, twined their fingers and he walked her out of the room.

Palpitations were attacking by the time they reached the morning room. It was the opposite of the more masculine rooms in the house. Decorated in peach and pale yellows, cushy furniture, the sunlight flowed through the big windows along the back and one of the side walls lighting the room in a soft glow. A white brick fireplace with bookcases on both sides took up the third wall.

Standing with his back to the door, Kenan was gazing out one of the windows. The sunbeam fired his hair that was identical to Stassi's mahogany locks.

"K," Volt murmured.

Kenan turned around, and his green eyes, also identical to hers, softened at the sight of his sister. He had left home a boy at sixteen, he was now a man at twenty-eight. Stassi scanned him greedily. He was so handsome. Tall with powerful broad shoulders. He had scars like Volt carried, he also wore his self-confidence the same as Volt.

Both men reeked of warrior strength and aggressiveness. Also, they both masked secrets behind their cool eyes. Her brother, like Volt, had an air of suppressed vitality, masculine virility, and the ever-present danger that clung to their strapping bodies and enigmatic eyes.

Kenan took a step towards his sister, then paused when Stassi visually stiffened. "Stassi," he murmured quietly, his gaze soaking her in. "God, little sister, I've missed you so much, so damned much."

The anguish in his voice snapped Stassi out of her muse and before she knew it, she was running to him, flinging herself into his arms. His arms wrapped around her and he hugged her so tightly it almost hurt. Silent sobs and tears gushed from her eyes soaking his shirt. Both men were dressed alike in black jeans and black thermals.

The siblings stayed in a clinch for a few minutes until Volt softly cleared his throat.

Kenan lowered his arms and his hands wound around her wrists, he held her back to look at her. His eyes were damp and warm. "Babygirl, damn, you sure grew up. You are a woman now. A beautiful, no, a stunning, breathtaking woman." He glanced quickly at Volt then back to her. "No wonder the mission is carrying on. I see why you-"

"K," Volt grunted, cutting off his thought.

Their words brought Stassi back to awareness. She stepped away from her brother, brows drawn in a frown. Still, she couldn't get enough of looking at him, drinking in every aspect of his manly body, handsome face. "Um, Volt said you had something to tell me," she said flatly, tugging her wrists loose.

"Why don't you two sit." Volt motioned towards the sofa, several large chairs were placed semi-circle in front of it with a glass coffee table in the middle.

The hurt of the past flooded her, shaking her head, Stassi wanted Kenan to spit out what he had to say then leave.

Kenan and Volt shared a look. Volt traipsed over to Stassi, lightly took her arm and pulled her to the pale yellow sofa covered in tiny flowers and gave her a small push making her sit down, which annoyed her but she let it go. Kenan moved to one of the pale yellow chairs and took a seat.

Volt sat in a matching chair. The siblings glanced at him, Volt stared back. He was staying even though it was none of his business. He must have decided they might require a referee. A woman Stassi hadn't seen before came through the doorway.

Carrying a large silver tray, the woman looked only to Volt who nodded at the coffee table. A white top made her wide shoulders wider and the black slacks made her long legs look longer. She wore the sturdy black shoes of a servant. Brown hair laced with silver was tied in a high bun lending severity to her already gaunt face.

She set the tray on the table and picked up a silver coffee carafe and poured coffee into three china cups on saucers on the tray. She directed her attention to Stassi. "Cream or sugar, miss?" she asked with stiff politeness, one brown brow raised like a boomerang over a dark brown eye.

"Anastasia, Kenan, this is Rosalee. Rosie, this is Anastasia Athens, and her brother Kenan," Volt introduced them.

"Just a dollop of cream, please," Stassi murmured politely.

Rosalee poured some cream from a small white pitcher, set a spoon on the saucer and handed it to Stassi then turned to Kenan. "Sir?"

"Black, please," Kenan gave her a kind smile. She poured the cup and passed it to him then without asking his preference, she poured a cup of black coffee and handed it to Volt. Indicating the tray, she announced, "There are pastries, and Sadie's homemade strawberry scones with clotted cream, and delicious sugar cookies," she muttered, "that *I* baked."

Embarrassed at her bragging, the cheeks on her narrow face spotted with pink. "Uh, please, help yourself." She turned to Volt and asked, "Anything else, Mr. Saldano?"

Volt dismissed her with a nod. "That's good for now, Rosie, I'll let you know if we require something else. Just see to the deck being prepared for our lunch." He immediately reached for a bear claw, not bothering to put it on one of the little china plates he chomped half of it in one bite.

"Yes, sir." She nodded briefly and left the room. Silence pervaded at her exit. Kenan studied Stassi while she deliberately avoided looking at him.

"Okay," Volt said. "K, you have the floor." He spoke to Kenan, but settled his attention on Stassi.

Her back rigid with tense nerves, she perched on the edge of the sofa clutching the saucer with both hands. Her skin still pale from her episode with Callen had become almost translucent. Ini's hits and Callen's assault had harmed her more than they thought at first.

She'd spent the night in the hospital with Volt and Jubal as sentries. No one was getting to her. Volt brought her to his home the next day. She was staring at the bear claws on the tray.

Taking a sip of his coffee then setting the cup and saucer on the coffee table, Kenan cleared his throat. "Ah," he started then cleared his throat again. "Stassi, I need to tell you how it was when we were growing up. It-"

She jumped to her feet, her face filled with angry color brightening the pale skin. Setting the coffee cup on the table, her voice shook with antagonism. "You don't have to tell me about our childhood, I was there, remember? Oh right," she sneered, sarcasm ringing in her now shrill voice. "You weren't there, so you wouldn't know about *my* childhood. You hid, you ran away, you abandoned-"

"Anastasia," Volt said quietly. "You promised me you'd give him a chance to talk. Settle down."

Shooting him a furious glare, Stassi plunked back down on the sofa. "Go ahead, although I doubt you have anything to say that I want to hear. You said it all when you hid while our father beat the hell out of me."

"Anastasia," Volt warned.

Throwing him another glare, she shut her mouth and glowered mutinously at her estranged brother.

Kenan shifted uncomfortably in the thickly cushioned chair. Leaning forward, he clasped his hands and rested his wrists on his knees. "Stassi," he paused, stood up and started again. "We know why he beat you, you resembled his abusive hated sister. He kept it under wraps while he campaigned, but he had mental issues. I'm thinking he was probably bi-polar or borderline personality disorder."

"That doesn't excuse what he did to me, or that you and mom let him," Stassi declared angrily over the sob caught in her throat. Volt coughed not a bit discreetly, and she slammed her back against the back cushion of the sofa, crossed her arms and closed her mouth with a mulish expression. She knew she was acting childish but she didn't appreciate being forced to face her brother and she wasn't going to make it easy on him or Volt.

Kenan's lips pulled in, he observed his sister with compassion, regret, and a great sense of loss. "Stassi, it wasn't as it seemed. Dad told mom and me if we interfered he would ah…he would hurt you worse. Mom and I tried to pull him away from you one time and he swore if we didn't stay out of it he would see that you…" his gaze lowered to the floor, he blinked, and when he looked back up at her his eyes were wet.

"He said he would make you disappear. He threatened to sell you into sex slavery, or that he would give you to some total stranger and we would never see you again. Still, one time it was so bad, he'd beaten you horribly, we called the police. The next day you were gone."

He sucked in an agonized breath before going on. "He wouldn't tell us where you were. He had friends in the police department, they always believed him over us. He told them mom was a hysterical ninny that was just trying to get him in trouble, and I was a juvenile delinquent that should be locked up."

Stassi's stared at him in wide-eyed incredulity. "No, no, that can't be true, I would have remembered-"

"The first time he sent you away you were three. The second time five. That time he didn't bring you back for over a month. Mom and I were petrified we'd never see you again. Dad hinted often he could easily kill you and bury you where your body would never be found."

"I don't remember going away from home for…" her mouth fell open as she thought back. "I remember when I was little, dad took me to a- a camp. There were other people there, no children. Dad said I needed to learn how to camp. But I stayed inside every day with an old woman who plunked me in front of a television and otherwise ignored me."

225

She stared blankly thinking about the memory and what Kenan was telling her. Blinking away the memory, she fiercely accused him, "You might not have been able to stop him, but you could have stayed and been my friend, my support, someone I could cry my heart out with. But no, you left me, joined the Army. Mom barely ever said two words to me. I was…" she sniffed back a sob, "alone. Terribly alone."

Kenan swiped his hand over his eyes, his shoulders hunched. "I wrote, Stas, Mom told me Dad tossed the letters, declined my phone calls. You have to understand, when I was sixteen I tried one last Hail Mary, one last time to save you. I called the police, but his friends came."

His chest expanded with a heavy breath. "He told them it was me that had beaten you. They wanted to arrest me but Dad told them he would take care of my punishment, and they left. Mom and I were helpless to go to neighbors or teachers, anyone, because Dad would make the cops believe it was me that was hurting you, I'd go to jail, and he would get rid of you.

"The next day I went to wake you for breakfast and there was a huge machete stabbed into your bed by your head. It staked a note that said if Mom or I interfere again it will be the last time. He made me join the Army when I was sixteen. He said if I didn't leave that you would be murdered or sold. I had no choice, pipsqueak, you know he meant it. He always did what he threatened.

"He said I had to stay away. He didn't want to lose his punching bag, beating on you kept him from getting into fights with other people that could cost him his job. After he died, and again when you left home, I tried to reach out to you but you refused any contact with me." His head dropped, hiding the dejection in his damp eyes.

Kenan said softly, his voice filled with regret, "I know now I should have forced it. I should have done what Volt did, forced you to see me, listen to me. But," he sighed, "I was afraid. Afraid of your anger, your pain of what we did to you. I was afraid I would make matters worse." He shrugged. "Yet, now I see I couldn't possibly have made things any worse than they were."

Glancing at Volt then back to her, his expression scrunched with aching loss and remorse, he sat back and grew quiet.

No one said anything, the trio sat quietly, the men waiting for Stassi to speak. When she didn't, Kenan said, "I kept tabs on you, Stas. I know when you went to university, your degrees, your job at Exbiotics, that aborted relationship with Glenn Dyke. He never told you I hunted him down and he spent a month in the hospital."

Her eyes rounded in shock, then they thinned in satisfaction. "Thank you," she murmured almost inaudibly.

"I'd do it again, Sis, a hundred times to a hundred people that hurt you. When I learned of your abduction by Nero Lamontagne, I was out of the country, it would take me too long to get to you. Volt," he nodded at his friend, "has more expertise in locating, hunting people and rescue, extractions. So I called in a favor. Although," he grinned at Volt, "I'm sure he would have done it regardless. Once he learned an innocent woman was being assaulted and imprisoned, nothing would stop him from getting her out. I sent the best to save you, Stassi."

Still she said nothing, her expression unreadable.

"Anyway," he went on. "I would have brought you with me to heal after Lamontagne, but Volt insisted he could keep you safer. He gave me daily briefings on you. When that bastard Callen, that fucking teacher," contempt dripped from his wrathful tongue. "If I'd known he escaped prison I would have gone after him right then. I didn't know about his assault on you. I had just left for the Army and didn't find out until much later when I started doing searches online about you."

Volt spoke up, "He will never bother her again, K."

Kenan acknowledged his understanding of what Volt was implying.

Kenan stood up, stuffed his hands in his pockets. When she still didn't speak, Kenan said sadly, "Well, I guess that's it then. If you want to stay with me, Stas, I will take you in a heartbeat. But, uh, I guess you don't want to have anything to do with me. I understand, honey. I'll stay out of your life, but I won't stay blind to it. I will always know where you are, what you're doing." He looked over at Volt's impassive face.

"Ah, okay then, I should be going," he said stiffly. Lifting his jaw to Volt he grabbed his jacket off a chair and started for the door.

"No, wait, Kenan." Stassi got up and hurried after him. He turned, his face wrought with grief and remorse.

Stassi threw her arms around him. "Kenan," she cried against his chest, "I understand, you had to do what you did to ultimately save me."

His voice shaking with emotion, hopefulness and anguish wired in his voice Kenan uttered, "Can you ever forgive me?"

Stassi leaned back and wiped her eyes with her palms. Her smile tremulous. "There's nothing to forgive. You did the only things you could, your hand was forced. I…I've missed you, so much, I love you."

Kenan embraced her, his face lowered to the top of her head and they wept.

"Your mother is next, Anastasia," Volt commented too softly for her to hear as he slipped out of the room to give the siblings privacy to reunite.

Chapter Twenty-Eight

"I need to go back to work, Volt," Stassi insisted just stopping short of stomping her foot. She confronted Volt in his office. Two weeks had passed and she was feeling much more like herself. The marks around her neck and other bruises had pretty much faded.

Volt tapped a few keys on his computer then looked up at her. "I told you, when I determine it is safe for you to do so, I will take you," he shifted his gaze back to his computer, dismissing her.

Irritation at him brushing her off like she was a servant, Stassi plopped her hands on her hips and glared at him. "I'm bored, Volt." Knowing she sounded petulant made her more irritated and it showed in her voice. When he didn't give her his attention but stayed pecking away at his computer she snapped, "Volt!"

His head down, his eyes rolled up to her. With a sigh he closed the lid on the laptop and sat back in the big black leather chair. "How can you be bored, Ana? You have everything you need right here. Your computer, phone, books, TV, movies, when I'm here I spend all my time with you."

This was true, Stassi admitted. He left periodically on business, whatever that was, she didn't know because he didn't share. Apparently what he and her brother did was a big, fat, deep, dark secret and she hadn't the clearance or whatever to be filled in. That irritated her as well.

However, when he was at the house, he indulged her every desire, played rounds of backgammon, monopoly, scrabble, they watched movies and sometimes just sat and talked about everything and nothing. Mostly she talked because apparently his personal life was also a big, fat, deep, dark secret, and she resented that he refused to share any part of it with her. He avoided her questions about his family, relationships, friends, yet he had no reservations about quizzing her on her own past, and present.

He knew everything, he had a sneaky skillful way of drawing out her own dark secrets. Most of them he already knew. Voltang Saldano, a veritable stranger knew more about Stassi than anyone else in the entire world. He knew about what Marcus Callen had done to her when she was a child, how her parents had handled the assault, *they hadn't*, how she had been estranged from her brother and mother due to her father's abuse. She told him about people at work, Charlie, his wife and baby Cody that Volt had rescued and had returned safely to them.

After a few cocktails one night she told him about her time with Rufus. Unfortunately, that night Volt had to rush in and awaken her from a screaming nightmare where the red-headed demon was chasing her with a butcher knife.

Wearing nothing but sweatpants, Volt had held her, and rocked her until she'd fallen asleep. The familiarity of being in his strong, gentle, comforting embrace confirmed that it was Volt who had held her, fed her that first time when he'd brought her home from Lamontagne's vile clutches.

She had even spilled about her supervisor, Brant's pursuit of her. This had drawn both Volt's brows and mouth down, but he hadn't made any comment about it.

What was eating her was that she was feeling closer and closer to Volt. She remembered his kisses, and longed for more. He was attractive in a tough sort of way, he was funny, and she'd caught what she'd thought were heated looks from him when he didn't think she was aware. His touches lingered on her more and more, and she found herself not pulling away, and feeling… a longing when he moved away.

Of course she had little experience on which to judge a man's interest in her, so she was probably wrong. She was only a target, as he and Kenan had referred to their rescues or extractions, she was only a job to him. He was probably just as frustrated as she that he felt the responsibility to keep her safe with him. After all, he said he'd rescued her for her brother's sake.

Volt had freaking ice water in his veins. For once in her life Stassi was yearning for a bit of intimacy. Maybe. Shaking off that thought, she said, "I need to work, Volt. I can't laze around like this, I need to be busy, have a purpose. You won't even let me go outside. I've been dying to see the lake behind the house. It should be safe enough for me to row a boat or canoe or something on it."

His wide shoulders rose with the deep breath he took in to keep his patience. "I have told you, it isn't safe for you out of this house. Land, water, it's all the same, access to you."

"But if you were with me," there was that petulance again. Yes, he had been spending time with her but the past few days it was almost as if he was avoiding her.

"Snipers, Ana, they can fire from a mile or more away and strike you. You know that I don't have as much security as usual this week because I had to send most of my men on a mission. The perimeter may not be as secure as normally. You need to stay within the protection of the house."

"Fine," she huffed. "But what about work? I would surely be safe at the lab?"

He lifted the lid on his laptop and returned his attention to it. "I won't say it again, Ana, you will stay here until I determine it's safe for you to go anywhere. Nero Lamontagne is still out there, for fuck's sake," his eyes rose to her for a second then snapped back to his computer, she was again dismissed.

Stassi stood there fuming, he ignored her. She swung around and stomped out of his office. She didn't see his hooded eyes following her out, or the thoughtful sigh before he returned to his computer.

Storming from room to room looking for something to do, the place was enormous, Stassi tried walking off her pique. It didn't help, she thought as she wandered into the library. Standing in the center of the room, she marveled that Volt had a library in his home. He had apparently rented the sprawling house as a base as soon as he agreed to help Kenan find her.

The house was rented, but everything in it was Volt's. She had asked him wasn't he eager to return to wherever it was he came from, he had shrugged and told her one place was as good as another.

Stassi roamed the comfy room with paneled walls lined with books. Most of the books were in neat rows, but there were many tucked in crooked, a few lay on their side on top of other books. Volt's crew hung out often at the house, it appeared some of them enjoyed reading.

A corner room, it had two walls of glass French doors and large windows that let in bright light that was perfect for the cozy groupings of cushioned chairs and divans that were clustered in front of the windows. Stassi noticed a table had a half finished jigsaw puzzle laid out on it.

She flit aimlessly around the room, pulling books out, flipping through them then stuffing them back on the shelves. She pushed a few puzzle pieces around. Eventually she strolled over and stood at one of the glass doors.

The sun wasn't streaming into the room today. Grey wooly clouds heavy with unfallen rain hung low misting the land in a thick fog. Late morning yet outside it was gossamer murk. The lake darkened from the leaden fog silted into a black haze.

Stassi could just make out the pier like a fork's tine thrusting out over the still water. The part of the dock closest to the house was shadowed in dark amethyst, a dim light from a lamp on a post near the water crossed a line of pewter beam over the end of the planks.

Staring out dreamily, Stassi loved fog. It covers the world in secrecy, eclipsing everything in gauzy colors, obscuring trees, houses, roads. Like being in the center of a dark blurry Impressionist painting. "That's it," she declared under her breath.

Disengaging the alarm, she unlocked one of the glass doors and stepped outside. Breathing in cool, damp air, a slight chill tickled goose bumps up her arms. Thrills of exhilaration rumbled through her at finally being outside and enveloped by the mist.

She made her way across the lawn her boots swishing through the dewy grass to the dock. She was perfectly safe, the fog was so thick no one could see her.

Thinking she should have grabbed her jacket, the goose bumps of excitement were turning into quills of cold. Rubbing her arms, she walked quickly to the pier. As she trod over the damp wood planks the ankle boots made slight clumping sounds in the deep silence.

Standing at the edge of the dock she could smell the briny water. Veiled in the clouded twilight, brisk wind played with her hair and ruffled her blouse. She tried to peer through the gloaming atmosphere, make out the water or surrounding trees but could see no further than a few feet out.

The lone lamp by the shore slightly lit the pier but out at the very end it appeared as if late evening. She had heard people describe the mist on the water was like watching smoke twirl and dance on glass. Stassi felt like she was standing on water hovering in a thick shadow of mystery.

A sound caught her attention. Her head cocked. Was that a twig snapping?

Turning around, she called out, "Who's there? Volt, is that you?" She hoped like heck it wasn't Volt, he would kill her for sneaking out here. Not sneaking, she scolded herself, she had every right to go about as she pleased. Another sound lifted the hairs on the back of her neck.

She tried again. "Hello? Is someone there? Please answer me!" Angling an ear to listen, she heard nothing but the wind rattling the trees. And it rattled her nerves. Time to go.

Hoping it was just a small animal lurking in the bushes, her heart racing, Stassi picked her way back carefully over the slippery wet planks. If she fell and hurt herself it might be hours before anyone found her, or worse, she could slip and tumble into the lake.

Hurrying with caution down the steps of the dock, the damp grass swished along her boots as she walked as fast as safely possible across the lawn.

Then the muffled night was broken by the crack of a gunshot. She froze. Should she hit the ground, stay still, hide, or run for the house?

Chapter Twenty-Nine

She chose running. Stassi was only yards from the lake when an arm belted around her and she was jerked back against a hard chest. One scream pealed out before a large hand clamped hard and rough over her mouth.

"Shut up, bitch before I clock you one."

Dread filled her belly, the voice was horrifyingly familiar. Stassi jabbed her elbow in the man's ribs as hard as she could and kicked him in the knee.

He grunted and moved his hand from her mouth while he stumbled trying to catch his balance. Stassi wasted no time. Screaming at the top of her lungs she ran as fast as she could to the house-

She heard his footsteps stomping right behind her just before he grabbed a fistful of her blouse and yanked her backwards. In her ear, Vinca Nivelli cursed as he released her blouse to get his arms around her. "You're gonna regret that, woman, wait until I get you-" Loud voices carried through the fog.

"Anastasia!" Volt shouted. "Where the hell are you? Answer me!"

He sounded furious, but Stassi would rather face his fury than Vinca Nivelli or Nero Lamontagne's. Stassi twisted and threw her body making it harder for Nivelli to get a good grip of her. She screamed, "Volt! Help me, I'm at the lake!"

Footsteps pounded over the grass towards them. With the thick fog visibility was almost zero. "Talk to me, Ana!" Volt yelled, he sounded closer.

She opened her mouth and Nivelli violently shoved her to the ground. Landing hard on her stomach, the wind knocked out of her lungs, she couldn't speak, but thankfully she could hear Nivelli's boots racing away from her.

"Dammit, Ana, call to me, I can't see you!" Volt demanded, but she couldn't suck in a scrap of air. Then, she heard panted breaths and hard footsteps and he was there.

"Shit, Ana," he growled, dropping down to the ground. His hand landed heavily on her back, he muttered curses, then commanded, "Baby, talk to me," worry etched into his furious tone. "Are you okay?" Very gently he grasped her shoulders and carefully rolled her onto her back.

She stared blinking wide-eyed in fright, her chest hitching as she fought to suck in air.

"Oh, shit, the wind was knocked out of you. Take it easy, try to take a real slow breath." Volt lifted her torso off the ground and cradled her in one arm while smoothing her hair back with his other hand. "Come on, baby, you can do it, relax a little, do it slow."

Several men materialized from the fog. Volt barked at them, "Find whoever it was, they have to still be on the property." The men silently vanished back into the haze.

Blinking anxiously up at him, Stassi struggled for a minute then she was able to suck in a gasp of air. A few coughs as she drew in more air and Volt stood up with her in his arms. Looking down he kicked something in the grass. "Fuckin' night vision goggles, hell."

Tramping to the house, he lowered his head to Stassi, asked her, "Did he hurt you? Do you have injuries?" The roar of motorcycles departing ruptured the quiet.

She shook her head, she was trembling all over. "N- no. I think he was going to take me again, Volt," the words rasped in fear.

"Again?" Volt strode furiously to the house. "You know who it was?"

"M- Mr. Lamontagne's man, Vinca Nivelli," she gasped.

Holding her high and tight to his chest he reached the house. Quickly passing through a side door where a man stood guard, Volt set her briefly on her feet. While still cradling her against his body, he closed the door and reset the alarm. "I want a quick scan of the house, make sure no one is hiding and check all doors and windows to see they are secure. Check all the alarms as well," he instructed the guard. The man said nothing, just bowed his head with a short jerk and took off to do as Volt bid.

Lifting her back into his arms Volt strode down a long hallway. He pushed the partially open door with his elbow and went inside. Gently, he deposited her on the edge of the bed. Whipping his phone out he hit buttons.

Stassi covered her face with her hands while she struggled to calm down. Volt's voice was muffled coming in through her stunned ears. She glanced around. They were in a large, masculine decorated bedroom. Filled with heavy furniture, she assumed it was Volt's bedroom. Feeling like a weak invalid sitting there on his bed shaking like a leaf, she lumbered to her feet.

"It was Nivelli, Lamontagne's muscle," Volt said into his phone, pacing the length of the room, back and forth. Nodding sharply, he mumbled, "Yeah, I figured as much, heard the bikes. Call some more men in, I want tighter security."

Pawing at his chin, he growled, "I know most of them are out, Jubal, call half of them back. Hire mercenaries we've vetted before to stock up the men on the mission. I want my best men back here."

Stuffing the phone in his pocket, he raked both hands through his hair and stopped pacing right in front of Stassi. Fury darkening his face and deepening his voice, he said, "I warned you about snipers. One of them was positioned quite a distance away in the woods with a night vision scope. Likely hiding up in a tree he took out a sentry patrolling, then that Nivelli fucker slipped in through the cover of the dark dense fog."

His hands flung out and he gripped her upper arms giving her a furious shake. "Goddammit, Anastasia, I told you to stay inside, you will damned well listen to me!"

"Is he- your man, is he okay?" she shivered the words out.

"What? Yeah, yeah, shoulder through-and-through. We heard the shot and I went immediately to get you, and, lo and fucking behold, you were nowhere to be found. Why the devil did you leave the house?"

Her teeth knocking together from his rough shake, Stassi said defensively, "I was bored, Volt, stop shaking me!"

"Bored?" Fingers squeezing he shook her again, his face a livid mask of rage. "You risked your life because you were bored? Dammit, I should throw you right over my knee and smack the hell out of your ass for that stupid, stupid jaunt. How many times have I told you to stay inside and to listen to me? How many?" He shook her again. "You could be right back in the sadistic clutches of that son of a bitch, so stupid, so-"

"V- Volt," her teeth clicking she cried, "you're hurting me."

"Hurting you?" Volt shouted in exasperation. "You don't think Lamontagne won't hurt you if he gets his filthy hands on you? My God, Anastasia, you want to experience another

Rufus? Think about what he could do to you before I could get to you!" His fingers tightened like bands of steel around her slender arms.

Stassi's shoulders rose up to her ears. "Okay, okay, I'm sorry, I get it, you don't have to beat it into me!"

"Beat it? Damned right I'll beat it into you to make you listen to me! I'll chain you to my goddamned bed, woman if I have to, to keep you safe." Volt shoved his face into Stassi's and lifted her up on her toes. His slit eyes firing bullets of rage.

"I said okay, Volt." She tipped her head up then winced at the crazed fury thundering off him in jagged bolts of incensed lighting. Where was that man who only moments ago had cradled her in his arms whispering soothing words of comfort, helping her to breathe?

"Calm down, Volt, let go of me, I just didn't think, I said I was sorry, let go. I just wanted something to do, you're always so busy and-"

His face screwed up tight, then his eyes bulged at her. "Something to do?" His fingers crushed. "Something to do? My God, Ana, I'm busy?" Laughing without a smile, he shook his head. He pulled her in close again, their faces an inch apart.

"Volt, you- you're scaring me, please let-"

"Ha, scaring you. I'm scaring you. You splay yourself out there alone splat in the middle of the open yard, why didn't you just pin a blinking neon sign on you, 'Come and get me, Lamontagne, I didn't get enough torture the first time around?'"

"Come on, Volt." She pushed and pulled but couldn't break free of his hands or his anger.

Shaking his head again, he said sarcastically, "Busy. I'm busy."

Laughing again, he barked coarsely, "I force myself to stay busy Anastasia so I can keep my bloody hands off of you. So I don't do this-" One hand curled roughly under the back of her head the other swept around to spread over her lower back and he jerked her up against him with a jolt.

Her lips parted from the blow and he slammed his mouth down on hers and ate at her in a frenzied fever.

It was like crashing into a charging train with lips. Sensual, full, hot lips consuming every inch of her mouth, her jaw, her neck, and back to her mouth. Stunned at his sudden kinetic ravishing, Stassi froze. At first.

His potent mouth savoring her lips, her tongue with masculine moans rumbling in his chest as if tasting her was the height of nirvana, his fingers gripping her tightly, not hurtful but to keep her from running from him.

Her hands went to his chest to push him away, he deepened the kiss, and Stassi fell, like a rock plummeting over a cascading waterfall into a rushing river.

And just like that, her mind emptied of all but the feel of Volt's hands on her body, his lips plundering hers. His tongue sucking and lashing at hers, Stassi accepted the tidal wave of sensations he executed upon her unawakened virtue, and she returned the lesson with gusto as she followed his lead and learned how to kiss. To really kiss.

Now she understood that the awkward fumbling, slobbering wallops from Glenn Dyke were not real kisses. No wonder she never wanted to go further with him, it had been like making out with a flopping, gasping fish.

Stassi always thought the reason she had never felt sexual was because of Callen's assault on her. He had stabbed her innocence leaving the holes gaping wide with a deep fear and revulsion of men, and when she finally braved intimacy with a man it had died a quick death by the name of Juliette.

Now Stassi understood, she had tried to make it work with the wrong man. She owed Juliette a heaving helping of thank you's.

Feeling Stassi responding in his arms, her immature tongue willingly, eagerly seeking his, her fingers in his hair, twisting, clutching, while she made the most alluring splendid sounds, Volt skimmed his hands down her back to her bottom. He squeezed lavishly, and at the encouraging sounds she made and her wriggling against his body, he stroked his hands up her sides, up her ribs to palm her breasts. Volt prepared himself for her to back off, push him away, but she didn't. Rubbing against him, she mewed into his mouth, and he was done.

"Ana, baby," he groaned and gripped the bottom of her sweater and lifted it, forcing her arms to rise with the sweater he pulled it over her head and tossed it. His blazing eyes latched onto her breasts molding over the black lacy bra.

Wrapping his hands around her ribs under her breasts he leaned back and looked at her. He saw Stassi's lids half-mast over unfocused green eyes, cheeks lit with heated pink, lips parted as her tongue stroked them as if trying to taste him.

"Ana, say you want this, you want me, say it," he rasped roughly, his voice harsh with lusting need of her.

Stassi didn't answer him, her head tilted back, a tiny line of green shone under the heavy lids that lowered further. She gripped his hair and tried to pull his head back down.

Resisting her attempts to get his mouth back on hers, Volt grated, "Anastasia, baby, I either need to stop right now, or you have to let me know this is what you want." After the trauma she'd endured in her life the last thing Volt wanted was for Stassi to feel he was forcing himself on her.

His hands stroked down and he tugged the button on her jeans open. "Baby," he whispered at her silence with urgency and hopefulness in his voice. "Just say yes, I'll take care of everything, I'll be gentle, slow. Say yes," he bent and gave her a sultry but short kiss, and her lips curved up in a sensuous smile.

"Yes," she whispered her reply, sounding so sweet and innocent to Volt, but all woman and that was all he needed.

"Thank God," he muttered and gave her a soft push, the bed hit her in the knees and she sat down. He knelt in front of her and removed her boots and her socks, then grasped her wrists and pulled her back to her feet. She giggled when he bent and very quickly dragged her jeans down and off. Kicking off his own boots, he reached for her. Suddenly self-conscious she shrank back, her hands covering the lace bra.

Smiling gently, Volt tugged at her hands pulling them from her chest, he murmured, "No, you are so beautiful, I wanna drink you in and then I'm going to make you mine, Anastasia. I've dreamed of seeing you like this, let me look at you." He pulled the straps of the bra down her arms then unclasped the back and drew it off her and dropped it. Before she could change her mind he slid his hands under her and lifted her, setting her carefully on the bed. "Don't move, baby," he told her.

Snatching his phone from his pocket he sent a quick text then tossed the cell on the table beside the bed.

Her big emerald eyes shimmered up at him as she watched him. Volt grabbed his shirt and pulled it up and off and threw it in one motion. His hands on his belt, he grinned at her verdant interest as she watched him with sexy wide-eyes. He withdrew his wallet from his pants, slid a condom out, then quickly removed the rest of his clothes and slid a knee on the bed.

She looked down at his manhood, he was heavy and hard and aching. Surprisingly she didn't look afraid, she beamed a soft smile up at him and the tight tension Volt felt in his chest slid away.

"Ready, Ana?" he asked as he rolled down to lay beside her. His fingers tucked in the lace trim of her panties he drew them down her legs and off.

"Yes," Stassi murmured with no fear in her eyes. "I'm ready, Volt."

And he initiated her into the wonderful world of being a woman, and the enjoyment and thrill of love making, and chased away any lingering fear of men. Well, of Volt.

Chapter Thirty

For several days Volt taught Stassi the beauty of true intimacy. They barely left the suite and Volt had Sadie bring their meals to them.

Tucked away in the bedroom, Stassi could hear Sadie's and Volt's murmurs from the front living room. Embarrassment heated her cheeks at the thought of Sadie, and everyone else, knowing she and Volt were having sex. Then she heard Sadie's teasing laughter and knew she was pleased that the pair had gotten together.

Stassi slid out of bed and showered while Volt chatted with Sadie. She heard him making phone calls while she towel-dried her long hair, and while she dressed, slipping on a pale blue sweater and jeans. After their first night together, without consulting her, Volt had all of Stassi's belongings moved to his room.

She stood in front of the mirror over a short dresser dragging a comb through an unruly curl and contemplated what the future was to be. Did Volt plan a relationship with her? He hadn't said anything in that regard, and, her shoulders slumped, she set the comb on the dresser, of course he had his job that was stationed overseas. He certainly would not have the inclination to carry on a long distance relationship with her.

"Huh," she grunted. Her long ingrained insecurities emerged and dug in. "Like he would want any kind of relationship with a little nobody like me. With his tough good looks and rocking body he probably has women in every port, every section of the world."

Her heart pitter-pattered when she realized she didn't want this to end. She didn't want to say goodbye to Volt. She also would never share a man. And why would he settle down with just one woman when he could have anyone he wanted? He was tough and dangerous, but half the women at Exbiotics had thrown themselves at him. Juliette had badgered her for his phone number.

With an unhappy sigh, Stassi sat on a chair and pulled on her socks and boots. She heard the front door of the suite close and then his footsteps coming down the short hall and she quickly dashed at a tear that had snuck out.

"You're dressed?" he said quizzically from the doorway. He was wearing jeans and an unbuttoned shirt. He'd thrown them on when he had answered Sadie's knock.

Getting to her feet awkwardly, Stassi stuck her hands in her back pockets and shrugged negligently. "Um, yes, of course. I heard you talking, I can tell you have business to attend to. I guess I can go fire up the computer and work on some chemical calculations I've been constructing." They had spent days naked in bed together, yet now she peered shyly up at him through long cinnamon lashes.

His head cocked, he said, "I'm not happy seeing you dressed." He stalked towards her with a grin. "Let's see what we can do about that."

"Oh, but don't you-" And he was on her. She tried to speak but that was difficult with her sweater being wrenched over her head. "Um, wait, Volt, you-" And her jeans were jerked down to her ankles and before she could say another word he lifted her and dropped her on the bed and removed the rest of her clothes and her shoes and socks.

She tried again, "Volt, I understand that you need to get working- oh!" Her lashes flashed up, he tore his shirt off and was out of his jeans in a beat and climbing on her. A string of condoms lay on the nightstand, he grabbed for one.

Volt's mouth descended on hers, he mumbled against her lips, "I am so not ready to let you out of my hands, Ana."

Hours later, they were sitting in the living room eating spaghetti and meatballs with salad and garlic bread on plates set on the coffee table. Volt finished his meal and sat back on the couch with a sigh, a beer in one hand. "So, Anastasia," he drawled laconically.

Stassi dabbed her mouth with the napkin and sat back with her soda. Taking a sip, she looked at him. He was sitting only a few inches away, it seemed he had to always be near her, touching her. Even after all the sex they'd had his eyes still smoldered with desire as they stroked over her body.

But she heard the serious note in his voice, her belly clenched, here it comes, the big brush off. Setting the soda on the table, she turned to fully face him, preparing herself for his sayonara. One leg curled on the sofa, the other hanging off the side, fingers twined tightly in her lap. "Yes, Volt?" She was proud of herself, her voice didn't quiver although she felt like she was dying inside.

Volt set his bottle on the table and turned to her. "I got word back on the samples of the bacteria we collected from Callen's lab."

Her brows rose. "Oh? You told me you had sent them to an independent lab you work with. What were the results?" She had at one point thought Volt had only rescued her from Callen's lair to get his hands on the formula for the bacteria, but when they returned to the States he had the formula sent to a government lab. They had decided together it was best the bacteria was studied by the government rather than some evil kingdom aspiring creep like Callen or Lamontagne.

The side of his mouth curved in an artful grin. "The bacteria is crap. Worthless rubbish." The grin widened at the incredulous look that came over her pretty face.

"I don't understand. I experimented with it myself, I know for a fact the chemical is valid. It did as claimed, it destroyed the gas, the oil on impact of any electrical device, batteries, whatever."

"You are correct, it is quite effective in its task, however, the bacteria rapidly breaks down, disintegrates in a short time period. That was the reason you had nothing left to study, it evaporates and there's nothing left, not even residue, as you found out. Twenty minutes after it's released from the vacuum packed container, by the time it even enters the ground it's already decomposing."

Stassi pondered this then said, "I admit I was stymied as to why we had nothing left to experiment with. I was careful to leave enough to use. When there wasn't any, I assumed I had calculated wrong, or I hadn't sealed the specimen properly and air degraded it. I even suspected perhaps someone had tampered with it, stole it. But this," she shook her head in dismay.

Her face scrunched in anger, she said with righteous vehemence, "All of this, the killing, torturing, kidnapping, beatings, all was for naught. The damned thing wasn't even viable."

Volt nodded. "Callen was allowing small demonstrations to buyers hoping to get them to pony up big bucks before anyone actually got their hands on the bacteria and found out it wasn't sustainable. By big bucks I'm saying millions, more likely billions he had hoped to bilk out of them."

Her chest rose and lowered with relief. "But this is great, Volt, it was wrong, the whole thing was horrible, a plague, but it's wonderful it's useless. We can all relax that world domination isn't going to happen through the dastardly bacteria and get on with other business."

"Yeah, well, your Mr. Crick called me. He wants you back. He wants you to work on developing the bacteria until it is viable, and he wants you to still work on creating the antidote."

Her brows sprung up in surprise then lowered in confusion. "Doesn't he know it's worthless?"

Volt drained his beer and set the bottle on the table then reached over and laid his hand on her thigh. Stassi noticed he didn't deliberately do that, it was almost automatic, he reached for her without thinking about it. Volt had always seemed a cold, remote man that Stassi found it hard to imagine this was how he normally acted with women he had sex with. He seemed more the hit and split kind of guy. A night or two of unbridled amazing sex and then he'd move right on to the next available female.

In her case, he was more or less forced to be with her because he was so adamant no one could protect her as well as he could. In her mind that was his ego speaking. His job he was so committed to, to the very end. She could see his motto would be that he would be damned if he let someone take her from him as easily as he had from others.

He was likely just using her for the handy sex. As soon as she was safe and out of his hair, and lair, she would not even be a blink of a memory for him. The grim, desolate thought sunk like a lead weight in her gut.

He answered her, "Of course he knows it's rubbish. I said he wants you to work on making it become what Callen had initially planned."

Her lips pushed out with a frown, she felt her stomach clench all over again. "I thought we were past this horrific intrigue, Callen's dream scheme. I thought with it being useless that the world was safe from the vile bacteria. I don't want to get drawn back into that dark web." Her eyes lowered in dread. She felt Volt's hand squeeze her thigh and she raised her gaze to his, and her stomach unclenched a little.

He smiled reassuringly at her. Volt smiled so seldom Stassi thought he was incapable of it. At least until the whole abduction episode was over and they'd stayed sequestered in his room. He smiled constantly then. If only she could see that smile forever…

She tipped her head back and took in his strong presence, powerful build of wide shoulders and thick chest, she'd learned his thighs and biceps were equally powerfully strong. He made her feel safe. Confidence exuded along with the ever present aura of danger in the enigmatic eyes and hard jaw. Warmth filled those dark eyes that smoldered at her.

"Ana, you don't ever have to do anything you don't want to. Crick would be unhappy, but he said if you chose not to be involved in the experiments with the formulas that he had other things for you to work on. He doesn't want to lose your brilliance." He smiled and said, "He means your brilliant brain, I like just your pure brilliance of being. Besides your stunning beauty, you truly light up the world."

Her face tinted pink at his compliments. Then it lightened with interest. Not commenting on his accolades, she asked, "Oh yeah? What other things does he want me to work on?"

The hand on her thigh moved up an inch. Volt cast a lop-sided smirk. "Way outta my league my tigress. He went on about nanotechnology and what effect nanomaterials might have on organisms and ecosystems. Something about green nanotechnology that are clean technologies that minimize risks of the manufacture of the nano products on environmental and human health risks, and also the hazards of using…what'd he call them? Ah, nanoparticles."

Okay, that sent prickles of excitement through her body. "Oh Volt, I love working with and studying nanoparticles! Oh, and quantum dots too!"

He grinned. "Yeah, I can see that, you're wriggling all over the cushion. You'll have to teach me about nanotechnology and all that shit. I only know the bare basics." His palm slid further up her thigh then over her pelvis to the button on her jeans.

With Volt's hands on her, Stassi's brain slid into fog-mode. Her eyes grew lazy along with a sensuous smile, she said, "Sure, some night when you can't sleep I'll regale you with all the things that make nanoparticles and what you can do with them, you'll be bored enough to fall asleep."

She giggled when Volt undid her pants then put his hand on her chest and pushed her to lie on her back. She went on with a small hitch in her voice, "The ancient Roman artisans used them to put a glaze of luster on their pottery."

Rolling over Stassi's petite form with his big body, Volt tugged her sweater up and covered her breast with his palm and murmured against her mouth, "I'm dying to learn what quantum dots are, baby," and he took her lips and tongue with the greediness of a starving man.

Chapter Thirty-One

Volt had argued endlessly with Stassi about returning to the lab and her home, but she eventually won out.

They had stopped first at her apartment to drop her things off then went on to the lab. Volt parked in the lot. As he turned the ignition off, he said, "Wait for me to come around and get you."

Rolling her eyes, Stassi said, "The danger is over, Volt. The bacteria is abortive therefore no one is going to come after me to create an antidote. And, since the government has the formula in its own labs now no one will be after me or anyone else to work on making it operative."

"Just wait for me," he ordered. Leaving the car, he paused and scanned the area. Stassi's door opening caught his attention and annoyance. He was there before she could get a foot out.

Holding the door so she couldn't push it open further and get out, Volt scowled at her. "Cripe, Stassi, let me do my job for once, will you?"

She felt like he'd slapped her in the face. A job, he'd said. Looking impatient, the thrust of her bottom lip came across as more of a pout. She was forced to move back inside the car. "Sure, Volt, I'm just a job. Fine, go ahead, do what you must."

It was difficult keeping the disappointment and dejection at the realization that she had only been a way for him to entertain himself while working. He did his task of keeping her safe while assuaging his sexual needs at the same time. Talk about being just a sex object. The reality hurt, it hurt bad.

Peering up at him through a fringe of lashes Stassi felt her heart splintering. The fact that she was only a job to him tore her up inside, leaving it wide open for all her old insecurities and self-hate to climb in and fester.

What a fool she'd been, she told herself harshly. He was suave and seductive, he played her like strings on a harp and she had been too naïve to see it. He probably wasn't even laughing at her ingenuousness, he was just using accessible sex, most likely thought it his reward for her rescue.

Now that the case was over, Stassi would return to work and school, and Volt would vanish as suddenly as he had appeared in her life. Clearly she meant nothing to him. To be honest, she didn't dare examine her own feelings towards the hard, tough warrior or whatever he was.

Ignoring her sulky compliance, Volt put a broad hand on the door to keep her from exiting. Again he scanned the building, the parking lot, the road leading to the lab and the perimeter. Seeing nothing alarming, he reluctantly pulled her door back open and allowed her to leave the vehicle.

Sliding out and to her feet with a, "Humph," Stassi shot him a glare. "Really Volt, it's over. Your job is done. You can call Kenan and tell him all is well and you can be off to wherever it is you came from knowing you did a successful job. You can put this whole episode on your résumé." She stalked away from him towards the building not seeing him blink at her hostile words before he started after her.

Catching up, Volt grasped the door handle and opened it for her to enter first and he followed her in.

Stassi swept inside but Volt caught her arm halting her. "Listen, Ana, we need to talk-"

"Stassi!" Brant boomed as he rushed towards the couple with his arms out. He quickly engulfed Stassi in a bear hug. Bending his head he tried to kiss her but she turned her face and the kiss landed on her cheek. Holding her tightly Brant murmured against her hair, "God, sweetheart, I've missed you so much, so damned much."

Volt stood stiffly, the tips of his ears turned red and the corner of his jaw worked but he stayed still, impassively observing the manager's overly friendly welcome.

Loud voices descended on them from numerous directions. Stassi had texted Charlie when they had neared the lab. Staff hurried to the lobby to greet Stassi, welcome her back to the fold. Volt was forced to step back as they encircled her shrieking and crying as they each reached out to have their turn at hugs.

"God, Stassi," Valentina King cried, her face was flushed with streaming tears. "We were so afraid we'd lost you again!" Pushing Brant aside she fell upon her friend with a bone-crushing embrace. Valentina's sobs rang loudly above the noise of the welcoming throng.

"Okay Val, let someone else have a piece of her," Charlie demanded. Moving from weeping Valentina's arms, Stassi turned and grinned at him.

"Charlie," Stassi breathed, her own tears springing. "I'm so happy to see you! Is everyone okay? Melinda? Cody?"

"Hell, Stas, I owe you everything. You saved my son's life. I don't know what would have happened to Mellie and me if Cody- if-" His voice broke in a despairing choke. His weak grin shone through tears pouring down his cheeks. "So, so grateful, Stas, you were so brave-"

"It's all good, Charlie. We're all here in one piece." Stassi let Charlie throw his arms around her and let him hug the stuffing out of her. They had spoken on the phone periodically and Charlie had bent her ears with his enthused gratefulness.

After Stassi and Charlie moved apart, chemists Donovan Crane, Jody Rickets and Troy Marshall peppered Stassi with welcome backs.

Donovan pulled her against him so fast her nose bumped into his long snout and his black glasses jostled up his nose. When Troy hugged her, Stassi could smell the booze on him, it smelled stale so hopefully it was left over from last night rather than he was imbibing early in the morning.

Over Jody's shoulder as the skinny girl gave her a quick hug, Stassi saw Juliette Moore and Dixy Lee had managed to separate Volt from the crowd surrounding Stassi.

Juliette hung on Volt's brawny arm and Dixy blinked big cow-eyes up at him with her mouth hanging open like she was viewing a super hero from the movies. Volt's head was lowered as he spoke to Juliette, he never looked up once at Stassi.

"Okay, everyone," Francis Crick ordered as he approached the boisterous group, "give her room to breathe," and he elbowed his way through the crowd for his own overly friendly and overly long hug. Stassi had to wriggle from his arms to break away.

"Welcome back," Karine Benton said coolly to Stassi.

Moving out of both Brant's and Crick's reach, Stassi smiled her thanks at Crick's willowy personal assistant. As usual, Karine wore her pink print dress clingy to her long legged model's form. Six-inch heels added to her lissome height, and her blonde locks were pulled tightly back in a meticulous chignon. Gold glittered from her ears, around her neck and off both wrists.

The two women had only briefly met on the few occasions Stassi had been summoned to Crick's office. They nodded politely to each other.

"All right, people," Crick announced, "let's get a move on. You're not getting paid to lollygaggle. Back to work, now, everyone." He made shooing motions with his hands.

The extraneous people flittered off but the close staff Stassi worked with stayed bunched around her.

His eyes glowing, Charlie reached his hand out to grasp Stassi's. "Really, Stas. You know we owe you big, me and Mellie. We will never forget what you did for us. You ever need anything, I mean anything at all, you tell me, Stas, and I'll do it. I'm there for you. Right?" He grinned at her, and Stassi smiled sweetly back at him.

"I said let's get a move on, people," Crick announced more loudly, frowning at Charlie. To Stassi he said, "I have projects for you to work on, I assume your…" he glanced at Volt, Juliette's lips were near his ear, his head was bent to her. "Ah, hero, told you about the concepts?"

Squeezing Charlie's hand, Stassi smiled at Crick. "Yes, sir, he told me about the nanoparticles you want me to explore."

"Yes." Crick nodded, shooing off more hangers-on. "Green technology. I want some studies on the use of less energy and renewable inputs. I'll be more specific when," he looked around frowning at Charlie and Valentina who had refused to leave. "Anyway," he huffed. "The material information has already been downloaded to your computer. You can get started right away."

"Um, okay," Stassi agreed, scanning the room she didn't at first see Volt. He was so tall, he was hard to miss, there- Stassi's lips pressed in a line. He was disappearing into a corridor with Juliette tucked against him.

Dixy Lee stood staring off at them, her cow-eyes rounded, she smiled like a mother who had just match-made her daughter with the perfect man. Her heart sinking, Stassi thought, "No, not perfect, but I thought he was mine." She shook her head thinking, "I'm such an idiot, no one woman will ever own that male."

Faster than Stassi could say persimmons, Crick ushered her to the labs and closed the security door behind them. No one that wasn't essential with high clearance would be able to pass through the door.

"There," Crick said, indicating a white laminated table, "your laptop. All the information is in it, what I'm looking for from you. Everything you need is in there," he motioned to double steel doors resembling cooler doors in a restaurant.

As if Stassi didn't have a shocked look on her face at the abrupt and speedy way he'd shepherded her to the labs and expected her to jump right into the job without even stopping at her desk first, Crick opened the security door. "You need anything, or any help, just call Karine. So," he stepped through the doorway, "welcome back and get to it."

Startled at his hasty exit, Stassi said, "Oh, but wait, Mr. Crick-"

He paused, one brow arched impatiently in question.

Feeling her face heating, she said, "My, um, Mr. Saldano. I didn't say goodbye. I think I-"

"Ms. Athens, you have been gone quite a while. It's about time you get started doing what we pay you for. Don't you think?" The brow arched further as if daring her to dispute his words.

"Oh, yes, but, I would still like to-"

"Yes, later, my dear," Crick uttered and closed the door. It automatically locked behind him.

"Well," Stassi exhaled loud and unsure. She headed to the computer muttering, "I guess that's it then. It's not like Volt was hanging around to say goodbye to me. I'm probably not even a tiny memory already. Might as well see what the project is."

She shuffled unhappily to the computer and powered it on.

Chapter Thirty-Two

A week later, Stassi locked her apartment door and climbed in her car closing out the chilly blast of wind. Turning the ignition on, she glanced around. She saw not a soul, not even another car. "I guess Volt called his men off."

She slumped in the seat and stared bleakly out the windshield. "It's truly over." Sighing, she thought she would feel a heavy burden lifted off her shoulders, a welling of relief that her life was back to normal with no evil scientists lurking in the shadows waiting to abduct her and force her to do their will.

"Yeah," mumbling to herself, Stassi backed out of the parking area and turned onto the street. "Why don't I feel happy, relieved, content?" Glaring at the road she traveled, she knew why she felt dejected instead of elated. Voltang Saldano. He'd gotten under her skin, way under her skin. She'd gotten used to living with him, seeing him every day. Sleeping in his big arms at night.

And the sex, her cheeks flamed at the things he'd taught her, amazing, wonderful, intimate things they'd done together. The area between her legs that just a week ago would go from zero to sizzling just from a hooded look and a sultry grin from Volt was now heating up at the remembrance of their times together. His audacious virility, the man could about make her climax with just a look. The way his mouth rose on one side and his eyes warmed and darkened when he gazed at her naked body ready to take him in. The car hit the expressway and she was soon flying along with a thousand other people.

"Well," Stassi sighed more heavily with a shake of her head, "it's really over," she said again, trying to convince herself that was what she wanted. "The guy didn't even call me. Even if he didn't know my number, he can find a person hidden away in the deepest darkest jungle in the most obscure country, he could certainly get my number. Besides," she grumbled, "he knows where I live, he could have stopped by."

Shaking her head again she grumbled peevishly, "But why would he? We meant nothing to each other. Just captive and rescuer. Everything is back to normal and he's likely off on some dangerous mission rescuing some gorgeous princess or something, while I..."

Stassi blinked back sudden tears as she exited the highway and started down the main street to the lab. She huffed miserably, reluctantly admitted, "But I don't want normal. I want Volt." Her heart seized with loss. The pain palpable. She couldn't bear the thought of never seeing him again.

"But, I have no choice. I'm not the type of woman that chases after men. It's in his hands, if he doesn't want to pursue a relationship with me, then, well, that's that. I need to shell up my stupid heart and move on. It's time to stop wallowing in self-pity. People always leave me," she choked back a sob.

"I should be so used to it by now. Really," she tried to stoke herself up, "I must go on with my life as if he was barely a ripple in the lake of my useless existence." Great. Her ego has hit rock bottom.

Pulling the car into the lot, she parked and shut the car off, but she just sat there staring at the lab. It was later than she usually arrived and everyone was either at work or in the field.

Her heart panged again, so hard with real hurt at the fact she would never see Volt again. He had lit her body on fire and that fire was going to blaze with or without him. There was no undoing what they had spent days, weeks doing. She couldn't put her awakened libido back in the box. So to speak.

Plus the platonic times they spent together were fun, mentally challenging, exciting sparks bounced off them as they played and conversed. She knew he had that dark, dangerous, mysterious side to him, but the Volt she'd spent time with stirred her on every level. Her heart automatically quickened every time he stepped into a room.

"Buck up, Stas," she commanded. "There are more fish in the sea. Now that I know there's not so much to fear from…sex…men, I'm sure I can find another…" she trailed off.

"Dammit," she cursed pounding the steering wheel with her fist. Anger suddenly fired up inside. "I don't want any other damned man. I want that son of a gun." But just as quickly the angry, flaming steam inside her furled off and dissolved leaving her feeling even more dejected than before as she lamented, "But, he doesn't want me."

She peered into the rearview mirror at her reflection. "What on earth made me think that l could catch and hold the attention of a man like Volt. He was a…yes, corny, but yes, he was, is a warrior. Brave and strong, and hot, yeah," she admitted. "The man is hot. But clearly not the man for boring ol' me." Heaving a sigh thick with despondency, Stassi opened the door and trudged to the lab.

She tried to shake off the gloom that was pulling her down, dragging her down like a cement block tied to her ankles into the deep fathomless sea. "It'll take a while to get over him," she whispered.

Smiling weakly at the few people in the lobby, Stassi knew she would never get over him. Volt had stolen her darn heart, and was never giving it back. She would never care about another man like she did him. "Dammit," she whispered to herself. "Get a grip, I'm acting like a high school teen with her first crush."

"Miss Athens."

She heard someone calling for her. Stassi looked up to the second floor.

Along one wall was an open walkway. Karine was standing there, one hand with long slim fingers curled over the railing. She called down to Stassi, "Mr. Crick would like a word with you before you begin." Her high heels clicked on the tile as she started along the walkway to the stairs.

Stassi stood where she was wondering why Karine was coming down to her instead of having Stassi go upstairs to Mr. Crick's office. She was also a bit surprised the model-like woman took the stairs instead of the elevator. Her heels were so high she had to carefully pick her way down the tiled steps. When she reached the first floor, she waved at Stassi beckoning to come to her.

"What on earth…" Stassi mumbled, where did Karine want her to go? She made her way across the lobby to where Karine had moved to a hallway.

When she reached her, Karine said, "Come with me," and she turned and strode down the hall.

"Wait, my jacket and purse, Ms. Benton, I just need a minute to drop them at my desk," Stassi spoke to the retreating receptionist.

Karine didn't slow her pace, just tossed a wave over her shoulder and said, "You're already late, Ms. Athens, you know Mr. Crick doesn't like to wait," and she walked faster.

"Late? I can't be late for something that- well, I mean I don't recall having an appointment with Mr. Crick. Did I miss a message or something from him?"

"Oh, you know how he is," Karine muttered as if that answered the question.

Peeling off her jacket, Stassi followed Karine down one hallway to another corridor and down yet another hall. "Ms. Benton," she huffed, keeping up with the quickly striding woman. Karine's lean legs were long and Stassi had to move faster to keep up with her.

What, is this a race? Stassi wondered. "Wait, listen, where are we going? Why would Mr. Crick be at the back of the facility?"

Karine just walked faster. Stassi marveled at how the woman moved so quickly in such steep heels, but she just kept powering on, her heels clacking faster and faster, must be all that model runway work. No wonder they were all so pin thin.

The two women strode rapidly down the long corridor until Karine slowed slightly. Stassi looked around at her surroundings. She had never been to the back of the building. There had been no reason. She didn't even know what was back there. "Ms. Benton-"

Karine stopped in front of a large emergency exit door. Without a word she pushed it open.

"Ms.-" Confused, Stassi followed her. "Where are-"

Karine suddenly turned and gave Stassi a shove and she stumbled out the door, her jacket and purse slipped from her astonished grasp and fell to the floor.

"Hey!" Stassi cried as she tumbled outside. She would have fallen if someone hadn't grabbed her arm and caught her up.

"Watch out, little, girl, being so clumsy you could easily get hurt." Vinca Nivelli grinned at her. His grip painfully hard, he jerked her away from the door. "Nicely done," he said with a wink to Karine.

The receptionist's face whitened. She whispered with remorse, "I'm so sorry, Ms. Athens. I had to." Karine put a finger to the side of her mouth and tugged it open, and Stassi could see a gaping hole where one of her molars appeared to have been removed.

"No! But Karine!" Stassi screeched as Vinca dragged her over the gravel lot. "Help me! Don't let them take-"

In one move, Vinca bent and tossed Stassi over his shoulder and hurried to a limo parked near the walkway, the vapor swirling from the exhaust pipe.

One of the back doors was propped open and Vinca threw Stassi inside. Climbing in right after her, he closed the door and the car took off.

Stassi hurtled across the inside of the limo landing right into the waiting arms of Nero Lamontagne. Gasping, she tried to windmill back from him yelling, "No!" But Lamontagne tossed his arms around her and lifted her to sit on his lap.

"Let me go!" Stassi shrieked. She couldn't believe it! Karine had led her right to the lion's cage!

Laughing with nefarious glee, Nero just wrapped his arms tightly around Stassi, so tightly her breath drew in a squeak. "Now, now, my sweet. Did you really think I would let you go?"

He moved one arm and gripped her chin jerking it up so their eyes were level. He was smiling, but it wasn't a friendly smile. Rage torqued from the depths of his cold, sadistic eyes.

"I demand you release-"

Nero gave her such a nasty shake her eyeballs rattled. "You thought to escape me? I don't give a shit the formula was no good. But you didn't comprehend that I own you, girl. I had plans for you. I was returning to my estate the day you killed Rufus. You were mine, and I was going to show you-" he broke off, his lips rolled from his tongue pushing ruefully at them from inside.

"Well, I will still show you what it means to belong to me." He gave her chin a fierce snap and sneered maliciously, "Oh yes, I will show you."

"No-" her screech was shut off as Nero slapped his hand over her mouth.

"From now on, little chemist," his voice a hard, repulsive edict in her ear, "you no longer have the right to talk. There will be only one time I'll require your mouth to be open and that will be when you are on your knees in front of me. Other than that," he squeezed his hand into a vising clamp sealing her lips, "your days of speaking are over."

He shoved his face in hers, his smile abhorrent, he said, "I won't have you gagged unless you try to talk. That will be up to you. There is nothing you could say that I would have any interest in hearing. So, from now on, this is your only warning, speak without my permission to do so and you will live every moment of the rest of your days bound and gagged."

Grinning at her he inquired, "Any questions, darlin'?"

Stassi opened her mouth, then at his snaky grin, she shut her lips. He clearly wanted her to speak so he could punish her as he threatened.

"Good decision," he told her, gave her a push and released her chin but kept his arm belted around her, holding her prisoner on his lap.

Vinca slid onto the long leather seat next to them. He gave her a cheerful grin that did nothing to hide the depravity behind it. Slapping a big palm on her thigh, he said with gusto, "This time I get my piece of you, chickadee." He leaned in and patted her cheek. "You ain't getting away this time, sweetness. Nero has you all to himself tonight, I get you in the morning, then we're gonna trade on and off."

Stassi twisted her face away from him and futilely pushed at the hand on her thigh.

Vinca laughed at her comical, completely useless efforts to make him unhand her. He grasped her wrists and glanced at Lamontagne with a grin. "You told a bunch of the soldiers that you would give them a reward for that last op." He turned to

Stassi and tugged on her wrists showing her how absolutely helpless she was. Snickering, he said, "I'm thinking you're gonna make a terrific reward to the fellas, am I right?"

There was nothing Stassi could say or do to stop them, to help herself. This time there would be no white knight to rescue her. Her brother thought the risk to her safety had been erased with the findings that the bacteria was worthless, so he would only be in touch with her remotely. She knew she'd never hear from Volt again, and that brought a piercing pain to her shattered heart. He probably would never even hear what had happened to her.

Still, she aimed her eyes out the side window seeking some kind of escape. It was tinted, no one could see inside, no one could see she was in distress, in dire danger.

The car started moving.

Chapter Thirty-Three

Expelling a burden-laden sigh, there was nothing to do but wait until an opportunity arose for her to initiate an escape. She had gotten away from Rufus, she would get away from these two horrible despots.

However, Stassi ruminated considering her situation, Vinca held her wrists, and Nero's hands started stroking up the front of her, what was she going to have to endure until then?

"Strip the bitch, Nero, then we can play with her," Vinca crowed in conquest, his smirk a slippery sneering leer. Sadistic anticipation gleamed in his eyes as he stretched her arms out to the sides to make removing her clothes easier access to his sick pal's now roaming hands that fondled, gouged, pinched, crushed and twisted with hideous enjoyment at the pain and humiliation he inflicted upon her.

Nero tugged the white blouse out of her slacks and shoved a hand up under it to cruelly clench her breast.

Stassi bit her tongue to keep from screaming, she refused to give them the satisfaction and amusement of her shrieks of terror and pleas to stop their assault. But she wasn't going down without a fight. She bucked and threw her body with all her might to break free of the repulsive pair of gangsters' clutches. She fought so hard she couldn't stifle the grunts and gasps of exertion.

Vinca's coarse laughter burned her ears in mortification.

Grinning in delight at the small woman struggling to fight the two huge males, holding her wrists, Vinca used them to twist her body to fully face Nero. Forcing her to straddle Nero's thighs, he viciously jerked her arms up behind her back barring any efforts she could make at stopping Nero from ripping off the buttons on her blouse.

She heard Vinca's satisfied snort at her cry of pain at the cruel wrenching of her arms.

Tearing the buttons off, Nero pushed Stassi's blouse apart. Carnal gaze on her heaving breasts, he slicked his lips with a slimy tongue and reached behind her to unclasp her bra.

She couldn't bite back her fright, Stassi shrieked, "No! No!" and twisted violently to avoid Nero's hands.

Nero barked as Stassi thrashed on his lap, "Hold her still, Vinca, or I'll have to tear it off."

"So, what's the difference? We weren't planning on having her clothed back at the compound anyway. Just rip everything off." Vinca gave Stassi's arms a savage jerk and growled, "Come on Nero, faster, I'm gonna explode if I don't give it to her soon. Get her pants off, hurry up, we can take our time playing with her tits and shit later."

"Yeah, yeah," Nero muttered sticking his hands inside the top of her pants he gripped hard to impatiently rip them apart.

Stassi bucked, shifting Nero's hands, but Vinca snapped her arms down causing her chest to thrust up, and lift her hips to Nero's greedy fingers. Her neck arched, her head fell back and she let out a desperate scream of pain at Vinca's ruthless brutality.

"Hold the fuck still-" Nero regained his grip on her slacks-and the limo unexpectedly braked hard, skidded then turned sharply tossing the trio across the bench seat.

Nero bellowed, Vinca cursed, Stassi scrambled to the door. Reaching for the handle as quickly as she could-

"Bitch," Vinca cursed, snagging a handful of her hair he jerked her away from the door as the car came to an abrupt, tire-squealing halt. The three tumbled off the seat to the floor but Vinca kept his hold of Stassi's hair.

Climbing up onto the seat she screamed and pounded at the window in the door with her fists but he pulled her back- and the opposite door flung open!

Nero was suddenly snatched out of the car and he was gone.

Stassi reached behind her to claw at Vinca's hands. A body thrust against Vinca shoving him into her and then she heard a thumping smash and a cracking bam then a crash as Vinca's head bashed into the window.

He let go of her hair, and she fell off the seat again landing on her knees on the carpet. She sat in stunned astonishment watching the horrendous mutilation being inflicted on Vinca.

Blood splattered over the window, and a hand grasped the back of Vinca's hair and he was repeatedly smashed against the glass again and again, even as the glass finally shattered, the pounding continued until his head was shoved completely out through the sharp shards of glass of the broken window.

It all happened so fast Vinca couldn't get a howl or a scream out. His face was shredded, blood flew around the limo and gushed from his entire head, or what was left of it.

Stassi scrambled out of the way as Volt gripped Vinca's shoulders and appeared to be trying to shove the man's entire big body out the window that was smaller than he was.

Stassi heard the limo driver cry for mercy as he was dragged from the car.

Eventually Volt realized he couldn't push Vinca completely through the window, he sat back on his heels and wiped his bloody palms on Vinca's trousers.

Vinca had been kicking and squealing like a stuck pig but now he lay completely still, his legs hanging limply inside the car, his head outside it, his shoulders wedged sideways in the frame of the window, and his arms trapped at his sides also wedged in the frame.

His big chest rising and falling with heavy rapid breaths, Volt swiped a hand pushing his hair out of his eyes and turned to Stassi. She had moved to the other side of the car afraid to leave the limo unsure what or who was outside of it.

Her rounded eyes dashed back and forth from Vinca stuffed in the broken window, the entire inside around him covered in crimson blood to the still enraged Volt who was struggling to calm his breathing. On her knees, her hand to her mouth, Stassi whispered, "Volt?"

He moved right to her and grasped her upper arms. "Baby, Anastasia, God, did they hurt you?" Worried eyes scanned her from head to toe taking in the ripped blouse.

One hand still over her mouth, eyes wide with shock and confusion she shook her head.

Volt swept a palm over the side of her face smoothing the hair back then grasped her arms again. "You sure? Do we need to go to the hospital?" His fingers dug deep into her arms, in his anxiety he wasn't accurately judging his strength. At her painful wince and shifting arms, he sucked in a heavy stuttering breath and loosened his grip.

"No, Volt, I'm fine." Cocking her head, her own pulse still racing at warp speed she smiled ruefully at him. "I'm fine because once again you arrived at literally the breaking point and saved me. How do you do that? Do you have some kind of a sixth sense or something? A little clanging bell goes off with an alarm that rings out 'Stassi's in trouble yet again'?"

At the twitching of his lips, a tiny giggle slipped out of Stassi relieving some of her tense terror.

"Damn, girl," Volt muttered and pulled her into his chest and wrapped his arms around her. His heaving sigh expressing relief that he was in the nick of time and he hadn't been too late to save her. That this time she wouldn't have to be sequestered away while recovering from terrible wounds and violations. His trembling palm cupped the back of her head, he pressed it into his shoulder and took a big breath letting it sieve out slowly.

They stayed like that for long moments listening to the commotion outside of the limo. Someone had called the police and sirens were approaching. People were gathering near the scene and cries of horror rebounded at the sight of Vinca Nivelli hanging in a broken car window with blood pooling on the ground beneath his macerated face.

Scuffles and shouts revolved around the car, Stassi heard Jubal calling out and she recognized Greco's voice as well.

Heaven knows what's going on out there she thought, and didn't care. She was safe and happy cuddled against Volt's strapping chest with his strong arms crushing her tightly.

The sirens grew closer and Volt leaned back but still held her.

"Really," Stassi asked, "how did you know I was here? There's no way you just happened upon us."

"Yeah," he agreed, drawing his large palm over her head and down the back of her hair in a long luxurious stroke. "We've stayed near. I knew Lamontagne wasn't the type of man to just let you go. Regardless of the efficacy of the bacteria, he wanted you. And he most certainly would have wanted revenge that you were able to escape him.

"He's a dirtbag gangster that thinks he's king of the world and no one would dare defy him or run from him, especially a gorgeous, helpless female, and I knew he would eventually come for you. He desires you and he also wanted to punish you, and he wasn't going to let you get away from him."

She jerked back but he held her tightly. Brows arched, she snapped, "What? You used me as bait? Volt, he could have killed me!"

"Chill, baby." Volt smiled taking the edge off his order. "Last time I took you from Callen while you were recovering I had a doctor insert a tracker inside of your-"

"What!" She pushed at him. "You put something inside my body? Where? How?" She anxiously patted her arms, her belly her chest, neck.

"Slow down, Ana," Volt told her. "It's in the back of your shoulder. It's the size of a quinoa seed. I couldn't take the chance of some asshat snatching you again and hurting you before I could find you and get to you."

Reaching her hand behind her back she felt all around her shoulder area. "But that wouldn't tell you I had been taken, that I was in danger."

Volt grasped her hand and pulled it down, set it on his thigh and covered it with his own. "It didn't. One of your, uh, coworkers, a Donovan Crane told me. I had cameras monitoring all over the place, but Crane's call was quicker."

Brows beetled in puzzlement, Stassi said, "How would Donovan know?"

Volt moved to sit on the seat, pulled her onto his lap and he leaned back. His arms encircling her, he told her, "In the very beginning, as soon as you were established at Exbiotics, Nero Lamontagne had Vinca Nivelli make Crane a little visit. Nivelli encouraged the skinny geek to spy on you and your professor. He reported regularly everything he saw and knew about you."

"Encouraged?"

He shrugged. "Violently encouraged."

"But why would Donovan betray me like that?"

"At first it was greed. Lamontagne paid him big bucks. But after Lamontagne abducted you and hurt you so badly," at the pained look that crossed her face, Volt combed his fingers through her thick hair in a soothing manner. He slid his hand around the back of her neck and stroked her skin with his thumb.

"After that, he got remorseful cold feet and refused to work with Lamontagne. But, he was stupid and assumed Lamontagne would back off. No, Lamontagne had Nivelli pay him another visit. This time when Nivelli left, he took three of Crane's teeth with him. And, uh, did some other things you really don't want to know about."

As the information soaked in, Stassi grasped the act of torture and cringed, her skin drew taut and whitened, her lips twisted. "Oh," she murmured. Gulping hard at the picture of Vinca Nivelli with a pair of bloody pliers wrenching poor Donovan's- She closed her eyes and shook her head. "But that doesn't explain why he contacted you."

Nodding, Volt continued stroking her skin. Cradled in the crook of his arm, his gaze stirring tenderly all over her face, his mouth softened, dark eyes warmed. "I had given everyone my card and spoke individually with each person. They were instructed to contact me if they saw anything, any strangers hanging about, any strange behavior from other staff, even from you. Crane called and told me he saw Karine Benton hustling you out the back corridor.

"He said no one went there except the material handlers and their manager when receiving extra-large deliveries in the depot. There was no reason for either of you women to be there. His call gave me the jump to get to you, the cameras wouldn't have picked up until you were being abducted."

A shiver rippled across her shoulders as Stassi recalled following Karine in confusion, then the horror of seeing Vinca Nivelli. He had moved so fast she couldn't get out a gasp before he grabbed her and hurtled her into the limo, into Lamontagne's waiting arms.

Her breath hitched at the recollection of when she'd realized her predicament with the two gangsters leering at her and the car starting to move.

Volt stroked his palm down her back in a calming motion, for both of them. Relaxing her, and to him, confirming she was safe and sound and in his arms.

He said, "It's over, baby. Anyway, Crane was terrified of what Lamontagne would have Nivelli do next to him if he defied him, but, Crane was also afraid of what he would do to you, and trust me, he was terrified of me as well. I made my position clear, if anyone allowed any harm to come you they wouldn't be alive to see the sun set.

"The stories of what we did to Rufus and the other soldiers had gotten around and my threats were taken seriously. So, Crane knew shit was up at Karine's odd behavior and he called me. As I told you, we stayed near and I had your tracker relentlessly on screen from the second I left you here. As soon as Crane called we jumped into action and raced after you. And, well, you were there, you know what happened next."

Her lips thrust out, eyes flitting agitatedly back and forth, Stassi pondered on everything he was saying.

"Baby," he murmured, curling a finger under her chin and lifted it so their eyes coupled. "Lamontagne had gone into deep hiding. You insisted on returning home and back to work. He could have gotten to you before I could locate him. I had to do something to get this crap off you so I disappeared and he made his move. You were never in danger, except for the damned time you were alone in this car with those two scumbag freaks.

"Even before Crane called me I saw your tracker move from the building and we came right after you. I..." He brushed her cheek with his thumb. "I was terrified of what they could, would be doing to you in those few moments you were in the car with them. I'm sorry-"

"Volt," she cut him off. "There is nothing to be sorry about. The danger has now finally been trounced. Lamontagne will be in jail like Callen, and Mr. Nivelli," she glanced over at the grisly mess that hung in the window, "if he survives he'll join them."

Her brows inverted in surprise at Volt shaking his head. "No? They won't go to prison? What is going to happen? I mean, will they go free? Volt, they can't-"

His thumb pressed gently over her lips silencing her. "I would never let those scumbags freely walk the earth again, baby. They will be…" his gaze lowered to her mouth then rose to her eyes.

"Ah, it's best you don't know what our plans are. Just be assured they will never be a danger to you or anyone else ever again. We don't trust the justice system to operate correctly. There are too many nuances. Too many technicalities smarmy shrewd lawyers could use to get them off. At the least, they would likely be given bail and you know that would be the last time they would see the courthouse or jail. I can't, won't, entrust your safety to a non-failsafe judicial system. I won't leave anything to chance that they could get to you ever again." He glanced at Nivelli, he hadn't moved even a finger.

Her shoulders lowered in relief. "Okay. You're right, I don't need to know. All I need to know is that I am finally, absolutely, 100% safe now. Am I?" Her back was to Nivelli. Stassi was so happy to be in Volt's arms she'd forgotten about him. Although there were some ugly sounds including heavy wheezing and sniveling coming from behind her.

A soft smile creased Volt's hard face. "Yeah, baby, you are. And I will ensure it is forever because you will always be with me."

Her green eyes widened, then lashes lowered in puzzlement. "What do you mean?"

"You forgot something else you need, Ana, and what I need." He lowered his head and pressed a gentle kiss on her lips, he smiled against her mouth feeling her confusion in her firmed lips.

"What do I, and you, need, Volt?" Her gaze was now on his mouth, her lids thickening and eyes shimmering with budding arousal.

His whisper wafting over her lips he said, "We need each other, Ana. I don't want to be apart from you ever again. I want you in my home, in my bed, in my life. What do you say?"

Her mouth grinned against his, she whispered, "I say I'm with you." She leaned back slightly. Self-doubt, her longtime friend rolled in again. Her tone growing serious, she said, "Um, what precisely are you saying? Are we going to- to date?"

"Hell no, baby." He touched their lips together. "I have no intention of us spending our days and nights apart. I plan to wake up to those lovely green eyes every morning for the rest of my life. You're gonna marry me as soon as we can arrange it. I want you to be my wife, Ana."

Her spine straightened, mouth dropped open. "Wife?"

"Yes, sweetheart, you'll marry me and we will live happily ever after together."

A small pout she said, "I'm not hearing you asking me, I'm hearing you telling me we're going to get married. Listen-"

"Whatever, baby, as long as it happens. I'll get on one knee later, but for now," the gently bussing lips on hers turned hard, hungry, and he went after Stassi. She was on his lap, his arms rolled around her body and he crushed her to him while he showed her what life would be like with them together. Hot, aching, sexy, loving.

It took forever before they heard Jubal, with laughter in his voice, telling them they needed to get a move on, the police were there and the paramedics were about to extricate Vinca from the window.

"Geesh, Volt, how can you make out with that bloody, hissing mess behind you?" Jubal grasped Stassi's hand and helped her out of the limo.

Volt slid out after her and to his feet. His arm wrapped around Stassi's shoulders. Smiling down at her he said, "You almost lose the most precious thing in the world to you, J, and you get it in your arms and it just freezes time. The rest of the world doesn't exist. Even raw meat hanging in the window."

"Volt, please." Stassi's nose wrinkled.

"Yeah, gross, bro," Jubal chuckled. The way he eagerly watched the paramedics and fire fighters trying to extricate Nivelli's huge body indicated he wasn't put off by grisly scenes.

Chapter Thirty-Four

Six Months Later

Stassi could hear the murmurings of their guests wafting up the stairs. Bursts of laughter and pure joy resonated from the floor below warming her heart.

Stassi's guests were people from Exbiotics, some from her university, and a group from her church. Volt's were men he worked with, his core team, and agents from other countries, they all brought their plus ones.

So, for two people who were considered unapproachable, cold, loners, the pair had managed to fill the chapel with tons of people that were thrilled to be a part of Stassi and Volt's marital joining.

She had put in a few months of work at Exbiotics and resumed her studies while she and Volt planned their wedding. She found herself constantly pinching her arm in fear it was all a dream.

But, even with all the delight of being Volt's significant other, the horrors of what had happened still pinged around in her brain firing off sparks of resurrected terror. She'd had moments of sheer panic whenever she caught sight of a big man that resembled Ini Madarov or Vinca Nivelli, or a burly redhead like Rufus. Thank goodness those panic attacks were receding and the bite of fright was less vicious each time.

The times she felt safest were when wrapped in Volt's strong arms at night. He had insisted she immediately move into the home he rented. In fact, by the time he brought her to her apartment to pack her things, she found he'd already had his team there and they had packed and moved most of her stuff to his place.

Apparently he planned on them marrying whether or not she agreed. Her bossy man, Stassi sighed with happiness. Of course there was no chance in hell she would have denied him. She was so crazy about her man, she would race him to the altar! Volt had even been the one to bring up children.

After several hours of lovemaking on a sunny Sunday he had asked her how many she wanted. Before she could even think about it, children had never been on her radar, not with her damaged view of life, Volt declared he wanted six kids, three boys and three girls, and furthermore, he'd wanted to get started on them right away.

He proclaimed this with a lascivious grin as he tossed the box of condoms in the trash with one hand and grabbed her with the other. In seconds he's stripped her and they started all over again, their laughter ringing from the rooftops.

They hadn't decided where they would put down permanent roots and build their own house. She was eager to see the strange country Volt originated from. He was still pretty closed up about his homeland, and he never spoke of family. But, Stassi figured she had time to finagle information out of the stoic man. She felt safe with him, he needed to learn to feel safe with her knowing his dark secrets.

Stassi gazed at her reflection in the mirror. The off-the-shoulder, heavenly white gown made of lace and pearls and diamantes twinkled around her body. She turned side-to-side to check and make sure everything looked right.

Twisting to check out the back, "Drat," she muttered. "I need to get Val to help zip up the back of this dress." The zipper was too long she couldn't manage it herself.

Trying to reach behind her to catch the bottom of the zipper, Stassi sighed contentedly at her reflection. "Never imagined I'd ever see this day," she mused at the pretty picture of her in diaphanous layers of snow white.

"And to think I'd sworn off men, never believed I'd dare to be in a relationship. It hadn't even been Glenn Dyke's full fault as the villain in their relationship. I had pushed him away, my insides were frozen and he wasn't the man to melt me. Now Volt," her lips curved in a fantasy smile.

She tugged vainly at the zipper but it was too low to pull up. Then she felt feminine fingers brush hers away and the zipper drew slowly up the curve of her back.

"Oh, Val, thank you. You got ready fast, I didn't expect you back so-"

"No, darling, it isn't your friend," a soft sweet voice said, sounding so familiar to Stassi. She hadn't heard that voice in so long. The zipper slid up and the clasp at the neck was clinched.

No, it can't be. Stassi swung around in astonishment. Her mother. Was here. Standing there, her gaze showering lights of love at her estranged daughter.

She didn't really look much different than she had when Stassi had fled her home. A few lines around the same wide green eyes as Stassi's. A strand of grey here and there in her almost shoulder-length russet hair. A couple of extra pounds embellished her slender figure. Sadness pooled though, deep, anguishing sorrow weighed those green eyes down.

Stassi could not pin down the feelings that rushed up and clogged her throat. Hate? Betrayal? Resentment? Pain? Anger? Loss.

What did she see expressed in her mother's sorrowful gaze? Fear? Anxiousness? Love. Hope.

Natasha Athens took a nervous step back from her daughter. "My dear, sweet Stassi," her voice shook as tears slid down her round cheeks.

"Mom?" Stassi was confused. Surprised. Stunned. She never thought she would see the woman who bore her ever again. Stassi had always hated her for her cowardly, non-motherly behavior as in making herself scarce whenever her father beat her. But, the last bit of ice that Volt hadn't melted in her heart heated to warm liquid.

Kenan had told her the truth of how it was while they were growing up. Her father had threatened to dispose of Stassi if either her mother or brother interfered in his abuse. They hurt her by keeping their silence, but they would have hurt her more if they'd tried to intervene.

Stassi could see the true love for her, and grave regret in Natasha's grievous gaze that glistened through the tears. "Mom," she repeated and held her arms open.

With a crying gasp, Natasha moved to her daughter and the women hugged, clung together and sobbed.

After long moments, they broke apart yet Natasha held Stassi's hands and looked at her from head to toe. Her watery smile curved in gratefulness, she whispered, "You are beautiful, my baby, so beautiful. I've missed you so so much. I-" she stuttered as tears fell. "I've missed you so much babygirl. There was nothing I could- Kenan could, our hands were tied, we just could not- will you ever forgive me?"

"I know, Kenan told me. I've missed you too, Mom," Stassi said with a sniff holding back her tears. She smiled at her mother. "I understand now. There is nothing to forgive, Dad forced you to keep out of the way, keep quiet. It's okay. It's all in the past. I hope," her head tilted shyly. "I hope we can be a family now. I want us to be a family. You, Kenan, me and Volt." She smiled shyly. "Volt wants children, your grandchildren."

Her breath caught, Natasha nodded as more tears fell. "Yes, baby, yes. I prayed for this day. Kenan brought me here today, I was so afraid you would…hate me, send me away-" her voice broke off with grief and regret.

"Oh, Mama, please don't cry. It's a new day for all of us. A brilliant wonderful new day. A wedding is a start, a new start, a beginning. A new beginning for us all. The dark dawn is finally breaking." She hugged her mother again.

"Hey, what'd I miss?" Valentina grinned as she entered the room.

Stassi looped her arm through her mother's and turned them both to face Val. "Val, this is my mother, Natasha Athens. Mom, this is a good friend of mine, Valentina King."

Val blinked, her eyes flicked to Stassi. She slanted her head in puzzlement remembering Stassi's angst when she briefly burst out about her family that night at the Brontysaurus. But Stassi's smile was gloriously happy, that was enough for Val. "Hi," she said proffering her hand, "nice to meet you."

Stassi slid her arm from her mother's so Natasha could shake Val's hand.

Natasha bowed slightly with a kind smile. "You as well, dear."

Music traveled up the stairs and into the room. Natasha said to her daughter, "I think we need to move along, your young man will think you got cold feet and ran off."

Grinning at her mother, Stassi said, "Trust me, if I did he would come after me and bring me back. So," she shrugged one shoulder happily, "I guess we'll skip all that drama."

"Been there and done that, huh?" Valentina claimed wryly.

Natasha's face was suddenly stricken with distress, she cried, "My poor darling, Stassi, Kenan told me the things that had happened to you-"

"It's over, Mom, I'm safe. The bad men have all been put away." Volt wouldn't tell her what happened to the men that had harmed her but he made sure she knew they would never see daylight again. At least those that still lived, he'd intimated. She told her mother, "I can live my life freely with joy and security."

Her lips pulling in tightly, Natasha nodded. She had no desire to bring a shadow over her daughter's important day. "Okay, honey. Now," she said, reaching for the veil, "time for the last touch."

Stassi stood still while Natasha and Val arranged the veil on top of her head. Half Stassi's mahogany hair was clustered on her head, the other curled down her back.

Her mother gently pulled the delicate veil down neatening it down Stassi's back. She smiled tenderly at her daughter. "You are so very beautiful, sweetheart. Your Volt is a lucky man."

Val snorted. "Have you seen Voltang Saldano, Mrs. Athens? Stassi is the lucky one. When he's not scaring the hell out of you, the man is the hottest hunk of manly meat to hit this burg in like forever."

"Val!" Stassi admonished her friend, her cheeks shiny pink.

"You don't have to tell me, Val, honey," Natasha said with a sassy grin. "I met the guy. He and Kenan came together to bring me here." She winked at Val. "You're right, man is prime meat!"

"Mom!" Stassi gushed at her mother, her cheeks growing brighter. "That's my future husband you're talking about!"

Natasha and Val laughed together, Natasha said, "Honey, this girl's got eyes, and he's eye candy, and I love candy."

Bursting out with laughter, Val, wiped at a tear. "Yeah, and I do love me some candy too!"

"Okay, okay, enough you goofs." Stassi rolled her eyes grinning.

"Mother." The girls turned to the door.

Kenan's eyes were on his sister. He blinked then said to his mother, "It's time for me to get you seated." He nodded to Val then spoke to Stassi, "I'll be back for you. Everyone is here, we're ready."

The edge of his mouth twitched up. "Volt is chomping at the bit. He told me if I didn't get you downstairs in the next five minutes he was coming up here and hauling you over his shoulder and bringing you down himself."

Natasha's brows arched at that, then she smiled. "Got yourself a macho tiger, huh, honey? Good for you. Okay," she held her arm out for her son to take. Then she said, "Oh, wait," and she hurried to her purse she'd hung on the doorknob. Kenan, Val and Stassi shared a puzzled look as she plucked the purse off the knob.

After rummaging in her purse, Natasha held her hand out to Stassi, her face lit with proud glee. A necklace draped from her fingers. Filigree chain, at the bottom dangled an antique setting, a diamond in the center glinted. She reached behind Stassi and clasped it behind her neck.

Patting the necklace, Natasha explained, "Val told me you had a borrowed penny in your shoe, and your garter was blue, you have diamond earrings and bracelet from Volt, those are your something new. And this," she touched the pendant that lay against Stassi creamy bosom, "was your grandmother's, her mother gave it to her. This is your something old."

She smiled proudly at her little girl, all grown up and ready to be somebody's wife. "We've lost so many years, baby." Her gaze swung regretfully, sadly, from Stassi to Kenan.

Filled with emotion, Stassi whispered, her voice breaking, "We'll make them up, Mom," she nodded to her brother. "We'll make them all up, together. Go on now, Kenan wasn't joking when he said Volt was an impatient man and he will darken this doorway shortly if we don't get a move on."

"Yes darling," Natasha chuckled and looped her arm through her son's and they headed for the door.

She had Kenan pause under the arch and she turned back to her daughter, her eyes glazed with love and shimmering tears. "I love you baby."

"Don't you dare ruin your makeup!" Val shrieked at Stassi as her identical green eyes shone with tears.

They all laughed breaking the tension and Kenan led his mother from the room.

Volt stood at the alter tugging on his sleeves, then he twisted a few buttons on his shirt then he straightened his bow tie, then glanced at his watch. She was twenty minutes late. What the hell, he looked to the entrance for the thousandth time.

What if she got scared? What if Stassi realized what kind of man Volt was, that he had so much blood on his hands, the things he was capable of doing that a normal man would shudder and shirk from. What if she realized what a hard, dominating killing machine he was and she ran out the back door and-

Kenan was walking Stassi's mother down the aisle. She smiled at Volt and Kenan grinned, and Volt's gut released a hair of tension. He nodded to Kenan and Natasha.

Hell, he could see where Stassi got her beauty from. Mrs. Athens was as lovely, delicate and sweet as his Stassi. He was looking forward to getting to know her better. Kenan strode calmly back up the aisle.

Volt pictured happy days sprawled on the carpet in the living room on holidays with Kenan and Natasha, and Stassi and their children playing delightfully- he shook his head and glanced down again at his watch.

Two more minutes and he was going upstairs after her and bring her ass down and get his ring on her finger. He didn't deserve the perfect woman that Stassi was, but he was a selfish son of a bitch and he was holding onto her. If that little girl thought she was not marrying him, if she was going to let a little fear chase her away-

He heard Jubal's light chuckle beside him. "She's coming, bro," he whispered, "the girl loves you, although God knows why she wants to look at your ugly mug for the rest of her life." Laughing at the scowl on Volt's face he nudged him with his elbow. "Quit fidgeting you impatient bastard," and he grinned at Volt's eyes narrowing at him.

"Listen, J, you asshole, hold down the fort, I'm going after her-"

The Wedding March started playing.

He looked to the door again and Stassi's friend Valentina was coming down the aisle dressed in deep amethyst. Her grin wide and pretty, she carried a bouquet of white peonies and purple delphiniums and lilac tulips. When she reached the alter she grinned at Volt and stood to the opposite side of where he waited.

Volt nodded to her but his attention was zeroed in on the entrance. He didn't see the rows of pews their friends were lined on, or the red carpet speckled with rose petals, he only had eyes for the beauty that was poised in the archway. Stassi clung to her brother's arm.

Kenan grinned large at Volt, and he started walking his sister down the aisle to his friend.

Stassi passed her bouquet of red roses, pink camellias, and purple astras strung with purple satin ribbons to Val.

When Kenan handed Stassi over to Volt, Volt lifted the veil that covered her face, he didn't smile, he couldn't. "Damn Anastasia," he whispered, "here I thought you couldn't get more beautiful. Baby, you are more dazzling than the stars that light up the heavens." He squeezed her hand. "You ready?"

She lifted her chin with a loving smile and he gave her a soft kiss that ended quickly at the minister's clearing of his throat.

Epilogue

The wedding went by in a blur, the reception a boisterous, cheerful festive party and everyone danced the night away. They ate rich food, richer cake, toasted the new couple with sparkling champagne.

People snickered at the big dangerous looking man that stayed protectively, possessively hovering over his new bride. His impatience to get Stassi alone glowed clear in the tender, lustful way he never took his eyes off her, his hands continuously touching her.

He allowed Brant all of two minutes dancing with his bride before Volt snatched her back into his arms with a frown to Brant.

Her small hands on his thick shoulders, Stassi giggled up at her cranky husband and gave him a light kiss. "Patience, my darling," she murmured against his lips, "another hour and we can politely exit our party. Now, dance with me."

****

Hours later, Stassi scolded him, "Volt, you're going to tear it, slow down."

He sliced the zipper down, yanked open buttons, and was struggling to push the clinging top part down.

His hands fell to her waist, his lips to hers, he muttered, "It's a wedding gown, baby, you're only getting married once, who gives a damn if it's ruined? If we have a daughter she will want to choose her own, it's way too fancy to be made into a regular dress. It's gorgeous, Ana, but I want you out of it, *now*."

Stringing her arms around his neck, Stassi giggled and kissed him. He was already hard and overheated, she pulled back before he just shoved her skirt up and- "Okay, Husband, let me help you."

Together they removed the gown, Stassi frowning when Volt wadded it up in his big arms and tossed it negligently onto a chair. "Geeze, Volt," she complained.

"You gonna nag me, woman, or you gonna help me?" Volt mumbled redundantly because he'd already whipped her bra off, her panties, and was rolling the white stockings down her legs.

Finally getting her naked, Volt lifted her and set her on the bed then stood back and stared at every gleaming, soft round inch of her creamy skin. "Damn, Ana, I'll never get tired of looking at you. You can have sagging skin and wrinkles and you will always be beautiful, my beautiful wife."

"Volt," now she sounded impatient. "I'll be old and grey if you don't snap out of it and get your clothes off and come here and consummate our marriage."

His face split in a huge white, rare grin and he stripped out of the tux as fast as he could then climbed onto the bed and pulled Stassi into his arms.

"Volt, the tux, you could have damaged it," she reproved him even as she molded her body to his and stroked her hands up his broad chest, her fingers tangling in the matting of hair.

"Ah, who cares, babe, I have ten more. I love you, Anastasia, my wife," he whispered as he covered her with his body.

Their lips meshing, Stassi murmured into his mouth, "And I love you, my darling husband."

The End

Louise Furley